MW01602457

THE BEST OF

The Norwegian Heritage

VOLUME II

COVER PHOTO: Gol Stave Church or *Gol Stavkirke,* the earliest stave church erected in Norway. Now in the Folk Museum in Oslo's Bygdøy Park, it was moved from Gol in Hallingdal about 100 years ago.

A full-size replica of this historic church is planned to be constructed at the Scandinavian Heritage Center in Minot, North Dakota.

THE BEST OF

The Norwegian Heritage

VOLUME II

Arland O. Fiske

North American Heritage Press

THE BEST OF THE NORWEGIAN HERITAGE
VOLUME II

Copyright © MCMXCVI
by Arland O. Fiske

All rights reserved. No part of this book, either in part or in whole, may be reproduced, transmitted or utilized in any form or by any means, electronic, photographic or mechanical, including photocopying, recording, or by any information storage and retrieval system, without permission in writing from the Publisher, except for brief quotations embodied in literary articles and reviews.

For permissions, or for serialization, condensation, or for adaptations, write the Publisher at the address below.

International Standard Book Number: 0-942323-23-8

Design and Production by
Creative Media, Inc.
Minot, North Dakota, USA

Published by
North American Heritage Press
A DIVISION OF
CREATIVE MEDIA, INC.
P.O. Box 1
Minot, North Dakota USA 58702
701/852-5552

Printed in the United States of America

DEDICATION

To

The Scandinavian Heritage Association

OF MINOT, NORTH DAKOTA, USA

*And to the many people
who are supporting its work.
May it help bind our
old and new world heritages
together.*

C O N T E N T S

C O N T E N T S

continued

Norwegians In The New World
continued

FOREWORD

"Arland Fiske is a good storyteller" said Dr. Sidney A. Rand, former United States ambassador to Norway and thousands of others apparently share his view. After his first volumes: The Scandinavian Heritage, The Scandinavian World, The Scandinavian Spirit, and The Scandinavian Adventure; which were all good sellers, we responded to many requests for a "strictly Norwegian" book and excerpted stories from the first three volumes to make up The Best of The Norwegian Heritage.

For the past half-dozen years it has been a best seller and readers have asked when they can expect more of these delightful and interestingly-told stories. Now, after a long wait, you have the opportunity to enjoy another smørgåsbord of stories with *The Best Of The Norwegian Heritage, Volume II*.

Arland, and his wife Gerda, make their home on Kabekona Lake near Laporte in northern Minnesota, obviously a good place for writing, and perhaps some fishing, too.

Allen O. Larson
Publisher,
North American Heritage Press

P R E F A C E

The stories in this book, Volume II of *The Best Of The Norwegian Heritage*, have been selected from the previously published "Scandinavian Heritage Series." The stories have been updated and revised, incorporating new information not previously available.

There are four groupings: The Olden Days in Norway; Visiting the Old World; Heroes of the Old Country; and Norwegians in the New World, plus a story on *News From Norway*.

Since beginning the publication of these stories in syndicated newspaper columns in 1983, I have been extremely gratified to learn how eager Scandinavian people are to know their ethnic heritage. While I would not trade my American passport for that of any other country, I also have discovered many values and strengths in our heritage which help me to appreciate the country of my first loyalty.

The love of freedom is what best characterizes the Norwegian spirit. Norway has been occupied by foreign powers, but it has never surrendered. In World War II, the government continued its resistance to the enemy from its base in England. Its people and resources were unsparing in dedication to gaining victory and freedom both for itself and its neighbors.

My reason for the research which resulted in publication of heritage articles began with a personal interest. Then my family became interested and finally a number of friends urged the publication of the stories. The reason for the publication was to give information on the heritage, to entertain with what has seemed to me to be interesting stories and to identify the enduring values cherished by people of Scandinavia. The stories have been written for the average reader who may not normally have access to this heritage information. I have been interested in both the well known and the lesser known people of our common heritage. I have chosen to communicate the heritage in story-form rather than in a textbook style of writing history.

It is also my hope that non-Scandinavians may find these stories interesting and edifying. Scandinavians number less then one percent

PREFACE

of the world's population, including those who have been transplant-
ed around the globe. We share the world with many people who have
the same love of freedom. We need to explore all the possibilities of
working together to make this planet a safe place in which to live.

Many people are in my debt for their interest, encouragement and
assistance in this writing project. My wife, Gerda, continues to be my
chief inspiration, together with our children and grandchildren. Allen
O. Larson, the publisher, and owner of North American Heritage
Press, has been most helpful through these years of working together.
Sheldon Larson devotes his excellent skills in designing the cover and
preparing the text for publication. My daughter, Lisa Gaylor, has
drawn the illustrations. I also appreciate the friendship of many Sons
of Norway lodges, especially Thor Lodge #67 of Minot, North Dakota, and Nordskogen Lodge #626 of Park Rapids, Minnesota. I am
much indebted to the publications of the Norwegian-American Historical Association. I express my appreciation also to Dr. Lloyd
Hustvedt and Dr. David Preus for their kind comments on this volume. Happy reading!

> – Arland O. Fiske
> Laporte, Minnesota
> June 23, 1995 – "Sanct Hans Aften"
>> Nativity of St. John the Baptist
>> Norse celebration of the Summer Solstice

PUBLICATIONS
BY ARLAND O. FISKE

The Scandinavian Heritage Series:

The Scandinavian Heritage

The Scandinavian World

The Scandinavian Spirit

The Scandinavian Adventure

The Scandinavian Heritage
Audio Cassette
(Twelve Stories From *The Scandinavian Heritage* Book)

The Best of
The Norwegian Heritage

Stories from
The Swedish Heritage

The Best of
The Norwegian Heritage, Volume II

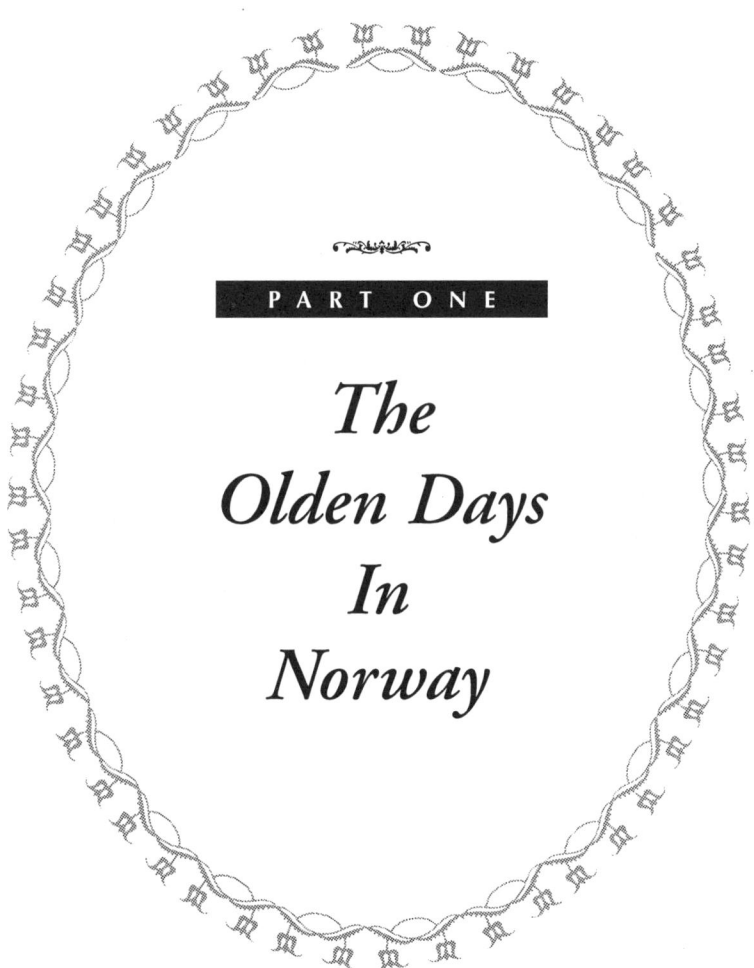

PART ONE

The
Olden Days
In
Norway

C H A P T E R

1

STAVE CHURCHES
AND DRAGON HEADS

D ragons live only in storybooks today, but to many people of the past they were real. The dragon heads on the stave churches of Norway have fascinated me. I've wondered what is the relationship between that beast of antiquity and the religion of the "White Christ" in the northlands of Europe.

I was surprised to discover the connection. Dan Lindholm has provided a scintillating study in his book *Stave Churches in Norway*, published by the Rudolf Steiner Press in London (1969). I discovered the book in a shop in Trondheim. Besides the story, there are over 110 pages of photographs which show the magnificent artistry, especially the wood carvings, of these elegant structures.

At one time there were over 1000 stave churches in Norway, today only about 30 remain, few in their original design. Strangely, they're catching on in America. The Borgund church from the Sogn region of western Norway was replicated in the "Chapel in the Hills" near Rapid City, South Dakota. It was dedicated in 1969 in memory of Rev. and Mrs. Anton A. Dahl, a pioneer Lutheran pastor in the Upper Midwest.

The stave churches, built out of wood, made their appearance before A. D. 1050 and continued to be built until the "Black Death" which struck Norway in 1349. This was an era of church building made possible through the introduction of the tithe by King Sigurd Jorsalfar (the Crusader). Every tenth calf born, every tenth fish caught, and every tenth sheaf of grain belonged to the Lord. The tithe was divided between support for the poor, the bishops, the clergy and a fourth was used for building churches. In this way, church construction flourished.

The wooden stave churches (stavkirker) were the center of worship for people in the hinterlands. Stone was used for building the cathedrals, the places where a bishop was in residence, like Trondheim, Bergen, Stavanger and Oslo. These stone edifices are some of the finest buildings in Norway, but it is the stave churches that have touched the hearts of the common people and have come to characterize the Norwegian spirit. It was possible for every community to have one of these since wood was plentiful all over the land.

The interior architectural design resembles a Viking ship upside down. A similar pattern of wood supports is used. The churches were built of a fir tree called "malmfuru," a huge tree with a straight trunk with a hard texture. The malmfuru has become extinct in Norway. The Douglas fir of western United States is the closest tree to it today and is the material out of which the "Borgund" stave church in the Black Hills is constructed.

A sermon in a medical book written in Old Norse offers an explanation of the stave church. "The church is created out of many parts in the same way as the Christian faith unites many nations and languages. Part of Christendom is with God in heaven, part in this world, so part of the church means the divine glory and part Christianity on earth. The altar signifies Christ. All gifts offered to God must be hallowed on the altar and in the same way our deeds are only pleasing to God when they are hallowed by the love of Christ." The rest of the sermon goes into detail about the symbolism of each part of the church: The doors, floorboards, benches, walls, roof, corner-posts, beams, joists and rafters, and the bell. It concludes: "Everything in the design of the church and the preparation for the service must be understood in its spiritual meaning and reflected in our inner life." The whole structure has an educational function.

What fascinates me most about these churches, however, are the dragon heads which stick out from the ends of the roof. Why did this symbol of ancient paganism adorn a Christian church? Some people suggest that their faith was a mixture of both the old and new religions. Admittedly, people do not make an instantaneous change from one faith to another. But Lindholm's research suggests something far more complicated and interesting.

The dragon is the symbol of evil and Christ is represented as the Conqueror. The stave church, according to Lindholm, "reminds one of the conquered dragon in a way that hardly any other building does." The Volsunga Saga about Sigurd as dragon slayer is woven into the architecture of these churches. "Sigurd is the conqueror of the dragon which greets us at the doorways," according to Lindholm.

When people enter the stave church they must face their enemy, the dragon, also called the "great serpent." This reflects the Genesis story of the temptation of Adam and Eve. The people of the Middle Ages felt no conflict between the biblical story and their mythologies. They grew into the Christian faith not so much by teaching, but through ritual and symbols. At first it was seen as magic, Christ was more powerful than his enemies. The liturgy was done in Latin which only the clergy understood, and not all of them.

Both Sigurd, the conqueror of the dragon, and the Risen Christ had their places in the stave church. Lindholm points out that the "heathen" pictures appear only on the outside of the church. The people of the far North could not relate themselves to the story of Abraham and the prophets as they first experienced the new religion. But they knew the story of Sigurd. The downfall of the pagan gods and heroes was represented to them in the "Gotterdammerung," as later described in Wagner's opera, "The Ring of the Nibelung."

It was curses and guilt that brought the destruction of the pagan world in this story. This is equivalent to the doctrine of "Original Sin" in Christian theology. That is why the Sigurd saga themes are carved only on the doorways to the stave church, to remind those who enter of the dangers of evil that threaten them outside of the church.

Art historians have been puzzled about the dragon image. The dragon image has appeared with variations all over the world, including the Chinese New Year celebrations. C. S. Lewis and J. R. R. Tolkien also used the dragon reminiscent of the Norse mythologies.

Usually the dragon looks like a reptile with wings. The Old Testament portrays Leviathan as a great sea monster which was overcome by the Lord. Germanic and Celtic artists also had a sea serpent. The classic battle was between St. George and the dragon depicted by a statue in the Storkyrkan cathedral in Stockholm.

The dragon image was so powerful an image that it provided the design for the Viking ships. Here it was used for the good of people. However, when the English, Irish and French saw these serpent-like ships approaching their coasts, it was the sign of the worst kind of evil.

The dragon's warning as people entered the stave church was to remind them that "a man could become a dragon when he was overwhelmed by excessive passion or growing desire," according to Lindholm. This reinforced the "Original Sin" teaching as taught by St. Augustine (354-430). "Everyone," according to Lindholm, "entering a stave church doorway had to face for a moment the image of the animal qualities hidden deep in man's being." The sword replaced the gods for the Norsemen. By the time of their "breakout" (about A. D. 800) many confessed, "we no longer believe in the old gods, but in our own swords, and in the power and measure of our own strength." Lust and revenge were the motivating powers within the Viking heart. That was the beast within them.

Their new religion taught the Norsemen forgiveness and mercy. But it took centuries before the old dragons were eradicated. The sermon from the medieval medical book concludes, "It is essential for us, dear brothers, to cleanse our hearts before celebrating the festivals so that God does not find anything displeasing there."

A second authentic replica of a stave church in America is being planned in the Scandinavian Heritage Center in the Shirley Bicentennial Park at Minot, North Dakota. It will replicate the church in Oslo's Bygdoy Park which was moved from Gol, Hallingdal, in 1886, by King Oscar II. It was partially remodeled into more classical form in its renovation. There are a number of near-replicas of stave churches too, including one near Spicer, Minnesota, built in the late 1930s. Maybe we'll see more of them.

CHAPTER

2

THE "PRIMSTAV"
(OLD NORSE CALENDAR)

I had to visit Haakon's Hall (Haakonshallen), a medieval castle in Bergen, to learn why my father always planted his corn by May 15.

The most fascinating part of the visit was to see a woolen tapestry, eighty feet long and forty-two inches wide. It was completed in 1961 by Sigrun Berg. Normally, it's hanging across the length of the wall where kings used to dine. But it had been taken down for cleaning and laid out over long tables, so I was able to study it with some care.

This tapestry is a "Primstav," normally made of wood and found hanging in the entrance of a home. The word probably derives from the Latin "Primatio Lunae," referring to the New Moon. This wooden calendar, also called a "clog almanac," was the way people kept track of time in the old days. There was a notch for each day.

The Primstav is laid out horizontally to show the two seasons, summer which began on April 14 along one edge of the board and winter beginning October 14 on the other. There was mid-summer day and mid-winter day, but no spring and autumn as we celebrate. When you finish one season, you just flip the board over.

Originally, the Primstav gave weather forecasts, planting and harvesting dates, pasturing dates for cattle, moving dates, to tell when fish will bite and such things as are in the *Farmer's Almanac*. Community life was organized around these dates. When Christianity came to Norway in the early eleventh century, thirty-seven new holidays were added to the calendar. Religious emphasis was given to the dates from nature. The Christian holy days usually remembered martyrs, the Virgin Mary, Christ or the Apostles.

Each holy day is marked by a symbol. April 14, "Summer Day," is a tree filled out with leaves, telling people to get ready for planting. It was also moving day for hired help. If it snowed on this day, it would snow nine times before full summer came. October 14, "Winter Day," has a mitten, showing that winter clothes should be taken out and put in order.

The most celebrated of the summer holidays is John the Baptist's birthday, June 24. Fires are lit everywhere on hillsides on the eve of this holiday. This was to protect people and animals against witches and evil spirits. The cows were taken to the seters ("outfarms"). If it rained, then it would be wet during harvest. The calendar symbol is a church building. August 10 was the last day for putting up hay or it would be worthless as winter fodder. By September 14 (Holy Cross Day), all crops were to be in barns for a blessing and cattle were turned loose to graze. Anyone who did not keep holy days was fined.

Some winter day when there is a snowstorm and the phone doesn't ring, I'm going to make a Primstav for my home. Maybe there is more wisdom in it than modern people imagine.

Now another of my childhood mysteries has been explained. I'm quite sure my father didn't know the origin of his beliefs that corn had to be planted by May 15 or it would not ripen. We didn't have a Primstav in our home. But he followed its advice, and our cattle and hogs always had their winter feeding.

Primstav.

CHAPTER

3

VIKINGS ATTACK LINDISFARNE (BRITAIN'S "HOLY ISLAND")

"From the fury of the Northmen, O Lord, deliver us." These words are alleged to have been prayed in the churches of France during the "Viking Age" (793-1066). While no copy of such a prayer exists, it certainly was the sentiment lifted up from the Christian altars in those fearful times.

The Viking "breakout" was a long time in preparation. Over-population, the inheritance rights of the oldest sons and the excitement of adventure combined with new technologies to produce such times. It came on June 8, 793. The target was Lindisfarne, a bare and windswept island to the northeast of York in England. Lindisfarne was the home of peaceful monks who went about their duties of chores, prayers and scholarship. The monastery was famous for its "illuminated gospels," considered to be the most beautiful book ever produced.

All of a sudden, the Viking longships appeared with their square sails and dragon heads. A contemporary historian wrote: "And they came to the church of Lindisfarne, laid everything waste with grievous plunderings, trampled the holy places with polluted feet, dug up the altars and seized all the treasures of the holy church. They killed some of the brothers; some they took away with them in fetters; many they drove out, naked and loaded with insults; and some they drowned in the sea." After Lindisfarne, every monastery and abbey in England, Scotland and Ireland was fair game for a raid. In another six years, France would also feel this new fury. In his book *The Fury of the Northmen*, John Marsden gives a vivid and brutal account of the era of Viking conquest.

VIKINGS ATTACK LINDISFARNE (BRITAIN'S HOLY LAND)

Lindisfarne was thought to be so holy that no harm could come to it. Missionaries from another holy island, Iona, on the west coast of Scotland, had founded this center of piety and learning. From the invader's point of view, it was easy picking. Monasteries were banks for the local wealth and had no guards or military fortifications. The attack on Lindisfarne sent shock waves across Europe. Besides, no one believed that the sea could be crossed over such a long distance.

After the attack, churchmen of the time claimed that there had been heavenly warnings: "...exceptional flashes of lightning, and fiery dragons were seen flying in the air," followed by famine. Alcuin, a famous English scholar teaching in the courts of Emperor Charlemagne in France, claimed that the attack came as a punishment for the sins of England! In addition to adultery, dishonesty and injustice, he also cited "long hair and flashy clothing."

But what made the raid possible? It was the Viking longship. It is fortunate for us that several of these ships have been preserved in the cold blue clay of Norway. These were buried in the earth as "coffins" for wealthy chieftains - often accompanied by slaves, animals and favorite spouse! One of these is called the "Gokstad" ship, found southwest of Oslo. It is now on display in Oslo at the Ship Hall in Bygdoy Park. Every traveller to Oslo should visit this museum.

The Gokstad ship was used for both peace and war. It could travel up shallow rivers and could be either sailed or rowed. Thirty-two oarsmen worked at a time. Double crews would ensure "non-stop" travel.

The "Hjemkomst" which sailed to Norway from Duluth, Minnesota, in 1983, was modeled after the Gokstad ship. Built in a potato warehouse in Hawley, Minnesota, by the late Robert Asp, it is seventy-six feet and six inches long. It captured the attention of the world during its famous "homecoming" voyage. Magnus Magnusson, the archaeologist and writer who created and narrated the PBS-TV series "Vikings!," said: "To my mind, quite simply, Gokstad is the most beautiful ship ever built." The Hjemkomst is now in a museum in Moorhead, Minnesota.

The attack on Lindisfarne raised some serious questions. First, did the Viking attacks prove that Odin and Thor were more powerful than the "White Christ?" Taken at face value, it would seem so. Yet in another 200 years, Norway itself would come under the sway of missionaries from England.

A second question: Is military preparation a contradiction to faith in God? Is it true, as a peace conference speaker said: "If God is on our side, why do we need the biggest weapons?"

The Gokstad ship is now a harmless museum piece, but it is also a grim reminder of the role which advanced technology plays in both peace and war. Lindisfarne, Britain's "holy island," might well be remembered as we struggle with the same hard realities in our time.

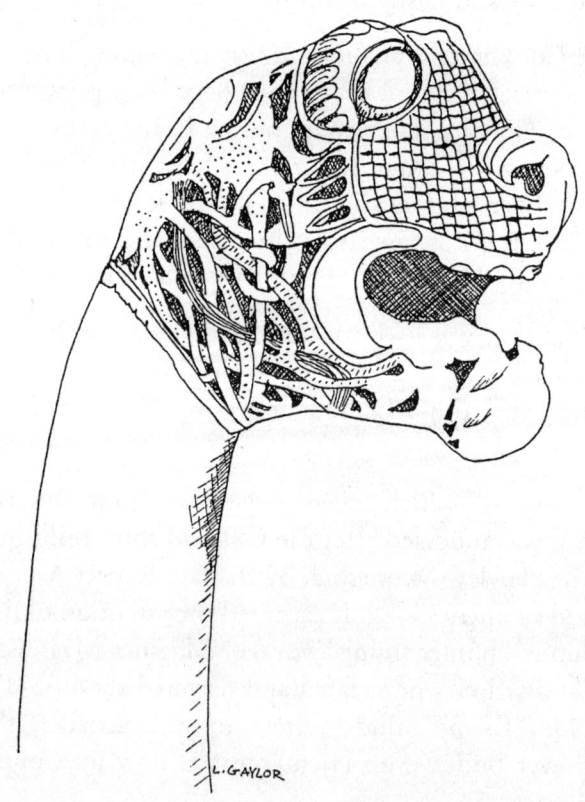

From the Oseberg ship, Bygdøy (Oslo).

CHAPTER

4

THE VIKINGS IN IRELAND

"Bitter is the wind tonight,
White the tresses of the sea;
I have no fear the Viking hordes
Will sail the sea on such a night."

This is how an Irish monk described the feelings of St. Patrick's land in the ninth century. Stormy seas meant protection from Norwegian and Danish invasions. Calm seas sent fear into everyone's hearts.

The Norwegian Vikings were the first to reach the green fields and heather of Ireland with a raid in A. D. 617. It was brutal, in the style of the times. Then followed 150 years of peace and friendly trade. But as the stories of this fair land were told during the long and cold, wintry nights of Norway's dark valleys, future invasions were conceived.

The "Viking Age" in Ireland began with a series of raids beginning in 795 near a place called "Dubh-Linn" (black pool). There the Vikings built a city about 837 to shelter their longships. Today it is called Dublin. It became the center of the earliest Norse kingdom, even before Norway itself was united under one rule. For 300 years, Scandinavians were an everyday part of Irish life. Before the era had ended, Ireland was transformed from a pastoral society built around monasteries into a land of cities and trade with minted coins. Even the name "Ireland" comes from the Norse "Ira-land." Many places such as Wexford, Waterford, Arklow and Wicklow have Norse origins.

Why did the Scandinavians come to Ireland? There are two main reasons. First, they needed room for expansion. The laws of inheritance gave the farm to the oldest son. Even today only about three percent of Norway's land is agriculturally useful. The landless sons and those desiring adventure looked to the sea and foreign lands for opportunity, just as later they looked to America. Second, piracy was not considered a dishonorable profession in those days. When the Vikings discovered that the monasteries served as the "banks" to safeguard people's jewels and precious metals, it was an easy matter for sea-hardened warriors to plunder this wealth. Many articles "made in Ireland" have been found buried in the cemeteries of Denmark and Norway. Norsemen brought much of the loot back to their wives who proudly displayed their husband's successes at sea.

The Irish referred to the Norwegians as "White Gentiles" (heathen) because they wore leather tunics in battle. The Danes were called "Black Gentiles" because they wore dark colored armor. The Danes preferred battle axes as weapons, while the Norwegians were partial to swords.

As often happens in war, many Irish collaborated with the enemy. A mixed race developed from intermarriage and the adoption of Irish children by the invaders. They were called "foreign Irish" and became notorious cattle thieves and soldiers for hire.

The Ireland into which these fierce Northmen came was an outstanding society of saints, scholars and kings. It is one of the ironies of history that the vanquished often have higher civilizations than the victors. It is not stretching the truth to claim that Ireland was the most Christian land of the Middle Ages. What made the Viking invasions so frightful in their early years was the attempt to establish the gods of Germanic paganism, Odin, Thor and Frey, with its system of human sacrifice. The Irish were not without tribal wars or other faults, but they were a model civilization amidst the barbarity of the times. *How the Irish Saved Civilization* by Thomas Cahill makes a good case for the Irish.

As the Norsemen settled down, they often fought alongside the Irish in resisting later Viking invasions. It is also true that many Irish were allies of the invaders. The Vikings, in time, became Christian and Dublin became a center of churches. Foreign mission work reached out to England, which had become paganized through Anglo-Saxon invasions from northwest Germany and Denmark. This ultimately led to the conversion of Norway itself by way of England. The flaxen-haired Celtic people of Ireland and the blonde and red-haired Scandinavians together have become the Irish of today.

There came a time, however, when the two cultures clashed in a decisive battle. It was near Dublin at the seaside city of Clontarf. Sigtrygg ("silkbeard"), the Norse king of Dublin, amassed 20,000 soldiers from many lands in the North Sea. He was matched by an equal number of Irish and Scandinavian allies. The Irish leader was the saintly and popular Brian Boru, the son of a chieftain named Kennedy. Brian, a devout Christian, was 73 years old but still a strong man. It was Holy Week and troops began to form lines on Palm Sunday. Brian did not want to do battle on Good Friday. The Vikings, fully aware of this, attacked. Brian, being faithful to his religious convictions, spent the day in prayer, guarded by a ring of shields. The Norsemen were better armed but had poorer field position. At the end of that day, April 23, 1014, Brian had won a crushing victory. But it was also a day of tragedy for Ireland. Brian and his sons, who had the ability to give stable leadership to Ireland's future, were all killed. As Brian knelt in prayer, a Viking warrior broke through the guard and struck him down. Ironically, the berserk Norseman had been prodded to the deed by an ambitious, charming but vengeful woman whom Brian had spurned in marriage.

Many Scandinavians settled in Ireland to become wealthy merchants and "Irish." Don't be surprised when you meet people who are proud to be Irish but have names that betray Norse origins.

A surprise ending to this story appeared in the *Chicago Tribune*, Nov. 11, 1980. Research on President Ronald Reagan's ancestry produced this report: "Reagan is descended from Brian Boru, an 11th century high king of all Ireland and the Emerald Isle's first national hero."

CHAPTER
5

ERIK THE RED

Ancient Iceland lacked the natural resources to build a society of culture. It had no forests, no metals and was not known for music. But Iceland excelled in literature and law. Its creativity was expressed in words. The long dark winters gave plenty time to write. The need to kill off most of their cattle provided adequate calf skins for vellum on which to record their stories. The coming of Christianity in 1000 gave them the Latin alphabet and a writing style.

It's fortunate that Icelandic people have had such literary production. Without their gift to the world, we might not have known about one of the most exciting chapters in human history, the story of Erik the Red and the Norsemen's discovery of America.

Erik was born in Norway. While yet an infant, his father, Thorvald, was exiled for murder and set sail for Iceland. When Erik grew up, he also got into a brawl and with his sword revenged the killing of two of his slaves (probably Irish). Iceland, being a land of law and order, banned him for three years.

To save his life, Erik sailed off into the unknown seas to the west until he came to a vast ice cap (715,000 square miles) which turned out to be Greenland. He explored until he found some grassy areas on the southwest coast. When the three years of exile were up, Erik returned to Iceland, a hero for his discovery. He told them that this new land to the west should be called "Greenland," knowing it to be a lie. But the sagas quoted him as saying, "Men will be more readily persuaded to go there if the land has an attractive name." He became a success in real estate!

After one winter in Iceland, Erik gathered twenty-five ships, crowded with 1000 people and domestic animals, and sailed to Greenland. Fourteen ships survived the journey. It was 995, the year that Olaf Tryggvason became king of Norway.

That same year, a young sailor named Bjarni Hjerulfson travelled from Norway to Iceland with a ship full of goods for trading. Upon arrival, he learned that his father, Herjulf, had left for Greenland with Erik. Determined to see his father, he sailed westward in search of the new land. Everything went wrong. Calm and fog set in. Then the north winds blew. When land appeared, it was not Greenland but the coast of North America, perhaps Cape Cod.

Bjarni did not allow the crew to go ashore, but kept on sailing past what may have been Nova Scotia and Newfoundland. Finally, he reached Greenland and was reunited with his father. They lived there for many years.

Erik was proud of his red hair and beard. It was the same color as Thor's, his hero-god. He also shared his pagan god's values. His three sons, Leif, Thorstein and Thorvald held a lot of promise. His one daughter, Freydis, was illegitimate. Leif was the most adventuresome of the sons and sailed off to Norway. While there, he fell under the spell (and the power) of King Olaf Tryggvason in Trondheim, who had him instructed in the Christian faith and baptized. Leif really didn't have much choice. Olaf was a determined evangelist. But it was an opportunity for him to get ahead.

When it was time to return to his family, the king said, "You are to go to Greenland on a mission for me, to preach Christianity there." Leif was more than a little alarmed to face his Thor-worshipping father with such news. He told the king that it would be a hard task. But the king replied that he had not seen a man better fitted for the job, saying, "You will bring it good luck!" That's how he got the name "Leif the Lucky." The king also held several hostages and sent "protection" to insure the success of the mission.

Leif's mother, Thjodhild, became a quick convert and had a church built near her house, under the rule of a priest sent by the king.

His brothers also accepted the new faith, but Erik remained a staunch pagan. To him, the new religion threatened the very foundation of Viking society. Thjodhild, his wife, refused to live with him again. That was his penalty for "unbelief." It may also have been her revenge for Erik's illegitimate daughter.

Leif was burning with curiosity about the new land which had been sighted by Bjarni Hjerulfson. He bought Bjarni's large ship and assembled a crew of thirty-five. Leif begged his father to lead the expedition. Erik, however, pleaded that he was too old, but was finally persuaded. On the way to the ship, his horse stumbled and Erik fell off, claiming that his foot was injured. Turning to Leif, he said: "You, my son, and I may no longer travel together." He was talking both about voyages and religion. Erik remained a loyal pagan to the end. This meant he couldn't be buried with his family in the consecrated ground of the church cemetery.

Erik had some admirable qualities and some not so good. But there is no doubt that he was a brave man and a good colonizer. The communities he established lasted about 400 years. Then they disappeared during the "Little Ice Age" of the fifteenth century. But without his courage and adventurous spirit, "Vinland" may never have been discovered and Columbus may not have taken his journey westward in 1492. There is a claim that Columbus spent time in Iceland gathering information about Vinland before sailing off to the "New World" which has become a home for so many of us.

CHAPTER

6

THE TALE OF THORFINN KARLSEFNI

When Leif Erikson could not make a second voyage to Vinland, the leadership for the explorations fell to Thorfinn Karlsefni. One the most distinguished of the great Norsemen, he had descended from an illustrious line of Danish, Swedish, Norwegian, Irish and Scottish ancestors. A cousin of Leif, it has been claimed that they were both distant cousins to George Washington. He belonged to a select group that they called "Great Vikings," since he was the master of a ship which had crossed the ocean and had become wealthy from his trading voyages.

A hundred years earlier, these Norsemen would have obtained their wealth by raiding monasteries and churches, but since the coming of Christianity to Norway, Iceland and Greenland, they now became rich through trading. They used to endure by "Thor's luck," now they sailed with "Christ's help."

Some historians claim that Thorfinn Karlsefni was the greatest of all the Norsemen, even greater than Leif Erikson. His accomplishments would not dispute this claim. Leif lent him his buildings in Vinland and he set sail with men, women, cattle, sheep and pigs. It should be noted that a thousand years ago, these animals were only about half the size and a quarter of the weight of those today. Selective breeding has greatly increased their size.

When they arrived at Leif's Shelters, it wasn't long before the "Skraelings" (Native Americans) came to trade with them. Just as the bargaining was going good, Thorfinn's bull came charging out of the trees, bellowing loudly. The visitors fled with their bundles of fur and other skin wares, but returned in a short time again for business. The one thing that Karlsefni would not trade to them was weapons. They treated the Indians to a taste of milk and they were so utterly taken by it that they gladly gave up all their valuable furs for another taste. After this episode, they built a strong fence around the encampment and a palisade around the main house.

Thorfinn's wife, Gudrid, an unusually beautiful and talented woman, gave birth to the first European child born in the New World. They named him Snorri. When I first read about this in the sagas, it hit me like a thunderbolt. I was reared on a farm in southeastern North Dakota and had been active in 4-H and farming. Among the County Agents in our area were two brothers of Icelandic descent named Thorfinsson, one of whom was named Snorri, after the first European born in this land. I'm still impressed with the connection.

It was inevitable that an armed clash would come between the Norsemen and the Skraelings. It happened one day when a Skraeling tried to steal some weapons and was killed. Knowing their fear of his bull, Karlsefni used the animal to charge into the enemy camp. It produced the desired effect.

Exploration of the new land was the Norsemen's chief interest. They spent four winters in Vinland, with part of the group tending Leif's Shelters, and the rest searching the coastlands. They were careful never to allow those who went on ahead to get too far away. King Olaf Tryggvason had given Leif two Irish slaves that were swift runners. They were loaned to Thorfinn for exploration. After scouting forty-eight hours, they'd return with grapes, wheat and other discoveries. One expedition, led by Thorhall (a Thor worshipper), became lost and landed on the west coast of Ireland where they were enslaved and killed.

Frederick J. Pohl has identified the New York harbor as one Thorfinn's points of exploration. He traces their journey past the coasts of New Jersey, Delaware, Maryland and Virginia where they looked in on every bay and river. One of these, Pohl claims, was the

James River, the site of an English colony 600 years later. Journeying southwards, they encountered more natives, some friendly, others not. Where possible, they traded. Once again, Thorfinn's bull ruined the party as he charged out of the woods and the Skraelings fled. This time they returned with a secret weapon of terror. They put a hornet's nest into a skin and flung it with a flexible pole. The noise of the enraged hornet's sounded like enemy war cries.

The Norsemen retreated in disarray at this unexpected turn of events. One of them, however, stood her ground. Freydis, the powerful daughter of Erik the Red, picked up a sword of a fallen countryman and challenged their advance. In good Viking style, she slapped the weapon against her bared breast with such a gesture of defiance that it was now the Skraeling's turn to flee to their boats. It was not easy for these Norsemen to be put to shame by a woman. So they claimed that the enemy's secret weapon came from a supernatural power.

Not everything they reported is easy for us to believe. One of these stories is about a "uniped," a one-legged man who kept following them on shore but escaped their chase. They believed that he had slain Leif's brother Thorvald.

Returning to Greenland and then to Iceland with a cargo of wood and furs made Thorfinn an even richer man. It also inspired many more young men to travel to Vinland. According to the *Greenlander's Saga*, after Thorfinn died and his son was married, Gudrid travelled to Rome and joined a convent.

C H A P T E R

7

LEIF ERIKSON DISCOVERS AMERICA!

Who really discovered America? As a child, I was taught in school that it was found in 1492 by an Italian named Christopher Columbus. There was also a rumor in my home community that a Norwegian had found it long before that Columbus fellow, whoever he was. Recently, Great Britain's Royal Geographical Society reports that a Welshman, John Lloyd, who was trading with the Vikings in Greenland, reached America in 1475 while searching for the fabled "Northwest Passage" to China. Because the trading was illegal, the information was kept secret at the time and later passed on to John Cabot.

Thor Heyerdahl has claimed that Columbus was a navigator on a Danish-Portugese expedition which reached America in February 1477. He based this conclusion on a study of one of the oldest maps of Greenland. It showed two Portugese flags in Norse villages on Greenland. He believes that "the expedition took the men and women of the Norse settlements as prisoners and later sold them as slaves," according to a story in *Nordstjernan*, (July 6, 1995), America's oldest Swedish newspaper.

This can become quite an emotional issue. Andy Anderson, founder and president of the "Leif Ericson Society" in Chicago, began a truth campaign to set the record straight. He published a book entitled *Viking Explorers and the Columbus Fraud*. There is no question in his mind where credit ought to go for finding this New World. In fact, he musters up quite a few arguments to assert that the whole Columbus story is a case of mistaken identity. He claims that the real

"Columbus" was a Jewish seafarer from Spain named Christobal Colon. As you can guess, Anderson is not the darling of Italian-Americans.

What is the case for claiming that Leif got here first? There are three main sources. First, Snorri Sturluson, the famous Icelandic saga writer, wrote of Leif: "He...found Vinland the Good." Second, a story called the *Tale of the Greenlanders*. And third, the *Saga of Erik the Red*. These writings do not always agree on all points. Erik (Old Norse did not have the letter "c"), also spelled "Eirik," was the father of Leif who was called the "Lucky." Erik had been outlawed in Iceland because of his pagan ways with the sword in settling personal disputes. Fleeing Iceland, he established a colony on the west coast of Greenland which grew into 280 farms. Norsemen continued to live in Greenland for over 400 years. That's longer than they've been in North Dakota!

America may have been first seen by Europeans when a Viking boat was blown off course en route to Greenland from Iceland. The Viking ships did not do too well against hard winds with their single sails, though they rode the waves well. The leader, Bjarni Herjolfsson, did not stop to explore the land but turned back to Greenland to tell his story to Erik. Leif bought Bjarni's ship and with a crew of 35 set sail westward about the year 1003. Their first landing was among glaciers, probably Baffin Island, which he named "Helluland."

The second landing was named "Markland" or "Land of Forests" and was likely Labrador. The place which lived on in their memories, however, was named "Vineland" or "Wine-Land," because so many grapes were found. On board ship was a German winemaker. He became ecstatic at the sight. Wine was expensive in Greenland because it had to be imported from Europe. Here was a paradise of unlimited grapes and abundant salmon in the lakes and streams. (It has recently been claimed that the word translated "grapes" in the Vinland documents should be translated as "berries." This would remove the objection that the Norsemen were mistaken about the location of their short-lived colony).

Leif returned to Greenland and became its ruler. He is also credited with converting the people to be Christians. Leif himself became a

Christian while visiting King Olaf Tryggvason in Norway. Olaf was an uncompromising evangelist.

The task of colonizing the New World was taken up by Leif's brother Thorvald. All went well at first. But on his first contact with "Native Americans," there was bloodshed. The Norsemen acted arrogantly. One of the natives escaped and returned with an attacking force. An avenging arrow killed Thorvald and the rest fled in their boats. He was the first European to be buried in America.

Besides the saga accounts, is there any other evidence that Norsemen set foot on American soil 500 years before Columbus? Attempts have been made to locate Norse settlements all the way from Hudson Bay to Virginia. But there is only one place which many scholars agree is clearly identified. It's on the northern tip of Newfoundland called "L'Anse aux Meadows." Helge Ingstad, a Norwegian Arctic explorer, began excavating in 1961. His findings were confirmed by Dr. Bengt Schonback, an eminent Swedish archaeologist. Evidence of buildings, jewelry, tools, slag iron and coal have been found.

A much publicized map purchased by Yale University has turned out to be highly controversial. Many claim it's a fraud. In 1898, a stone slab written in runic letters was found near Kensington, Minnesota. It told of thirty Scandinavians who had journeyed inland and met tragedy. Many scholars, however, reject the genuineness of the stone. But this has not discouraged nearby Alexandria from erecting a monument to display for tourists. Perhaps other runic slabs will be found and Leif's claim for finding America will turn up some new wrinkles.

CHAPTER

8

THE "VARANGIANS" IN THE EMPEROR'S COURT

In the world of a thousand years ago, no city was as exciting as Constantinople. It was the center of trade, culture and political intrigue. The Byzantine Empire, as it was called, was based on the belief that it was an earthly copy of the Kingdom of Heaven. Just as God ruled in heaven, the Emperor was to rule the earth and carry out his commands. Byzantium was no democracy, but rather a rigid autocracy in which the will of the Emperor was supreme. It was the dream of every traveller to visit the city which called itself the "second Rome."

The Vikings were there too. They were known as "Varangians," another name for Scandinavians in that part of the world. It was natural that the exotic tales of this city would fire the imaginations of people as far away as Iceland. Anyone who made such a trip and brought home souvenirs was a hero in his homeland.

The Swedes pioneered the travel routes across Russia down into those lands. Their name for Constantinople was "Mikligardur," the "Great City." They came first as traders and later as warriors. Magnus Magnuson calls those Vikings the "super-technocrats of their time." They led the world in metalwork and ship building. They also had a quick eye on how to make money. The modern name "Russia" was actually another name for the Sweden. In those days, Russia was called "Greater Sweden." Once having settled in the cities along the Russian rivers and having built others (for example, Novgorod), they pushed down by the thousands to attack Constantinople.

The Varangians came to trade in furs and slaves. They forced the Emperor to give them these rights. It was not long before they had won a place in the Emperor's court as the "palace guard." Powerful monarchs were always eager to hire mercenaries. The Vikings became the Emperor's elite "enforcers." Emperor Basil II, who came to power in 976, made the Swedes from Russia into a separate regiment of "lifeguards." Even Chinese writers, who visited the "Great City," told about "the tall, blue-eyed, red-haired men" that they had seen. While most of the Varangians were Swedes, many Norwegians were also "soldiers of fortune" among them. They were often given the tasks which were not for the "nice minded."

The military had the highest priority in the Byzantine government. Discipline was extremely severe. Flogging and cutting off the nose or ears was standard punishment for disobedience or cowardice, as well as blinding and execution. An unlucky general might be paraded through the city on a donkey dressed in women's clothes as a mark of shame and disgrace. The Varangians had their own officers that were responsible to the Emperor for which they were paid a salary. "Booty" was one one of the benefits of a military campaign. The Emperor took one seventh, the officers took half of the balance and the rest was given to the soldiers. As you can guess, there would be cheating. The greatest of all the Varangians was Harald "Hardrada." It will take another story to tell about him. See the author's *The Best of the Norwegian Heritage*, vol.1.

CHAPTER

9

SIGURD THE CRUSADER

It's hard to fine a more colorful Scandinavian than Sigurd ("Jerusalemfarer"), son of King Magnus Barefoot. It was an exciting time to be a Christian ruler for those were the years of the Crusades to wrest the "Holy Land" from the hands of the "Infidels."

Sigurd shared the rule of Norway with his brother Eystein. They were only about thirteen or fourteen years old when coming into power. Eystein ruled the north and Sigurd the south. It was decided, however, that while Sigurd was off to wage the "holy war," Eystein should be in charge. It worked remarkably well.

Sailing with sixty ships in 1108, Sigurd first paid a visit to King Henry of England, the son of William the Conqueror, also of Norse descent. Sigurd's crusade does not seem to fit into any of the nine noted Crusades, but he did fight a series of battles with the "heathens" in Spain, Portugal and the islands on the way. (It is not correct to call Muslims "heathens" by today's definition, as they hold a monotheistic view of God. They also had a superior civilization to the Christians of western Europe). According to Snorri Sturluson in his "Sagas of the Norse Kings," Sigurd's terms of peace were: "No man he spared who would not take the Christian faith for Jesus' sake." The people back home responded generously with gifts to support the cause. The crusades were profitable to the victors. Great amounts of booty were carried away in the Viking ships.

Sigurd stopped in Sicily to make Duke Roger into a king. Roger was one of the Norman rulers in Italy and Sicily. In Palestine, he was met by the Christian King Baldwin who spread valuable clothes on the road for the "red carpet" welcome into Jerusalem. Not only was Sigurd given a magnificent feast, but he was given a splinter of the "holy cross" on condition that he would promote Christianity with all his power, secure an archbishop for Norway and collect a tithe. The fragment of the cross was to be placed by St. Olaf's body in Trondheim. This induced many more pilgrims to Trondheim to venerate St. Olaf's relics.

Jerusalem behind, Sigurd sailed for Constantinople to visit Emperor Kirialax. Again precious cloths were spread over the road to impress the visitors. Sigurd had the horses of his royal guard shod with golden shoes and gave instruction that one fall off in public view. They were to act as though nothing had happened. Upon leaving, he gave his fleet to the emperor and many of the Northmen joined the imperial guard. He made his way home across land, being entertained by Christian kings along the way. At age twenty-three, he returned from three years of crusading, the most famous king of the North.

The Crusaders have left their mark in Palestine. I was impressed by the magnificent churches they built and by the ruins of the castles left behind from their 200 year period. The Lutheran Church of the Redeemer in Jerusalem today worships in a Crusader building. When I worshiped there in 1985, the service in the chapel was led by Pastor Calvin Storley of Minneapolis who has Norwegian ancestry. Sigurd would have liked that.

The Crusaders were finally defeated by a Kurdish warrior named Saladin who re-captured Jerusalem for Islam in 1187. While motivated by pious intentions, the Crusades remain one of the greatest scandals in the history of the church. King Sigurd, however, became the most renowned hero of the North. He died at age 40 and Snorri wrote that the "time of his reign was good for the country; for there was peace, and the crops were good."

CHAPTER

10

MARGARET, "MAID OF NORWAY"

Great importance often hangs on slender threads. Such was the case in Scotland as the fourteenth century began. In the days when royal families were the rule rather than the exception, succession to power was often marked by violence. Many times unexpected events occurred which changed the destiny of nations. The birth of Margaret - "Maid of Norway" - was carefully noted by the ruling houses of the North Atlantic. War and peace hung in the life of this little girl.

Margaret's grandfather, Alexander III (reigned 1249-1286), the king of Scotland, had three children, two sons and a daughter named Margaret. His wife, also named Margaret, was the daughter of England's King Henry III. This meant that there was peace on the border of those two countries. Alexander's two sons died childless. His daughter, Margaret, married King Erik II of Norway. Their only child, a daughter born in 1283 in Norway, was also named Margaret. She became the Queen of Scotland at age three when King Alexander died. This Margaret has been remembered as the "Maid of Norway."

Scotland and its surrounding islands were a favorite place of Norwegian adventurers in those days. Large numbers of Norsemen lived in Caithness, Sutherland, the Isle of Man, the Orkneys and Shetland Islands, as well as in the eastern part of Scotland. They came mainly as settlers and traders.

Events of history often do not work out as planned. About twenty years earlier, the king of Scotland wanted to buy the Hebrides from King Haakon the Old of Norway. Haakon refused and the Scots attacked the islands. Haakon responded by assembling a huge naval armada. Norway was the greatest sea power of the North at that time. No decisive battle was fought, but the winter storms came and the scattered fleet sailed home. Haakon died and the new king, Magnus, agreed to the sale. To seal the "Treaty of Perth" (1266), a royal marriage between Norway's Prince Erik and the Scottish Princess Margaret was arranged.

The year 1286 began with frightful storms. Waves up to sixty feet high have been known to have rolled across the North Sea in such times. It was so bad that March 18 was predicted to be the "Day of Judgment." In defiance of this prediction, King Alexander held a royal feast on that date about twenty miles away from his home. On the way home in the dark of night, his horse slipped over a cliff and the king was killed. He had just been married a second time to a French princess named Yolanda. Having no heirs from this second marriage, little Margaret of Norway became the prize that every royal marriage-maker in northern Europe would conspire to catch.

The struggle began. England's King Edward I, Margaret's great uncle, wanted to protect his interests and keep his border peaceful so he could wage war in France. He wanted to arrange a marriage of his youngest son to the young Queen who was then only three years old. His son, also named Edward, was only two. Scotland's ruling classes were assembled to swear allegiance to Margaret on pain of excommunication. But since no woman had ever been the ruler of Scotland, many were uncomfortable with the idea. The king of France, eager to undermine England's power, wanted to protect Yolanda's interests. This alarmed Edward.

It was agreed that Margaret was to sail to Scotland and take up residence as the Queen, although six guardians would run the country - two earls, two bishops and two barons. In May 1390, Edward's ship arrived in Bergen to bring the royal child to England. Erik refused to let her go.

To make certain that Erik would agree to the royal marriage between Prince Edward and child Queen Margaret, Edward loaned Erik 2000 pounds of sterling silver. There was another problem.

According to the rules of the church, this marriage was illegal because they were too closely related. Margaret's mother was Edward's niece. Pope Nicholas IV was persuaded to give his permission and everything seemed all set for Margaret to go Scotland with the support of the English.

In September, the time came for Margaret's voyage to the royal marriage in Scotland. The ship stopped at the Orkney islands which were ruled by Norway. The autumn seas were stormy. Little Queen Margaret, perhaps being homesick, became ill and died in the arms of the Bishop of Bergen who had accompanied her. She was just seven years old.

When news of Margaret's death reach Scotland, the contending parties for power chose up sides. Bloodshed was inevitable. By this time, there were many pretenders to the throne, but it finalized in a contest between two people: John Balliol and Robert Bruce. Both claimed the right of power after Margaret's death.

Robert Bruce is one of the most famous names in Scottish history. He also had Norse blood, having been descended from Lodver, a Norwegian earl of the Orkneys. His ancestors had joined Duke William of Normandy in his conquest of England in 1066. As a result, the Bruces were among the Anglo-Norman elite with the inside track to power. Robert's father had accompanied Edward, while still a prince, on a crusade to Palestine. Robert was known as one of the three "most accomplished knights in Christendom."

After twenty years of destruction and bloodshed, Robert Bruce led the Scottish forces to victory over the English at the Battle of Bannockburn (June 1314). An equestrian statue of Robert stands on the site. Since his death Scotland has been joined to England. An excellent book on the struggles of Scotland in that time is *Robert the Bruce: King of Scots* by Ronald McNair Scott (1989).

For a short time it appeared that the thrones of Norway and Scotland would have a common ruler. Except for the frailty of her health and the stormy sea voyage which struck her down, Margaret might have become the mighty Queen of the North.

The Norwegians and the Scots have a long and interesting history. Edvard Grieg's paternal ancestry goes back to Scotland. And there have been many others. The name Margaret, spelled in various ways and which means "pearl" in Greek, is common to European royalty. There was even a "St. Margaret" of Syria in the third and fourth centuries, but historians are not certain now that she ever existed. "Margaret" came into Scandinavian history from Scotland.

Margaret I (reigned 1388-1405) combined the thrones of Denmark, Norway and Sweden. The present Queen Margaret II of Denmark (since 1972) is highly regarded by her people and throughout the world.

The royal name Margaret also belongs to our family. My paternal great-grandmother proudly bore that name. I never knew her, but a Norwegian historian who did has praised her in a published poem.

The present King of Norway, Olav V, was baptized "Alexander Edward Christian Frederick," combining the names of kings of Scotland, England and Denmark. Then he was given the name of Norway's "eternal king" upon arrival in Norway as a two year old boy.

Can you imagine so much history hanging in the balance of the life of a little girl? Just suppose that Margaret - "Maid of Norway" - had lived. The events of a nation would have been quite different and many lives and much property may have been spared destruction.

A young Queen Margaret ponders her future fate.

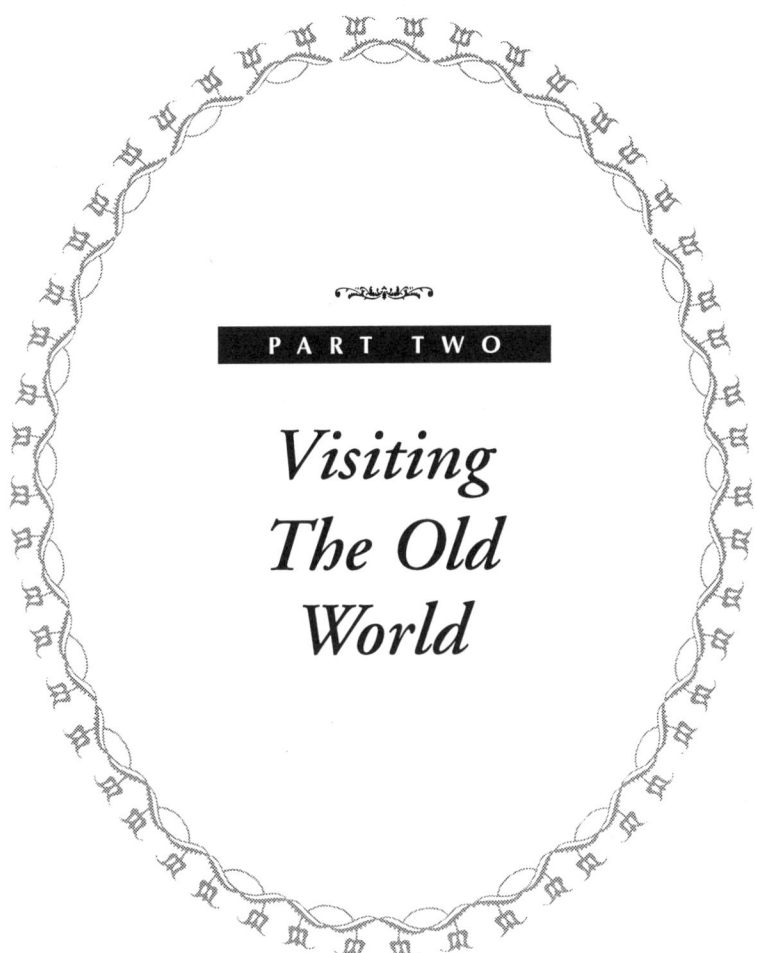

PART TWO

Visiting
The Old
World

11

A CHRISTMAS TALE FROM TELEMARK

The "old times" in Norway, about which we children of the immigrants often fantasize with nostalgia, was in many ways steeped in the Dark Ages. They had, however, a magic that is lost in our world of high technology. They didn't have either our conveniences or world view. They often lived a lifetime in the valley of their birth until the nurturing earth reclaimed them.

It was a world in which the imagination was allowed to grow without the limitations of scientific verification. The woods, valleys, rivers and ocean were alive with mystery. People who lived up in the mountains didn't worry much about world issues. They usually didn't hear of them until they had become history. Their world was often limited to a sojourner who lived by his ability to tell stories which regaled the listeners and held them spell-bound through the long and dark hours of winter.

The story of Jon of the Black Croft (a croft is a small enclosed field) is such a tale set in the mountains of Telemark, to the northwest of Skien. The magic of the tale centers near Morgedal, one of the beauty spots in that land of the North.

Jon's father had built his cottage on a high plateau overlooking the prosperous valley below. The farmstead consisted of a cottage, a low stable and a hay shed. Above the buildings were forests of fir trees. Like so many others, Jon's father went to the Lofoten Islands to risk his life in the hope of getting a good catch of cod.

Normally, the fish didn't start to run until the New Year, but sometimes they were lucky and the catch would begin a few weeks before Christmas. They called this "Advent fishing." The seas were often stormy. Many a man and boy did not return to home and family again. As a reminder of those out at sea, a model ship was hung above the nave or chancel in the parish church.

Jon's father also took to peddling and trading in the years of his youth before settling down to wife and child. Jon's mother had now been a widow for many years and she feared for her son's future with the poor catch of cod in the Lofotens. The drought and poor prices for produce offered no encouragement either. But she kept on working, making clothes of "vadmel," homespun cloth. These could be ornamented with silver buttons fashioned from coins.

Jon's mother wanted him to emigrate to America where so many of their relatives had gone. But since she would not go along, Jon would not go either. Nothing she could say would persuade him otherwise.

He half-believed in the magic of the "old times" that could turn a person's fortunes around. Out of the dim past, the Nokken, Hulder and Fossegrim (sprites or fairies from the rivers, woodlands and waterfalls) might still emerge to dazzle the eyes of a weary traveller with a lovely farmstead if one acted quickly to claim it. His dream was to claim the legend of the "enchanted valley." It could become his if it ever appeared before his eyes and if he would immediately hurl a piece of steel into the wall of the building pictured in the mirage, and then recover the steel while it was still burning hot. The legend of the enchanted valley was an aspiration to people of Jon's time as Eldorado was to Spanish explorers in America.

It was Christmas eve, one of the most magical times of the year. The Yuletide menu at the Black Croft for Jon and his mother was spare that year, the cod harvest yielding hardly a thing. But yet they shared with the pastor and his family such as they had. Jon went into the woods to find trees for their cottage as well as the parsonage, plus some juniper branches to be strewn on the floor for fragrance.

When Jon delivered the tree to the parsonage ("presthus"), he was welcomed cordially, despite their difference in social classes. They did not send him home empty, but filled his stomach with julekakke and fattigmand, favorite pastries to this day among Norwegians. The return trip on skis up the mountain side was slow because he was given a bundle of yule-sheaf (grain) for the birds and a side of pork for his Christmas dinner, plus two silver marks, equivalent to a day's wage in the woods.

It was dark when Jon returned home. His mother was out in the stable milking the cows. Jon finished the chores and gave each animal an extra measure since it was Christmas eve. Legend had it that when the farmer locked the barn that Holy Night all the animals and feathered creatures were given the gift of speech to praise the Christ-Child. Then they went to sleep facing Bethlehem. The wise farmer would also remember the "Julenisse," the jolly bearded Brownie, with milk and porridge, or else a strangled animal might await him on Christmas morning.

On the way from the stable to the cottage, he stopped to look into the heavens for the Bethlehem star, like a lantern in the distance peering over the wooded mountains. Upon entering the cottage, Jon was greeted by the light of the Yule Candle and the fresh scent of juniper.

On Christmas morning Jon was up early to attend matins at the parish church. The rich and the wealthier classes came in their cutters pulled by prancing horses ringing with bells. Skis were the transportation of the poor. Jon racked up his skis and entered the candlelit nave.

As Jon left the church, he met Kirsti, a friend of the pastor's lame daughter, Ingeborg. They hadn't seen each other since confirmation. She had stayed at the parsonage to help with the household duties while being instructed for the rite of passage. But her home was not in that parish.

Several years went by and Jon was now twenty-five, looking for work as he hiking near Morgedal (the home of Sondre Norheim, father of modern skiing). A lost kitten, pure white in color, caught his eye as he travelled in the dusk. It was lonesome and hungry, like Jon.

This formed a bond of companionship. Around the next bend was a farmstead. In the fading light of day he recognized a voice, but not the face.

It had been several more years now since he had seen Kirsti and he could scarcely recognize her at first. The kitten was hers too. It turned out to be a happy meeting as well as a welcome meal. Kirsti's father was unable to do farm work. He walked with a cane and moved about the farmstead with care, his sight having failed. He had advertised for help, but no one responded. The harvest of hay was too much work even for a strong girl like Kirsti to cut, dry and stack, and to feed the cattle when winter came. So Jon found a job waiting for him.

The hay harvest went well until Kirsti hit a rock and bent the scythe. In attempting to straighten it, the blade broke. As they returned to the farmstead, the landscape took on a new appearance before Jon's eyes. It was like magic, the magic of the mountain fairies. Kirsti walked ahead while Jon was held spellbound by the vision. Right in the midst of the glowing sun, Kirsti appeared as radiant as a princess. Was this real or was this an illusion conjured by the Hulders?

Quickly, Jon took a piece of steel from the broken scythe and hurled it into the farmstead. Then he hurried with all his might past Kirsti and her aged father. "Do you believe in the tale of the Enchanted Croft, Kirsti?" he shouted. "If you truly do, then come and help me find the sign. They found the piece of broken blade firmly lodged in the stable wall. It was too hot to touch.

In his excitement, Jon exclaimed, "Now I have won the farmstead, field and the magic princess from the Hulders, Kirsti!" She stood staring at him in amazement, wondering what all this meant. Reality returned to Jon in a moment and he said apologetically to her, "But twas only a fairy tale, Kirsti. This only happens in the world of make-believe that the poor boy wins the prize. Only in storyland does Aske-ladden get half the kingdom and princess to wife. In real life the cotter's son wins only poverty and hard days."

Jon was about to walk away in his disillusionment when Kirsti called: "But wait, Jon. Perhaps it is no fairy tale. What if I told you..."

He turned to look at her again and realized that the legend of the enchanted croft was for real.

It was stories like this that kept life interesting and made the imaginations sparkle in the "old days" of Norway. If you were to visit the enchanting scenery of those mountains, rivers and valleys, you'd begin to wonder, as only children are able, that maybe the fairy tales are true.

I'm indebted to Olav K. Lundeberg's book *The Enchanted Valley - A Story and Legend of Christmas in Telemark in the Old Time*, published in 1937, for this fascinating tale. The book was about to be discarded from a church library in Arlington, Ohio, where my son Paul was interning. Recognizing its worth, he sent it to me in time for my Christmas reading. Keep your eyes open for libraries about to discard old books. You may find a gem.

CHAPTER

12

UP IN THE SETERS

The closest place you can get to heaven in Norway is up in a "seter." It is not, however, to be confused with the "Garden of Eden." The seter is a "summer cheese farm" located in the mountains. A third of the farmers used to have seters.

Farms in Norway are usually small, sometimes less than ten acres of tilled land. Only a few are really large. A hundred acres is a good sized operation. But often attached to the basic acreage, where the farm buildings are located, is an outlying pasture and woods. These also provide a place for hunting and fishing.

In the past, children and old women stayed up in the seter with the cattle, sheep and goats from early spring until freeze-up. This was before school attendance was compulsory. It was a lonesome life and there was plenty of time to think, usually about home. They would also put up hay. There would be a little cottage or chalet called a "hytte" (pronounced "hitta") for shelter and a "stabbur" (pronounced "STAH-bur") for storing cheese, butter and supplies. The stabbur is an unusual looking building set on rock pillars to keep out the rodents.

Seters were previously used only in the summer for grazing farm animals, but today skiers come for winter holidays and especially at Easter. Now that there are good roads, snow removal equipment and snowmobiles, the seters have become very popular. But make no mistake, it can be chilly up there in the winter, forty below or colder. Even in summertime, you'll be glad if you brought a warm woolen sweater. Especially in the evenings.

It's an eerie feeling to be up so high. When travelling in Norway, you are either going up or down and usually there are mountains hovering above. Almost everything is below when you are in the seter country.

These summer pastures are usually owned by a group of farmers down in the valleys. Since grass seeding began only about 200 years ago, it was required to have these outfarms. Farmers were not allowed to keep flocks at home during the summer. That would use up the winter supplies. They still guard every blade of grass growing by the buildings. I was going to see the house in Surnadal where my great-grandmother had lived. Eager to get there, I started walking across the field. My host quickly called me back and said we had to follow the road. All the grass is saved to feed flocks and herds.

We saw some large goat herds up in the summer pastures and signs advertising "geitost" (goat cheese). Some of the people in our group wouldn't miss a chance to eat it, while others simply couldn't appreciate its taste. These summer pastures are an old way of life in Norway, but now many of them are returning to nature.

If you ever visit Norway, be sure to allow some time to travel through these highlands. Then listen to Ole Bull's "Seterjentens Sondag," a song of the "Seter Girl's Sunday." You'll hear her sing: "I gaze on the sun, it mounts in the skies, the hour now for church time is nearing. Ah! would I were home, amid all I prize, with the folk on the highway appearing." She yearned for the church bells, but only heard cowbells. She was lonesome and it would be a long time till freeze-up.

CHAPTER

13

CHURCH LIFE IN NORWAY

There are three significant periods in Norway's church life: The High Middle Ages (1000-1300), the Reformation era beginning in 1536 and the Modern period from about 1800.

Norway became a part of "Christendom" through the conquest of King Olaf Haraldson ("St. Olaf") starting in 1014. In this period, the Christian religion became the law of the land and the church a vast land owner. Dissent was dangerous. Pilgrimages and the crusades were held to be the surest way of gaining salvation.

The Reformation came to Norway first at Bergen through the Hanse merchants from Germany. By 1536, Lutheranism replaced the authority of Rome. The King in Copenhagen appointed the bishops and took over the church lands. He also had St. Olaf's casket removed from Trondheim to Denmark where it is thought that the jewels were removed and the silver melted down for the king's treasury. His remains were buried somewhere either in the cathedral or on the grounds. That ended the cult of Olaf and the pilgrimages to his grave.

The "Great Awakening" of the Norwegian church began with a farmer from southeast of Oslo, Hans Nielsen Hauge. Born in 1771, Hauge grew up in a pious home and parish. It was, however, a brooding and melancholy faith with lots of emotion and sentimentalism. Hauge's problem with that piety was its lack of ethical seriousness.

Much like John Wesley's conversion, Hauge claimed a spiritual breakthrough when he was twenty-five years old, telling him "you shall confess My Name before men." Hauge was faithful to his vision. He preached his message of faith and moral earnestness in every community which he could reach. Though opposed by the authorities, he made a mark on Norway unequalled by any other person, bringing an awakening to the land which deeply influenced immigrants going to the New World.

Until the Oslo University opened in 1813, Norway's clergy were trained in Copenhagen. Among the outstanding church leaders in the 19th century were Prof. Gisle Johnson, Icelandic background; Prof. Carl Paul Caspari, a German Jew who converted to Lutheranism; and Bishop J. C. Heuch, who wrote an excellent book on pastoral care. Norway has had its share of the "liberal" and "conservative" struggle. As a result, two theological faculties in Oslo prepare candidates for the ministry, one independent ("Menighetsfakultetet," "congregational faculty") and the state university.

Foreign mission work has been a passion for the church in Norway. South Africa, Madagascar and China were early areas of activity. The mission societies raise significant sums of money for this work.

Fortunately, the leaders of the church came to an agreement in the 1930s, just in time to be united against the Nazi occupation which tried to control the clergy. The best known leader was Bishop Eivind Berggrav, whose family traced its roots to Germany. A "reformed liberal," he took a strong stand on the church's confession of faith and became a symbol of resistance for the whole nation. Under his leadership, the church took many risks to protect the Jewish minority during World War II. He came to Minneapolis several times during the 1950s for conventions of the Evangelical Lutheran Church which had Norse background.

Despite many predictions that the church of Norway has suffered a demise, my own observation is that the church is deeply rooted in the consciousness of the people and has its greatest influence whenever the nation feels itself in danger.

CHAPTER

14

THE OSLO CATHEDRAL

It was not until adult years that I learned why my home congregation in Colfax, North Dakota, is named "Our Saviour's." Called "Vor Frelsers Menighed" in Norwegian, it took its name from the Cathedral Church in Oslo. The original Our Saviour's Church, consecrated on November 7, 1697, replaced Holy Trinity Church, built in 1630 and which burned in 1686. Before Holy Trinity's time, there was St. Hallvard's, built about 1100 and burned in 1624. In those days, fires were a constant threat to cities.

The present church building has been twice renovated. First redone in 1849-50, the latest renewal was completed in 1950 to celebrate Oslo's 900th anniversary. Two massive bronze doors designed by Dagfin Werenskiold portraying the Beatitudes greet the visitor. The hand carved altar, designed in Renaissance and Baroque patterns, shows the Last Supper and Crucifixion, with St. John and the Holy Mother standing on each side of the cross. At the top is a carving of the Risen Christ flanked by two angels. The pulpit was carved by a Dutch craftsman and was placed in the church in 1699. At the top of the canopy above the pulpit is the King's monogram - C 5 - standing for Christian V. By it are two lions. These carvings have become an inspiration to wood-carvers all over Norway. Woodcarving is a national hobby in this land of forests.

The first organ was built in 1711 by a famous Danish organ-builder, Lambert Daniel Karsten. It was renovated in 1930. In 1976, a new organ was installed which has 87 stops and five manuals plus pedal.

Sixteen stained glass windows are the work of Emanuel Vigeland, a famous name among Norwegian artists. Showing scenes from both Old and New Testaments, they were given as a memorial to those killed in World War II. There are also pictures of St. Augustine, St. Bernard, Luther and Calvin.

The most spectacular art work is on the ceilings. These were completed in 1950. They tell the story of the Bible. The paintings are based on the Apostles' Creed and can be seen from below at any angle.

A small chapel was completed in 1950. One of the stained glass windows was donated in memory of Crown Princess Martha (1901-54), wife of King Olav V.

Our Saviour's Cathedral is probably the most ornately decorated church in Norway. Every detail has been planned to help the worshipper meet Jesus Christ as "Lord of the universe."

In front of the church is a statue of the Danish King, Christian IV, who rebuilt Oslo after the great fire of 1624. Nearby is an open market. But let me advise you, if you go looking for the cathedral, follow your street directions carefully. None of the streets are straight. If you get lost, just walk down hill. It will take you straight to the harbor and then you can start all over again. The clock on the tower was installed in 1718, the oldest in the country and it still works.

If you are in Oslo on Sunday, try to visit Our Saviour's Church for a worship service and stay for a guided tour. It's part of the Scandinavian heritage. It's well worth an extra hour of your time.

Bronze doors at the entrance of Oslo Cathedral.

CHAPTER

15

DISCOVERING NUMEDAL

For years, Numedal was a place in Norway that I could not visualize, though I knew it must be there. It was important to me as the birthplace of Grandpa Hellik (1859-1931), who was born "Thoreson," but who, like so many other Norwegians, took the Scottish name "Thompson" in America.

My dream of visiting Numedal came true in September 1985. It was a beautiful morning as we drove from Oslo past Drammen on our way to Kongsberg where Jorun Teksle, the daughter of a third cousin, met us at the railway station. We followed her through the mountain valleys past the village of Lyngdal until we came to a cozy farm nestled above a valley.

Though they had never seen my wife and myself before, we were greeted as though we had always been the dearest of friends. And as you might guess, we didn't get away from the farm until we had eaten more tasty food than was good for our diets.

Besides meeting our long lost family, the most interesting part of the visit was to see a locally produced movie on the immigration to America. People of the community re-enacted the 1870s and 1880s. It fit right into the time when Grandpa Hellik emigrated to Kassen, Minnesota, in 1877. The movie showed how groups of immigrants formed their wagon trains, stopping by each farm along the way, as they travelled south to Kongsberg. There they re-grouped and got ready for the trip to Drammen to board a ship for the long journey to the New World.

It was a late harvest in Scandinavia when we visited Numedal. Cousin Kjetal Teksle was busy combining. It was slow going because there had been so much rain and some of the heavy stand had lodged. I was impressed with the well kept farms. One of the interesting buildings is the "stabbur." It's a house built of logs set up on rocks (to keep mice from entering) where food and clothing were stored. The top floor was used for summer living quarters. Some of the stabburs are up to 500 or more years old.

It's a strange and fulfilling feeling to trace roots. You look at the faces and see the profiles and likenesses of family in America. The moment we saw Jorun, we knew she was kin. For a moment I almost thought I was looking at my sister Florence when she was in her 20s.

The church is important to these country folks. Every visitor is taken to see the church and to take a walk through the cemetery. Grave stones are pointed out. You start to feel close to people you've never seen whose names are carved in rock. One of the things that impressed me most were the beautiful hand-made bunads (festive dresses) which daughters in the family wear for their confirmations and other important occasions.

If you make such a trip, you should be so lucky as to meet the local historian. On our way to the farm, we stopped to see Sigurd Vinger in Flesberg. His well organized notes will some day become a "bygdebok," a regional history. He asked me to find out more about family who were missing to him because they had gone to America. I asked him how far back he could trace our roots. He said, "to about 1400." That's an awful lot of history to absorb. It's scarry too, you never know what you'll find. But if the ancestors from Numedal were anything like the cousins we discovered on this trip, I'd like to meet them all.

CHAPTER

16

TROLLS AND MOUNTAIN ROADS

If you ever go to Norway, look out for the trolls. I've never actually seen a live one, but there's been so much talk about them that they must exist. The time to be on the alert is after dark.

I thought about this as we left Lyngdal shortly before sunset to drive to Hemsedal, north of Gol in Hallingdal. The distance isn't so far, but the roads are full of sharp curves. To save an hour of time, we crossed over the mountains at Rodberg instead of staying on the main highway through Geilo.

Saving an hour seemed like a good idea, but I had forgotten how sharp and narrow the switchback roads could be. By the time we got to Rodberg, it was pitch black. I breathed a sigh of relief when we had finally twisted our way to the top. But it wasn't over. Then we wound ourselves down until we came to a level road along the Tunnhovd Fjord. We could see farm lights along the way. I felt better by the fjord as I didn't think there'd be any trolls here.

We started to climb again as we took the fork in the road to Nesbyen. Now we were heading into troll country again. I drove carefully down the middle of the road. The last thing I wanted to do was hit one of those fearful creatures. There is no telling what kind of a spell they'd cast on us. A strange object lay on the road ahead. I slowed down, but not too slow. There it was, a large sheep sleeping on the highway. If we could get to Hallingdal and follow the river north to Gol, I figured we'd be safe. Since my earliest ancestors in America came from that valley, the trolls would probably be no danger.

After about three hours of frenzied emotions, we arrived in Hemsedal and found our motel. We hadn't seen any trolls, but we felt that they had been watching us all the way.

If you don't believe in trolls, just read the story of the "Three Billy Goats Gruff." The stories in Asbjornsen and Moe's book, *Norwegian Folk Tales*, illustrated by Werenskiold and Kittelsen, are powerful enough to convince any unbeliever.

Some people bring home troll statues when they go to Norway, but not me. I'm staying clear of them. When Paul Kemper was along on our Scandinavian tour in 1984, he showed great courage by having his picture taken alongside the figurine of an especially ugly one in Bergen. I've heard that trolls tried to get into people's trunks when they emigrated to America. Fortunately, so far as is known, none of them succeeded. People who claim some knowledge of these mysterious creatures say that they are ugly, have humped backs, crooked noses and wear pointed red caps. They live underground, often in fine houses of crystal and gold.

But why do trolls fascinate us humans? It's because they have magical powers, can tell fortunes and are able to make people rich, it's said. The way to scare them off is to play a stereo going full blast with rock music. They can't stand noise. Trolls don't trust anyone either, because Thor used to throw his hammer at them. They're not like the elves, called nissens in Denmark, whom farmers feed at Christmas to protect the cattle.

Ireland has its leprechauns, Germany its poltergeists, France its goblins and England its pixies. But none of them compare to the trolls for pure ugliness. Fortunately, they don't look like Norwegians. Besides that, they have tails. But my advice is, keep your eyes open!

Some friendly trolls.

CHAPTER

17

HOMECOMING TO HEMSEDAL

It was 11:30 p.m. when we arrived in Hemsedal, located about 150 miles northwest of Oslo. Normally it's pretty quiet in mountain villages by this time. But not on the second Monday of September when Norway elects parliament members. Just like Americans, people stay up half the night watching the returns.

It was a close battle. Unlike America, Norway has over a half dozen political parties that run hard races. When the voting is done, they make their deals to see which coalition will elect the Prime Minister. The conservative group, which included the Farmer's Party, barely squeaked through to hold power. The opposition was the liberal coalition which included the Labor Party. One of the big issues was NATO. Everyone I talked to favored staying in the alliance, but grafitti on the Oslo streets read, "NATO UT" ("NATO Out"). When the votes were counted, Norway was still in.

Unlike my other ancestral communities in Norway, we found no kin in Hemsedal. It's possible there may be some fifth cousins, but every known relative either went to America or left no heirs. One surprise is to learn how readily people changed their names a century ago. My great-grandparents from Hemsedal have Ole and Kari Bakken written on their gravestones by Walcott, North Dakota. Back in Hemsedal, they had been known as "Holle." It's not strange then that their children took different names in America. Most of them chose Johnson, except for son John who took Olson. He claimed there were too many Johnsons in the community. His mail kept getting mixed up with the neighbors.

The most interesting discovery in Hemsedal was a place called "Skinnfellgaarden" ("Fleece Court") about two kilometers from the village. It's a collection of old houses from Hallingdal where Vult and Martin Simon carry on a business of producing hand-made clothing from lambskins. You can buy anything from a headband to a full length coat. The unique feature of their product is the "krotingene," the printing on leather with old secret symbols used in Norway about 200 to 250 years ago.

The Simons claim to be the only people who possess the secret of making dye from boiling the bark of alder or birch trees and imprinting it on leather with wooden blocks. I bought a lambskin cap in an old Norse pattern which is unusually comfortable and warm and which weighs little more than feathers. It feels pretty good in North Dakota winters. The "kroting" on my cap is the symbol for life, taken from the picture of the spinal column. It was their belief that life was in the spine. It's my guess that this is an old Viking idea derived from the fact that if a person received a blow on the back with a battle axe, life would depart. That seems likely.

In our homecoming to Hemsedal, we met no one in particular but did catch a good view of the land of my earliest origins in America. It's a beautiful place for skiing, fishing and hiking. Ole and Kari, however, chose the prairies of the New World. I'm glad they did, but wish that mountain valley were a little closer.

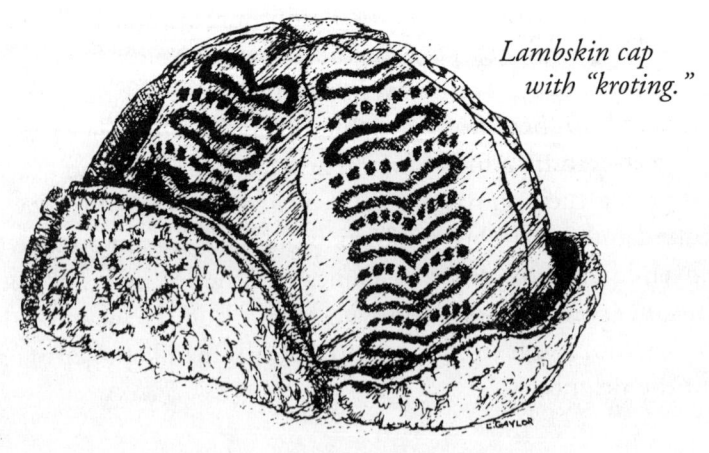

Lambskin cap with "kroting."

CHAPTER

18

JOURNEY TO SURNADAL

The search for "roots" has become a passion for our generation. My quest began long before the eventual journey to my ancestral homeland. There was a problem. We had incorrect information about my paternal grandfather's birthplace. It seems strange that he could have reared a family of seven children and failed to give them such vital information. The record of his death in the state capitol in Bismarck, North Dakota, lists Sunndal, Norway. A visit by an aunt to Norway turned up no trace of roots there.

A chance meeting with Prof. Kris Skrondal of Norway in 1976 renewed the search. We were seated across the table for breakfast at Luther College in Decorah, Iowa. Seeing my name tag, he asked, "Where does your name come from?" I told him that it was from somewhere in the Trondheim area. To my surprise, he said, "I know exactly where it is and have been there many times." Then he drew a map locating "Surnadal." I was not convinced, but it was too exciting to drop.

A couple of months later, a letter came from Prof. Skrondal inviting us to his home in Mosjoen, about 300 miles north of Trondheim. We arrived there in mid June 1977. After a visit to his "hytte" (cottage) near Hattfjeldal (in "Lappland"), we journeyed to Surnadal, a valley about 75 miles southwest of Trondheim.

The road sign at the bridge by Per Moen's store in Sande read "Fiske." Seeing our family of seven travelling in a VW Minibus, the Moens supplied bananas for our snack. Per took us to a Guest House on a dairy farm where Georg Solem lived. I later figured out that he was a fourth cousin to my father. While we prepared our supper in the kitchen, the Solems were watching "I Love Lucy" on TV with Norwegian subtitles. I had not expected my visit to be upstaged by Lucille Ball.

Georg told me that the main Fiske farm should have belonged to Alf Olsen Fiske (1773-1854), my great-great-great grandfather. (I didn't even know that I'd had a great-great-great grandfather.) He told me, "when Alf's mother died, his father remarried. The new wife talked him into giving the farm to her son, Peder." It was news to me. I still had some doubts. It is still remembered as a community scandal. Georg said: "It should not have been."

I was amazed at the fine fields on the Fiske gaard (farm). I thought all the farm land in Norway was poor. Above the door of the farm house it stated that it was built in 1821 by Peder Fiske. It was in excellent condition and the furniture was from the past century. Georg told me that he had descended from Peder and that my grandfather, Ole, and his father had been best friends.

That evening, I stood on a mountainside above the valley, still wondering. A strange feeling came over me. It must be the place! A visit to the nearby Mo Church left no doubts. I was "home" at last. The cemetery was well marked with stones bearing the family name.

Mo Church in Surnadal.

I could hardly wait to get home and tell my relatives about this discovery. What if the inheritance had not been botched? What if my grandfather had remained in the fertile valley of Surnadal? Where would I be today? Surnadal has become dear to my heart, but I'm glad Grandpa Ole immigrated to America.

CHAPTER

19

AT THE "PRESTHUS" IN ORKDAL

Orkdal is a peaceful valley by the sea, about twenty-five miles southwest of Trondheim. In the days of the Vikings, however, King Harald I Finehair (Haarfagre) fought a mighty battle with the people. Those that he did not kill, he forced to serve him, including their king. He went on from there to conquer all of Norway.

Our visit in Orkdal was to the "Presthus" (the priest's house). In Scandinavia, people refer to the pastor as a "prest" or "priest." The Sogneprest (head pastor of the valley), Kaare Rogstad, is a second cousin. The presthus in Orkdal is located on the "prestegaard," (priest's farm). The land is farmed by a hired family who live in a separate house. The profits are used to support the congregation.

The visit with Kaare's father, Stephan, gave a special insight into the war years. He had been a railroad conductor. Though life was difficult, he told me that there were many fine German soldiers stationed in Norway and that they were only carrying out orders. Not all Norwegians feel that way. It was interesting to find someone who did not harbor strong resentment to the occupation.

The farm was a special delight to our children because there were horses for riding. It was a modern mechanized farm, but not nearly as large as those in the great plains of the USA.

The house, built of wood, was long and large. One look at it and I wondered about the heating bill. The ceilings were at least ten feet high. The rooms were spacious, with living quarters and an office on the first floor. Bedrooms were on the second floor, with some of them used for guests. Dinner was served us in the family dining room, not the banquet room. It was a cozy setting with a large round table. We were surprised when the dessert (butter brickle ice cream) was passed around in a large serving bowl. "Butter brickle" seemed to be a special treat wherever we visited.

The church was built of stone and seated about 800 people. American tourists come home with a lot stories about church life in Scandinavia, many telling how poor church attendance is. This is not what we saw. The annual national mission conference filled the Orkdal church four times on the weekend that we visited. Among the guest speakers were some from foreign countries. I was impressed.

While Scandinavians do admit to having an attendance problem, tourists cannot really judge the situation, especially in the summer. We don't do too well in America during the vacation period either. I asked about the attendance during the fall to spring season. I was told that in Orkdal it is quite good throughout the year.

There has been a strong interest in world missions and relief by church members of Norway. On the last Sunday of October, a door to door in gathering across the whole nation is taken which amounts into the millions of dollars. To help promote the emphasis on missions and relief, The television stations carried special programs to help bring the message to the people. We learned some encouraging things by our visit to the presthus.

CHAPTER

20

VISIT TO STOREN

My search for roots took our family to "Eggen," about four miles east of Storen, which is about thirty miles south of Trondheim. Our family on my maternal grandmother's side traces its ancestry to the farm's beginnings.

When the "Black Death" struck Norway in 1349, two out of every three people died. Most of the survivors fled from the mountains and went to live by the sea. It wasn't until the 1700s or later that much of the interior was re-inhabited. That is why many of these farms date back to relatively modern times.

Such is Eggen. It presents a sharp contrast to Fiske farm in Surnadal, across the mountains to the west. Eggen is a typical mountainside farm. There is no flat land and rocks are everywhere. People took their names from the farms. My home community in the north part of Richland County, North Dakota, reads like a transplant of Storen. Names like Folstad, Sokness, Gylland, Skarvold (Score), Wollan and many others originate in that area of Norway. Another farm, just a couple of miles east of Eggen is Rognes. Members of that family immigrated to Astoria, South Dakota, and have given distinguished leadership as Lutheran pastors in America.

There was a light rain as we drove over the mountains from Orkdal. Fortunately for us, we found a line of cousins across the Trondelag who telephoned ahead to arrange our next visits. Driving to farms one has never seen before can be a test, especially over narrow mountain highways. Besides, there are a lot of emotional energies burned up when searching for roots. We knew, however, when we had arrived at Eggen. Cousin Ole was waiting by the mailbox holding an umbrella and a miniature American flag. He didn't speak a word of English. Neither did anyone else in the household, except for a daughter-in-law. It helped that my dialect is from that valley.

We were greeted at the doorway by Anders, the patriarch of the farm, a cousin to my father. I had been told that he looked a lot like my father who had died in 1969. But I was unprepared for what I saw. He was an almost perfect "look alike." I was so stunned that I became speechless and could hardly look at him. In silence he handed me a picture of my father's family. It was taken in 1917, just before Uncle Olaf went off to the war in France, from which he did not return.

A short distance away was a two story house built of hewn oak logs, seven or eight inches thick. I guessed it to be about 200 years old but it looked as solid as the mountains. It had been home for many generations of my maternal grandmother's family and is still in use. In such situations, one stands in awe. All of a sudden, the past comes alive in the woodwork, the landscape and in the profiles of the present inhabitants.

If you travel to the "Old Country" in search of roots, it will be easier if you are looking for "place" names. It is no guarantee that you will find blood relatives, but it will be exciting. It's harder if your name is Anderson, Jacobson, Johnson, Larson or Olson. But don't give up. And if you ever do find your ancestral sites, you will have one the greatest thrills of your life.

CHAPTER

21

DISCOVERIES IN TRONDHEIM

From earliest childhood, I had heard the wonders of the Nidaros "Domkirken" (cathedral) in Trondheim. A picture of this church, the grandest in Scandinavia, had hung in our living room since 1906. My mother had told me that new work on this building will go on "forever. When I saw it, I'd have recognized it anywhere.

It was an exciting moment to see this historic landmark which dominates the city from every direction. Here is where St. Olaf Haraldsson was buried almost a thousand years ago. I was surprised at the simplicity of the worship service, which showed the influence of Hans Nielsen Hauge. Just to be in Norway's first capital, founded by King Olaf Tryggvason (995) and to walk on its streets, was an awesome feeling.

It's in the homes that the visitor learns the secrets of a city. Fortunately, we had discovered cousins in Trondheim. Gunhild Krogstad, a cousin to my father, proved a most delightful host. She served us rommegrot. To my surprise, our children wanted seconds. In preparation for the trip, we were careful to teach them the polite words of greeting, appreciation and basic survival. My mother had taught them the Norwegian table prayer.

At Gunhild's house, we did it up right. To the tune of the doxology, we stood and sang the prayer: "I Jesu Navn, gaa vi til Bords at spise og drikke paa dit Ord; dig Gud til AEre os till Gavn, saa faar vi Mad i Jesu Navn. Amen." (In Jesus' Name, we go to the table to eat and drink at your word; to you, O God, be praise and to us the gift, so we receive our food in Jesus' Name. Amen.) Tears came to Gunhild's happy eyes when she saw that her American cousins had kept the faith learned in Norway.

We encountered two conflicting theories of what is best to do after eating a big meal. In Mosjoen, Prof. Skrondal had insisted that everyone must take a nap for at least an hour. But in Trondheim, the cousins got up from the table and took us on a brisk five mile hike.

One of the most interesting places to visit in this ancient city of the North is the "Folkmuseet" (Folk Museum). It was quite a shock to see some of the buildings which sheltered our ancestors. Cattle and people lived in adjoining rooms. I especially noticed the low ceilings and the short beds. The windows were few and small and did not have clear glass panes. The most interesting building of all is the "stabbur." It is a storage shed built of logs where food and grain are kept and is set on pillars of stone. The front step is at a distance from the threshold. This is how they keep mice out of their supplies.

The visit to Trondheim was returned to our house in Minot, North Dakota, in October 1983. Four of the kin came to attend the Norsk Høstfest, including Gunhild. It was her first trip to America. The highlight was to attend the banquet honoring Princess Astrid. We learned, however, that such company was not new to her. Twice before she had dined with King Haakon VII and King Olav V, when her husband had been honored for his lifetime of service as a sculptor on the cathedral. They liked the Høstfest's musical entertainment too, and thought Myron Floren was the "greatest."

C H A P T E R

22

A SURPRISE IN HATTFJELDAL

It was a cool and sunny morning when we boarded the train in Trondheim for the 300 mile ride north to Mosjoen. Snow capped mountains and green valleys surrounded our journey. We were met by our host, Inspektor Kris Skrondal, the Superintendent of schools in the area. After feasting on a meal of boiled salmon, we prepared to travel to his "hytte" (pronounced "hitta," meaning "cottage") near the Swedish border.

The trip took us through Hattfjeldal where the Samis ("Lapps") were holding a convention. They were easy to identify in their bright red clothes. We saw no tourists in this area. Norwegians moved back into the valley in 1823, 474 years after the "Black Death" struck the land.

The hytte was located in a narrow valley south of Hattfjeldal called "Susnadal." Only one road led into it. To get to the hytte, we had to portage our bags and supplies over a high swinging bridge. Below was the "Sus" river. It flowed with a fierce torrent. That is why it is called the "Sus," which means a "hissing sound." Huge slabs of slate were piled along the banks.

The valley was lush green in color and was humid and warm. Above were mountains that looked like they could be climbed in an afternoon. We accepted the challenge. It wasn't long before we reached the snow level. The water in the mountain streams was the purest that I've ever tasted. It had melted from the glaciers above. Then we reached the level where there were no trees, only rocks and wind. We pressed on but soon realized that this called for winter clothes. Snow flurries became a blinding blizzard at times. And everytime we thought we had the crest in sight, a new ridge of mountains appeared. Our son, Mark, made it to the top and planted a stake. I returned below for a sauna and a plunge into a stream that came down from the glaciers. The near freezing water was a shock.

The language of this isolated valley was very difficult. It may just have been the dialect. One day a man stopped by who looked after the hytte in Skrondal's absence. The next day, we saw him again while driving on the road. Another man and woman were with him. Our host told us that the woman was married to both men. That was a new encounter for me. We asked how the community felt about this. He assured us that they were accepted by the people of the valley, but that it was the only situation of its kind known to him.

As we returned to Mosjoen on St. Hans Eve (June 23), bonfires covered the mountain sides in every direction. This is their custom on the night before the first day of summer. They stay up all night and have a big party. We were near the Arctic Circle where the sun made just a little dip below the mountains and soon reappeared.

We have never forgotten that beautiful valley with its torrential river, the swinging bridges, the reindeer herds and strange customs. If I ever get to that part of Norway again, I'd like to see it one more time. Besides that, they serve the best rommegrot I have ever tasted.

CHAPTER

23

WHO ARE THE "LAPPS?"

The first time I saw a "Lapp" was in Hattfjeldal, a Norwegian city near the Swedish border, a short distance below the Arctic Circle. There was no mistaking these people in their bright red clothes. There are only about 37,000 Lapps in the world and they live in the frozen regions across the north of Norway, Sweden, Finland and the Soviet Union. Twenty-two thousand are in Norway and 10,000 in Sweden. We later met a beautiful girl in Helsinki who had a Lapp grandmother.

The Lapps call themselves "Samek"or "Samer." They prefer the name Sami in America. The word "Lapp" may once have been a term of contempt. They are small of stature, quick of movement and have a Mongol appearance. Their language is related to Finnish. Four groups of Lapps are identified: Mountain, Forest, River or Lake and Sea Lapps. The Mountain Lapps have changed the least through time. (They don't have television!) They are totally nomadic and have large herds of reindeer.

Reindeer hides are a big sale item in the department stores and in the open market places. If you travel on highway E-6 in the summertime between Trondheim and Oslo, you will find a Lapp encampment near Dombas in the Dovre Mountains. It's their way to get in on the tourist trade. For about $35 you can buy a beautiful hide.

In ancient times, Lapps were thought to be connected with witchcraft. Viking warriors wore protective leather armor tanned by the Lapps. It withstood the blows of both sword and axe. Lapps were also thought to cast spells and curses on people. One could not be too careful around them. In Knut Hamsun's "Growth of the Soil," a Lapp caused a child to be born with a hare-lip. Cunning minds made up for their smallness of size.

The ancient religion of the Lapps was "animistic." They believed that "spirits," capable of being good or evil, lived in nature. Sacrifices were made to oddly shaped stones. Bears were venerated because they stood on their hind legs and for their assumed wisdom. The "intermediaries" in religion were called "noaides" and used drums to produce seances. By means of ecstatic trances, noaides traveled to the other world for help.

Some Lapps became Christians as early as the thirteenth century. It was not, however, until the eighteenth century, in the age of "pietism," that the conversion of the Lapps to Christianity became a serious undertaking. Thomas von Weston, a Norwegian pastor, was called the "Apostle of the Lapps."

In Sweden and Finland, a Christian movement called "Laestadianism" developed. Named after Lars Levi Laestadius, a Swedish Lapp clergyman, the Laestadians declare "absolution" to each another during the worship service. Their meetings become highly emotional. They do not use loudspeakers for preaching as they believe the Holy Spirit speaks only through the natural voice.

After the "Black Death" (1349), northern Scandinavia was abandoned by its regular inhabitants. The Lapps and their reindeer moved into this vacuum and were the only people until the 1820s in some areas. Formerly exploited with unjust taxation, the Lapps are now given government protection and public education. If you ever travel in "Lappland,", keep your eyes open, you may see some of these interesting people and their reindeer.

In recent years, some Norwegians have discovered that they were really Sami. Some of them told their families that they were "Black Norwegians" and preferred to conceal their Sami identity. Many of these folk now have accepted their new ethnic identity with great interest.

CHAPTER

24

A Short Stop In Oppdal

Trains are a good way to travel in Scandinavia. Not only do they run on time, but the the cost is reasonable. The government subsidizes them so that fewer automobiles will be needed. The train ride from Trondheim to Oppdal is about seventy miles and is uphill all the way. The climb continues over the Dovre Mountains and past Dombas. Then there is a steady descent through Gudbrandsdal all the way to Oslo.

Our visit to Oppdal was an unexpected delight. Johanna Korsnes, a cousin to my father, and her husband, Fredrik, were retired sheep ranchers living on their farm near Driva, about ten miles south of Oppdal. Two taxis met us at the depot for our ride to the farm. Since taxis in Norway are not limousines, we could not take our luggage along. We were advised to stack everything in a corner, "No one will touch them." Though there was no choice, I was more than a little skeptical.

When we arrived at the farmhouse, Johanna, named each of us seven travellers as we entered. We had sent her our names, but I still don't know how she did it. I was impressed. Looking toward the west from the farmyard, I saw more snowcapped mountains than I could count. It was June 27. Below were green valleys.

We were served a full Norwegian dinner of which roasted lamb was the main course. It was a delicacy. I inquired if they had butchered a lamb from their flock. "Oh, no," was the reply. "We bought it at the meat market in Oppdal." "But why," I asked, "do you do that when you raise sheep?" The answer was simple. "We can buy fresh meat at the market for less than we are paid for live lambs." They explained:

"It is because the government takes money earned from petroleum and subsidizes the farmers. Otherwise, all the farmers would want to move to Stavanger and work for the oil company." With only three percent of its land agriculturally productive, Norway can't afford to lose its farmers.

We talked about their "socialism" with its free medical care, university education and liberal benefits to the retired and handicapped. I asked, "Do you think it would work in America?" "No," was the answer, "because your country is too divided. In Norway we are one nationality, speak the same language and are all loyal to the king."

We talked about America too. Some of the family had lived in the States for a while. In all the world I cannot imagine that America has friends more loyal than in Scandinavia. Even though the politicians may voice disagreements with our foreign policy, the people know that their freedom is dependent on a strong USA. They are well informed on news from the New World.

Soon it was time to return to Oppdal and board the train for Oslo. The taxis were on schedule to pick us up for the midnight departure (though it wasn't dark). Sure enough, our belongings were just as we had left them. Not a thing was missing or had been touched. It was a short stop, only eight hours, and the taxi fares cost forty-five dollars. But it was well worth it. Meeting long separated relatives, the delicious lamb roast, the view of the mountains and a briefing on the Norwegian economy has not been forgotten.

25

A JOURNEY THROUGH NORWAY'S WESTLANDS

If you want to see nature in its rugged best, join me on a trip through the Westlands of Norway. As we go north to Stavanger, with the ocean on our left and rocky fields on our right, we see stone fences built between fields. As we get closer to this city called the "Oil Capital of Norway," the land becomes clearer and well built farms appear.

But you haven't seen anything yet. Travelling north from Stavanger to Bergen, we cross four beautiful fjords. Sweaters and jackets are needed. The wind is chilly as we cross the Boknafjord. We lean on the rail and watch the farms on the hillsides. A little later, we go down into the cafeteria for our second cup of coffee and a pastry. It takes about an hour and forty-five minutes to get to the island of Karmoy which has the burial tomb of Norway's first national king, Harald Haarfagre. In the city of Haugesund, we visit Olaf's Church which dates back to Norway's earliest Christian era. Journeying further north, we travel on the the Hardangerfjord and across a heavily wooded island called Stord. After more ferry rides, we finally arrive at Bergen. There we visit the open markets by the harbor where fresh fish, flowers, reindeer skins and souvenirs can be purchased.

The ride northeastward to Voss takes us through twenty-nine tunnels carved in rock. Some of these are a mile and a half long. The cost for building such highways dazzles my mind. As soon as we are through the tunnels, a new engineering wonder appears, switchbacks. Here the road takes us over the mountains instead of through them. No roller coaster compares with the thrill of these highways which switch back and forth on the mountainside. We look downwards for thousands of feet before finally going over the top. The bus can't always make the turn. We hold our breaths while the driver backs up a bit and then moves onward. We meet other cars and busses. Someone has to pull over or back up. We're grateful for a calm driver and the Volvo motor coach with its well tuned engine and its air brakes. The most exciting of these switchbacks is "Trollstigen," meaning "troll stairs." Our tour guide, a theological student, plays "Ave Maria" over the public address system on these roads.

We arrive at Voss, birthplace of Knute Rockne, the great Notre Dame football coach and stop by his statue. Some of our friends fill up on more coffee. By this time, we are using both cream and sugar as Norwegian coffee is the real stuff. Others go to Goldsmed Hoel's jewelry shop for presents to bring home. We cross more switchbacks. We stop to pet the goats up in the seters (high mountain summer ranches). The goats are friendly and love to be fed tobacco. In the distance is Jostedalsbre, Norway's largest glacier.

We see people in bathing suits soaking up the sun on chaise lounges on top of the snow banks. Its lonesome up here. You feel like you are on top of the world. To get down, another set of switchbacks beckons. It's wild country. It's the other Norway and you can never forget it.

Travelling in view of glaciers, we arrive at Balestrand, a favorite vacation place for Germany's Emperor Wilhelm II. Even today German tourists come in large numbers. Across the Sognefjord is Vangsness, the birthplace of Vice President Mondale's great grandfather. The name Mondale, however, comes from nearby Mundal. It turns out that Frederick of Vangsness married Brita from Mundal, moved to her side of the fjord and took her name. There's a rivalry in the valley today. Both places claim him. It's 1984 and people want to know if we will vote for their favorite son to become president. They hope we will.

At Balestrand we attend an English service in St. Olaf's Chapel. It's a good way to begin the week as we travel through breathtaking scenery. At the very top of one mountain range is a quaint red guest-house called "Rorvik Fjellstove." It advertises "Kafe-Rom" (Cafe-Room). We drink coffee and sample pastries while sitting on a balcony overlooking the winding roads by which we have just travelled. Two hours later, we arrive at Skei where we buy homemade woolen gifts to take home. We save the sixteen percent tax by having our purchases shipped to America. While eating lunch at the hotel, we visit with the owner, Jon Skrede, who was a member of the "Fjellklang Spele-mannslag," a local orchestra which had played at the Høstfest in Minot.

At the end of another day of spectacular scenery, we come to Hornindal where rummagrot is a part of our buffet dinner. We cross the Geiranger Fjord, the most photographed place in Norway. We see a Soviet passenger ship. I decided to tease our Norwegian tour guide by asking, "What are the Russians doing in our waters?" Giving me a strange look, he replied: "Your waters?" "Yes," I said, "we're all Nor-wegians here." We spend a night in Molde, Norway's "City of Roses." Then we travel eastward through Surnadal on our way to Trondheim. Please excuse my excitement as we go into this valley. It was here that my ancestors lived near Mo Church for hundreds of years until "Amer-ica Fever" carried Grandfather Ole off to the Red River Valley.

Finally there is Trondheim, the ancient capital. Unlike the Viking days, its harbor is serene and peaceful today. The center of attention is Nidaros, the great cathedral. It's the largest and most famous church in Scandinavia. Here St. Olaf was buried. Before the Reformation, pil-grims came from many lands to see his jewel-laden casket and to seek healing from his remains. Under the Lutheran rulers, the casket was moved to Denmark and melted down into crown treasury. The relics have disappeared, but people still come to visit. Olaf the Saint's body is reported to be secretly buried somewhere in the building. The stat-ues of biblical characters alone are worth seeing.

The old parts of many cities are being restored. New modern sub-divisions, however, are being developed. There are no skyscrapers. We don't have to strain our necks to see the tops. Besides, who would want to hide the landscape?

Norway is a place of endless beauty, but we just hadn't seen its full grandeur until we have travelled through the Westlands. I hope you can see it for yourself sometime.

A fjord scene in Western Norway.

CHAPTER

26

MOLDE, "CITY OF ROSES"

It was on an August Monday afternoon when we arrived in Molde, the "City of Roses," on Norway's west coast. This community of 21,000 people barely survived the ravages of World War II. All but a few scattered houses in the center of the city were destroyed.

The Allied forces were undefeated when the British and French evacuated their forces for the defense of their own homelands. Enemy aircraft struck day and night to destroy Norway's struggling army at the end of April 1940. King Haakon VII barely escaped from Molde on the British cruiser Glasgow amidst burning docks and buildings. The Norwegian troops were left behind without weapons or supplies to hide in the countryside or be captured. This is still a sore spot in the memory of Norway's Resistance fighters. They felt betrayed by their allies. By May 1, the fighting was all over.

Today Molde is a peaceful place, having been rebuilt into a beautiful and modern city. It's located in one of Norway's most scenic tourist areas. I enjoyed walking down to the docks and watching the huge luxury liners come into port as they travel between Oslo and North Cape above the Arctic Circle. Some day, I'd like to get on one of these boats and visit all the coastal cities. Molde, however, is in an area with beauty uncommon even in a country which is famed for its scenery. Roses have been planted to help forget the war years and they grow everywhere to gild this lily of the North.

We were fortunate. Ocean clouds often roll in to darken the skies of Central Norway, but we saw the region in bright sunshine. The air felt clean, as if it were filtered. Out in the surrounding countryside of fjords and mountains is an unspoiled vacation land enjoyed in both summer and winter. Hiking and skiing are popular pastimes especially in these parts. Off in the distance, the snow covered mountains glisten whenever the sun shines. You can spend a whole day in one spot and have a change in the scenery every few minutes as the sun circles around the horizon.

The Town Hall with its copper facade stands in the center of Molde. There you will see a statue of the Flower Girl with her basket filled with roses. The Romsdal Fellesbank (community bank) stands at the main corner of the business district, covered with ivy. Nearby is the Veoy Church which stands as a symbol of faith in the heart of the community.

An annual jazz festival is held in the summer. Folks dancers come to perform for large crowds. Besides these, theatrical productions, music, art and a large selection of sporting and recreational activities make Molde a virtual paradise.

Sailboats in the bay make a beautiful picture. There is also a Fisheries Museum. Visitors can get a vivid impression of the difficult life of the coastal fishermen. Fishing boats are displayed which once provided the catch for Norway's large export of fish.

If you travel in this area, be prepared to use the ferry boats. Each county runs its own transport system. They operate efficiently and on time, with the aid of government subsidy.

Molde is about 150 miles southwest of Trondheim, the main Norwegian city north of Oslo and about forty miles south of Kristiansund. About twenty miles north is the village of Farstad. This had special interest to my friend Idar Farstad of Minot who was on our tour. Cousins met him in Molde and took him to see his father's birthplace.

If you go to Molde and don't have relatives to host you, I recommend eating at the Alexandra Hotel. Better food you can hardly find. But don't be in too big a hurry to move on, stop to smell the roses.

CHAPTER

27

A VISIT TO THE BERGEN AQUARIUM

We humans come in a variety of sizes, shapes and colors, and think of ourselves as pretty special in God's eyes. But we are alike to the point of being boring in comparison to the almost endless variety of life forms that live in water. I learned a lot about this from my visit to the aquarium in Bergen, Norway.

After 10 years of planning and building, the Bergen Aquarium was opened in 1960. It's located at Nordness Point, formerly a strong fortification, and about a fifteen minute walk from the "Bryggen," which used to be the headquarters of the Hanseatic League in western Norway. Nearby, in the midst of the old military installations, is the Institute of Marine Research. It's a 10-story building, containing about 100 offices and laboratories. You can also see a place called "Witches Hill," where Anne Pedersdotter and others were burned at the stake.

Bergen has one of the few aquariums in the world that has unlimited supplies of clean, natural seawater. About 800,000 gallons a day are pumped from about 500 feet deep in the nearby ocean. It's not necessary to filter it as the undercurrent off Nordness Point constantly keeps it renewed. About five miles of pipelines, built of neutral plastic materials, bring both fresh and salt water to the aquarium.

Nine large tanks on the upper floor and forty-two smaller displays on the lower floor give an idea of the many kinds of fish which surround Norway's long coast line. The outdoor pool contains seals, porpoises and walruses.

Light, air and water are essential to all life and these are adequately available in this aquarium. When walking through it, you get the feeling of being beneath the surface of the water because the glass in the side walls is at a 135 degree angle. This hides the glass from the viewer.

We first visited the cod family. Mixed in were varieties of catfish. Diagrams were displayed to show where these fish can be caught along Norway's coastline and how to catch them. I'm amazed at how "scientifically" these creatures are designed. Our modern submarines and aircraft have nothing on the sophisticated equipment built into a codfish. Its pelvic fins are used to find food on the ocean floor. It can detect prey under a flat stone and turn it over. The lateral line on the fish is used to detect noises. It serves as an "early warning system" to tell whether the vibration comes from an oar, the surf or an engine. Sound travels five times as fast under water as in the air. Let fishermen take note!

Other tanks displayed fish that live beneath a wharf, on the sandy bottom or in the deep sea. I never cease to wonder at the anemones, sea urchins, starfish and sea cucumbers. I took special interest in the salmon family and flatfish. One aquarium consists of sharks and rays. There are eight species of sharks in Norwegian waters, some of which are too large for an aquarium. One of the nuisances of the ocean is the Conger Eel because it becomes tangled in fishing nets. Sometimes it's mistaken for a sea serpent. The Crustaceans (lobsters, crabs, crayfish and prawns) have so many thousands of species that no museum can include them all. The prawns begin life as males and become females when fully grown.

How long can a fish live? The halibut can live sixty or more years. Herring may get to be twenty-five and cod as old as thirty. Others may be only two or three years. The age of a fish can be read from its scales, its ear stone or vertebrae. Before fish are put into the aquarium, the air in their swim bladders is removed. They are then re-pressurize in the aquarium.

Fish are as different as people. Some are trusting of their feeders, while others take months to become friendly. There is a lot to learn at an aquarium.

The sea, however, is not as safe as it used to be. Humans have dumped so much petroleum, chemicals, radioactive waste and garbage into it that large areas are no longer safe for life. Maybe the fish in the aquariums are the lucky ones.

CHAPTER

28

THE LIGHTHOUSE AT LINDESNES

Lindesnes is located at the very southern tip of Norway. The shoreline is extremely rocky where the North Sea has washed against it for untold ages. At the top of the rock formation is a lighthouse which warns ships as they pass by between Bergen and Oslo.

It was a warm and sunny day when we were there. The wind, however, was blowing a chilly breeze which required jackets as we walked to the top of the lighthouse. To our delight, we saw the SS Norway, the world's most luxurious cruise ship, a few miles out on its way to Oslo.

Down below the lighthouse is a dugout in solid rock. During World War II, the Nazis had placed artillery there just in case the Allied Expeditionary Forces should try to invade Norway at this point. The guns are gone, but the man-made crater is a grim reminder of those dark days. Up to 425,000 Nazi troops were tied down for the defense of Norway which Hitler might well have wished to have had on the Russian front. The German soldiers, however, much preferred Norway, despite the dangers waiting by its roads. Visitors to Norway today can't help but notice how well "Fortress Norway" was guarded by its unwelcomed guests.

Today Lindesnes is a peaceful place where flowers and heather grow wherever there is soil on the rocky surface. On the way down to the parking lot, there is a kiosk, a little shop, where refreshments and postcards can be purchased. There is also a house by the path where souvenirs are available including a certificate that will be signed by an attendant. It certifies that you really visited this most southern point of Norway.

Its a long way from north to south in Norway. North Cape is 1100 miles from Lindesnes ("as the crow flies"). The coastline measures 1645 miles with an actual 12,500 miles when the fjords and larger islands are considered. The widest distance across Norway measures 270 miles.

To get to Lindesnes from Oslo, you drive over a scenic highway that travels past Drammen, Tonsberg, Larvik, Arendal, Grimstad and Kristiansand. This includes some of the oldest settlements in the country. As you come near to Grimstad, you will see on the right hand side of the road the farm of Knut Hamsun, a Nobel prize winner in literature. The countryside is lush with vegetation in the summertime. There are plenty of rocks in southern Norway, but when you get to Lindesnes you realize that the community is built on solid rock. The road past Flekkefjord and Egersund leading to Stavanger and Bergen has some extremely rocky areas.

On your way to Lindesnes, be sure to visit nearby Kristiansand. It's a good place to buy fresh fruit and flowers as you travel. It has a charming open air marketplace and a stately cathedral right in the town square. It's a few more miles and takes a couple of hours to visit this scenic place, but it is well worth it. Brave warriors and kings have climbed these paths. If you close your eyes for a moment, you can almost imagine that these mighty men have come back for another look at the beautiful ocean that glistens in the sun. You'll never forget it.

CHAPTER

29

OSLO,
FRIENDLY CITY OF THE NORTH

The most picturesque approach to Oslo, Norway's capital city, is by boat. As you travel up the Oslofjord from Denmark or Germany, Sweden is clearly visible on the right and Norway on the left. The shorelines come closer together and the houses appear in beautiful settings on the mountainsides. Finally, there is Oslo harbor, with the most temperate climate of any capital in northern Europe.

In spite of its far north location, the temperatures in Oslo are pleasant even into October. During the winters, however, sunlight becomes scarce, especially in the valleys. But in the summer, it never gets entirely dark during the days of the "midnight sun." The longest day of the year is celebrated on June 23, St. Hans' Eve or the "Birth of John the Baptist." People light bon fires and many stay up all night to celebrate.

Oslo began as a tiny trading community in 1048. It grew quickly because of its fine harbor. The mountains to the north give it protection from the Arctic winds and the sea to the south brings moderating temperatures from tropical currents. Fire has destroyed the city many times.

In 1624, the Danish ruler, King Christian IV, rebuilt the city close to the Akershus Castle (built about 1300) and renamed it "Christiania," after himself. In 1925, the old name "Oslo" was restored.

When Norway became free of Danish rule in 1814, Sweden's kings became their monarchs until 1905. They agreed, however, to respect Norway's new constitution of May 17, 1814, and to establish Christiania should be Norway's capital. So the king had a parliament in both Stockholm and Oslo, but he rarely ever appeared in Norway. Today, one out of every eight people in Norway lives in Oslo, about 500,000 of them. It's recognized as one of the world's most beautiful capitals.

Several things impress me about Norway's chief city. First, it has a vivid sense of history. The name of almost every street has a part of Norway's "who's who" written into it. Whether it is "Karl Johans Gate" (pronounced "gahtah" and means "street"), Halvdans Svartes Gate," "Ibsens Gate" or "Gyldenloves Gate," whole volumes could be written about every man after whom a street is named.

Second, the neatness and cleanliness of the city is impressive. There is also the feeling of personal safety as one walks the streets. This is rare in the large cities of the world today. I would suggest, however, obtaining a street map which is available free in most hotels and department stores. It's an old city which grew with no anticipation of 20th century traffic and automobiles. There is excellent public transportation to every part of the metropolitan area.

The third thing which my wife (of Danish ancestry) and I find to be enjoyable about Oslo is the people. They are friendly and polite. Their life styles are different from Americans, not having as much emphasis on night spots and eating out. If you stay in a hotel or guest house, your breakfast ("frokost") will probably be included. These, like the ones we ate at the Continental and Bristol hotels, are such a big spread that there is little need for a noon lunch. However, bakeries and coffee shops offer delicious open-face sandwiches and pastries that delight both eye and stomach.

Everyone who visits Oslo should see Frogner Park and the huge life-like granite statues by Gustav Vigeland. Bygdoy Park which contains the Viking ships, a Folk Museum, the Kon-Tiki Museum and more is worth an afternoon, if not a whole day. Conducted tours are helpful, but they usually don't allow enough time at each of these interesting places. Up on the mountainside to the northwest of the city is Holmenkollen, called the most beautiful ski jump in the world. By the harbor is Akershus, the ancient castle, with the Resistance Museum from World War II. The Oslo Cathedral, "Vor Frelsors Kirke"

("Our Savior's Church"), consecrated in 1897, is a work of art on the inside. A statue of King Christian IV stands on a plaza out in front. Lovers of art will want to visit the National Museum of Art and the Edvard Munck Gallery.

Two buildings dominate the skyline: The City Hall and the Royal Palace. The "Syttende Mai" (17th of May) parade travels from the palace to the "Storting" (parliament building) on Karl Johans Gate alongside of the "Student's Park," site of the old university campus.

Norwegians are proud of their capital city. And if you ever visit it, you'll fall in love with it too.

PART THREE

Heroes
Of The Old
Country

CHAPTER

30

NORWAY'S ROYAL FAMILY

Norway's royal family was well known to me as a boy growing up on a North Dakota farm. A large picture of King Haakon VII and Queen Maud, together with the ministers of state and the Domkirken (cathedral) in Trondheim, dominated our living room wall. Only later did I learn about George Washington and Abraham Lincoln. The picture now hangs in my house as a reminder to our children and grandchildren of their heritage.

It was November 25, 1905, when the new king and his family arrived in Oslo to begin a reign of almost fifty-two years. Just a week before, the Storting (parliament) had elected Denmark's Prince Karl to be the first real king of Norway in 525 years. Ninety-one years of rule by Swedish kings ended in a political impasse. Oscar II gave up his claim to Norway in frustration.

It was not a foregone conclusion that the new Norwegian Government would be a monarchy. Many leaders had "republican" sympathies and wanted a president. Two reasons prevailed to elect a king. First, it was tradition in Norway to have royalty. Second, most of Norway's neighbors had kings and this would make for peaceful borders.

Prince Karl took the name of Haakon VII. The Haakon VI (1350-1380) had been Norway's last "Norwegian" king. When he died, his Danish born queen, Margaret I, controlled the government until her death in 1412.

The new king brought the world's oldest royal family line to Norway. King Haakon had descended from Denmark's King Gorm (died about 940). The earlier Norse kings had descended from the Swedish

"Yngling" family. They appear to have been driven out of Sweden and moved to Norway in search of a land to rule.

The new queen, Maud, was the daughter of England's King Edward VII. He did some political arm twisting to influence Norway's decision. Their son, Alexander, was renamed "Olav." Since he was just two years old, he would be reared as a genuine Norwegian. This remembrance of Norway's "saint" king was a good sign for the future. Their royal motto is "Alt for Norge." They have kept their promise.

The new king was dearly loved and many Norwegian-Americans began to name their sons "Haakon," just as they had previously named them "Oscar." During World War II, he worked courageously in England for Norway's freedom.

Crown Prince Olav and his Swedish wife, Crown Princess Martha, were very popular both in Norway and America. She was the great, great granddaughter of King Karl Johan of the French Bernadotte family who had come to Sweden as Crown Prince in 1810. Karl Johan's statue stands in front of the palace in Oslo. In their 1939 tour of America, Olav and Martha were greeted by large crowds of admirers whose respect and enthusiasm was worthy of envy by any president or governor.

When Olav became king in 1958, there could have been a question whether he should be called Olav V or VI. Prof. Karen Larson of St. Olaf College published *A History of Norway* in 1948 in which she had already listed five Olaf's as kings of Norway. When the announcement was made, however, it was as Olav V. The Olaf listed as king by Prof. Larson from 1103-1116 has lost his place in history. (The reader should be informed that the letters "f" and "v" are interchangeable in phonetic spelling. Modern Norwegian prefers "f" to "v" in proper names. That's why the royal name is "Olaf" in ancient times, but "Olav" today.)

Olav and Martha had three children: Princess Ragnhild, born in 1930; Princess Astrid, born in 1932; and Crown Prince Harald, born in 1937. During World War II, Crown Princess Martha and her children were in America, spending a great deal of time with the Roosevelts at their home in Hyde Park, New York. When she died in 1954, Eleanor Roosevelt wrote to the palace in Oslo: "We in this country will not forget Princess Martha. She will always mean to us the finest qualities that a woman can have - courage, patience, kindness and generosity."

Crown Prince Harald was an able understudy of his father, preparing for the day when he will have to become the head of state. Like King Olav V, he is also a sports enthusiast. Crown Princess Sonja has become very popular in the United States from a recent visit. Crown Prince Harald became King Harald V after the death of his father on January 17, 1991.

Midwestern USA was favored with a visit by Prince Astrid (Mrs. Johan Martin Ferner) at the Norsk Høstfest in Minot, NDorth Dakota, October 21-23, 1983. Her visit was to honor the children of Norwegian immigrants who, while loyal Americans, have never lost their deep feelings for the land of their heritage. I watched as the Princess was presented to the audience. There was a hushed silence and emotions ran high. I saw many tears of excitement stream down faces in that crowd of thousands.

Princess Astrid is the mother of five children and lives in Oslo. After her mother died, she often accompanied her father, King Olav V, on visits throughout Norway. She came to the Høstfest as his personal representative. Long live the King Harald V, his royal family and their motto: "Alt for Norge."

CHAPTER
31

HANS EGEDE,
"APOSTLE TO GREENLAND"

Sometimes the questions of little boys drive them to adventures that no one could have imagined. Such was the case of Hans Egede ("EG-gi-der"). He was born Jan. 31, 1684, at Harstad, on an island off the northwest coast of Norway. Hans' father, the Resident Magistrate of the district, had grown up in a parsonage in Denmark.

Life on the island was hard, but it proved a good training ground for Hans' future. Though his parents were desperately poor, they managed to send him to the university in Copenhagen. Norway didn't get a university until 1813. He loved history, mathematics and astronomy and had an aptitude for languages. Combining a fierce determination to learn and a stubbornness that refused to quit what he began, Hans graduated in just 18 months and was ordained before his twentieth birthday.

After his wedding to Gertrud Rasch, Hans was assigned to a little fishing village in the Lofoten Islands. There he remembered stories from childhood about the Norsemen who had settled Greenland 700 years earlier during the days of Leif Erikson. It had been almost 300 years since there had been contact. Were any of them still alive? Hans had to find out. An "inner Voice" told him to go to Greenland and search.

It took thirteen years before Hans got the backing of King Fredrik IV and a group of Bergen merchants who wanted to trade with the Eskimos. The war between Denmark and Sweden could spare no ships or money for the expedition. To prepare for his work as explorer, colonizer and missionary, Hans gathered information on Greenland by talking to sailors.

For fifteen arduous years Hans labored on the west coast of that ice covered island. It was not easy. He won the confidence of the Eskimos, but the "angokoks" (witch doctors) plotted to kill him. Hans called their bluff and put them out of business. He found ruins of ancient Norse settlements, but no trace of the people. Because the Dutch traders burned down one of his settlements and threatened death to Danes, troops were sent from Denmark. This did not prove to be a blessing. Quarreling and drunkenness got the best of them during the long winters. Sometimes they nearly starved before the supply ships arrived in the summer.

Hans began Christian work among the natives and set up trade in furs, whale oil and fish. The hard winters, however, claimed Gertrud's life. Eventually, Hans returned to Denmark where he was in charge of a school to train missionaries for Greenland. He turned down the offer to be bishop of Trondheim. His two sons took over the missionary and trading work and his two daughters married pastors in Denmark.

In Godthaab ("good hope"), the capital of Greenland, a towering statue of Egede stands on a hill overlooking the city. Hans has been called the "Apostle to Greenland" and his family is still dearly loved by the Eskimos. Each time I've flown past Greenland, my eyes have strained for the settlements started by Egede. But from 40,000 feet in the air, all one can see is water and ice.

C H A P T E R

32

HANS NIELSEN HAUGE AND "LIBERATION THEOLOGY"

The struggle of the working classes to break free from economic and political oppression has always been a part of human history. Most such attempts have failed either because of inadequate preparation or by brutal repression of the oppressors. Peasant movements, slave uprisings and social justice movements are not new, but they have received much greater attention in the twentieth century.

One would not ordinarily identify the Norwegian religious reformer, Hans Nielsen Hauge (1771-1824), with "Liberation Theology" of Latin America today. But there are some interesting points of comparison which may come as a surprise to the people who look upon Hauge as their folk hero as well as religious leader.

Liberation Theology emphasizes social justice, freedom from economic and political oppression, and calls for giving power rather than charity to the oppressed. This is in contrast to the classic Christian tradition of concern for liberation from sin and fear of death. Liberation Theology isn't satisfied with better things to come in the spiritual realm. It wants full freedom now in the present secular order. It wants a piece of pie now, not "pie in the sky by and by."

Sometimes Liberation Theology is confused with Marxist Communism because both claim to be concerned about the liberation of the oppressed lower classes. There have been times when Christians of this persuasion have made common cause with Communism, just as the Danish Underground did in World War II to oppose the Nazis. But once the revolution took place, Marxism created a new class of capitalists, as Milovan Djilas wrote in his book *The New Class - An Analysis of the Communist System* (1957).

While Liberation Theology is politically popular in the Third World, especially Latin America, it was also an ideological force behind the Civil Rights Movement in America and the opposition against apartheid in South Africa. The Feminist Movement and concern for the poor white also employs the dynamics of Liberation Theology. Liberation theologians claim that their goal is to liberate the oppressors from their need to oppress.

How does Hans Nielsen Hauge relate to Liberation Theology? I'm indebted to Rev. Kenn Nilsen of Jericho, Vermont, for calling this to my attention in an article he wrote for the *Trinity Seminary Review* (Columbus, Ohio) Fall 1987. Hauge was an activist who believed that Christians ought to be involved in the political process.

That's in contrast to traditional Lutheran quietism, or the belief that the church shouldn't offer direction or criticism to the affairs of state. Hauge became involved in community life and this got him into trouble with the bishops and sheriffs in Norway. It cost him both imprisonment and health, but the movement he started changed Norway to this day and strongly influenced the political views of the immigrants in America.

Hauge was influenced by the pietist movement identified with two German church leaders, Philipp Jakob Spener (1635-1705) and August Hermann Francke (1663-1727). Its goal was to fill the moral and social vacuum following the Thirty Years War (1618-1648) with a theology of the heart rather than the head, and was a challenge for moral integrity and care for one's neighbor.

Hauge was a self-educated farmer from southeastern Norway. He was a hard worker and gifted at manual skills. He also had a good business head. His outstanding skill was as a communicator. When Hauge talked, people listened. He was not a shouting sensationalist, but a serious and quiet conversationalist who drew heart-felt responses out of people. When Hauge was twenty-five years old, while working in the field, he was overcome by a deep spiritual conviction and he believed that it was his life's calling to preach the gospel to all Norway.

There was no lack of religion or preaching in Norway when Hauge began his travels. But the state church pastors educated in Copenhagen during the "Enlightenment" period tended to intellectualize the gospel, including the explaining away of biblical miracles. Some of the sermons preached at the time were entitled, "How to Grow Potatoes," "On Vaccination," and "Love of the Fatherland." A widening gulf grew up between the clergy and the people. When Hauge appeared, the people recognized him as one who spoke with authority.

Hauge's social ideas wouldn't satisfy a liberation theologian today, but they were radical in Norway during his time. He was a firm believer that the church was a people called by God and not an hierarchical structure. More than that, Hauge believed the church was made up of members to be equally valued. This meant that the rich farmer and his poor tenant were to be treated as brothers. He even believed that people should share all their worldly goods. This didn't sit well with the upper-classes in Norway. Most Norwegians were poor. The good government jobs were filled by Danes and Germans who were wealthy friends of the king in Copenhagen. Hauge naively believed that the ruling classes were as concerned about the need for social reform as he was.

Once his eyes were opened to the entrenched self-interests of the ruling class, Hauge wrote: "The worldly minded have become rich and powerful in the world, and by their wicked wisdom have made the good people their slaves while they themselves live in luxury, splendor, and sensuality." He further wrote, "we must encourage the weak." How? Hauge believed that cultivating the soil was the most honorable occupation. This way one did not oppress one's neighbor to gain a living.

Hauge was one of Norway's earliest folk leaders. But he was different from the revolutionaries. He believed that "if individuals, parishes, and states would deal in love with everyone and try to serve them, then peace would be established. All people could use their gifts with diligence to earn their daily bread. No one would have to rob or beg. No one need remain in idleness and ignorance. Everyone would have enough to do."

He started a paper mill and trained farmers in the skills of the business. A part of the daily schedule was Bible study and devotional meditation. The profits were shared. He also started a brick factory to benefit the workers. During the English blockade of Norway, the authorities had to let him out of jail so he could build a salt factory. When it was completed, he was put back in prison.

How was Hauge's work like the modern liberation movements? Both claim a biblical basis in their concern for the poor. Both criticized the civil and religious authorities for their neglect of the poor. Like Hauge, Gustavo Gutierrez, a leading liberation theologian from Peru, emphasizes "doing" theology rather than just "reflecting" on it. But there is one major difference. Hauge was "non-violent," while the Third World movement recognizes degrees of violence to obtain its goals.

Nilsen states "the irony is that the thrust of Hauge's work is now more likely to be embraced and appreciated by Roman Catholics in Central and South America than by Protestants in North America." While Nilsen cites no direct linkages between these two movements, they have a lot in common and we haven't seen the end of them yet.

Hans Nielsen Hauge

CHAPTER

33

THE "WINDJAMMERS"

I recognized it the moment I saw it. Right before my eyes in the Oslo harbor lay the "Windjammer," an ocean-going sailing ship that had gone the way of the dinosaur. Twenty-three years before, in 1954, I had seen the movie "Windjammer" at a theatre in Minneapolis. It was one of those serendipitous things. I had gone to the Mill City for business and discovered the movie playing in a downtown cinema. The fact that it was about Norway and Norwegians attracted me.

The "Windjammer," in this case, was a ship powered by wind that has become a school for Norwegian boys who want to learn the art of sailing. It's a point of pride for these teen-agers to be chosen for this experience at sea, even though work on board ship is difficult and can have some risks. But the very thought of it rouses the Viking spirit for adventure that has never left these people of the North. After leaving the Oslo harbor, they sail southwards along the coasts of France and Portugal and follow the southern route across the Atlantic until they reach the eastern shores of America and then sail northwards to make stops at major ports. The visit to New York was always a highlight as many of them have relatives living there. The whole East Coast population of Norwegians gets excited over their arrival and they are entertained royally.

I must admit that I hadn't known of the "Windjammer" until seeing the movie, but curiosity has since moved me to learn more about it. The only use of the term "windjammer" I'd heard as a child was as a jibe about people who were always telling tall tales.

The taunt of "windjammer," however, was probably not so far from the truth about the way steamship sailors referred to these proud sailing vessels. The steamship crews gave them this name because they didn't believe that these "monsters," as they called them, could actually sail. They claimed that they were far too clumsy to sail neatly into the wind, and that they would have to be "jammed" into the billowy gusts.

But the windjammers proved to be worthy competitors to the steam-powered ships for many years. In fact, many people with experience on the sea believe that they are the finest sailing ships ever built. Having acres of sail on their towering masts, they transported uncounted loads of nitrates, guano, coal, grain and lumber to all parts of the world. For about sixty years they gave the steamships a good run for their money. They outsailed them around the Cape Horn (the southern tip of South America) on their way to the west coasts of both Americas, to Australia and other distant ports.

The windjammers were successors to the famous clipper ships that had traversed the seas since the 1830s. Instead of being built of wood and iron as the clippers, the windjammers were constructed of steel and had improved equipment which required a crew of less than thirty, whereas the clippers needed fifty or sixty men while carrying a much smaller load. The windjammers were built up to 400 feet or more in length, being more than twice as long as the clippers. The windjammer masts had up to five or six large sails and rose up to 200 feet above the keel. The wire, chains and ropes used on them measured in miles. Even when dry, some of the sails weighed a ton. The "bottom line" for the owners meant more profits.

The windjammer era lasted for about sixty years, from the 1860s into the 1920s. There were attempts to make them profitable during the 1930s, but by that time steam had conquered. Then came the more powerful diesels. Several factors combined to end the windjammer's high place on the sea.

When the United States built the transcontinental railroads, it eliminated much of the need to travel around the tip of South America, which was a major run for the windjammers. When the Panama Canal was built, the steamers had the advantage of being able to go through the canal, whereas the sailing vessels had difficulty with such passages. Yet the windjammers were so cost effective that they lived until the advent of the much faster steam-powered ships. Wars improve technology and that happened in the shipping business too.

In their heyday, great pride was taken in the wind-powered vessels as they raced against their own records to shorten the time. In the early days, steamships moved at only about seven knots per hour. The windjammers could travel up to 16 knots. The clippers could go up to about 18. The windjammers had an advantage in bad weather. Steamers ran the danger of having their propellers sheared off, their smoke stacks crushed and their boilers doused with sea water. The windjammers kept right on course.

There were dangers at sea that needed improved equipment and better designed ships. The most serious danger was having the crew washed overboard by high waves. The high waves were estimated to carry over 700 tons of water as they hit the deck. The German shipmasters were the first to rig life nets along the sides of the deck when they entered stormy waters. The helmsmen were always in danger on stormy seas, and were sometimes lashed to the deck. Just working the wheel was dangerous enough.

These sturdy ships were also called "floating storage bins." It reminds me of World War II days when some of the aircraft - those of twin tail construction - carrying military cargo were called "flying boxcars." By today's standards these are, however, pretty small.

Competition between countries to move freight the fastest was keen. Two firms excelled. They were the German firm of Reederei F. Laeisz and the French Antoine-Dominique Bordes et Fils. They kept breaking each others records. The cargo could also be a problem, especially nitrate hauled from Chile for fertilizer in Europe. It was extremely heavy, flammable and noxious.

After World War I, the Versailles Treaty deprived Germany of its magnificent merchant fleet, both steam and sail. This blow to the country's economy probably contributed to the depression which aided Hitler's rise to power. The German ships in the American harbors at America's entry into the war (April 6, 1917) were impounded and sold. The German windjammers were given Indian names and sold to companies that tried to make a business of hauling lumber from the Pacific Northwest to Australia. Though bought for a low price, the new owners went bankrupt. Gustaf Erikson bought the best of the windjammers for $12,000 after their failure in America and sailed it to Sweden.

The windjammers are now extinct except as museum pieces and for the one in the Oslo harbor. Though it is used as a school for training young sailers, look for it in the Oslo harbor if you visit there. You just might be lucky enough to see it when it's in port. Then remember those "thrilling days of yesteryear" when they sailed the seven seas in majesty.

CHAPTER

34

JOHAN FALKBERGET, NOVELIST FROM THE COPPER MINES

Johan Falkberget and the city of Roros in Norway may be two of the best kept Scandinavian secrets. Roros is located on the eastern route between Trondheim and Oslo. UNESCO's World Heritage List includes Roros together with the pyramids of Egypt and the redwood forests of California as tourist attractions. It was founded in 1644 by Lorentz Lossius, a German business man, who was given permission to develop the newly discovered copper mines. The area had been virtually uninhabited since the Black Death days (1349) when two out of every three Norwegians died.

It was not unusual that German miners were invited into Norway by the Danish king, Christian IV. Norwegians were poor and inexperienced in mining. Germans, however, had been operating mines for centuries and many of them had the money required to get the work started. As a result, Roros is a community of people with Germans, Norwegians and Swedes today. This gives it a distinct racial mix.

Johan Falkberget (1879-1967) lived most of his life in the Roros community and it provided him with the setting for the majority of his novels. In his writings, Roros is known as "Bergstaden" ("mining town"). Its high altitude, sharp contrasts in climate, closeness to the Swedish border and its great church towering over the wooden cottages give it the background for fascinating stories. Falkberget's father was a mine foreman who also farmed in his spare time. Schooling was limited to a boy in such a situation as he was needed at home for work. The future novelist began working at the mines when he was eight. But he persisted and got whatever education he could. At age fourteen, he was writing articles for the local newspaper. He left the mines when twenty-seven and became editor of a newspaper in Alesund, but soon moved to Oslo.

His writings showed a deep social conscience which revolted against the oppression of the privileged classes over the working people. In 1922, at age forty-three, he returned to Roros to take over the family farm which he inherited. This provided the setting for his writing the history of his home community. "The Fourth Night Watch" ("Den fjerde Nattevakt," 1923) began his most famous series of novels.

The setting of this story is early nineteenth century and the principle character is Benjamin Sigismund (based on an actual person), the newly arrived pastor from Copenhagen. He was a handsome man with all the qualities of charm, except patience, which he eventually learned from an alcoholic klokker (deacon), who was the local blacksmith. His wife, Kathryn, was a sickly person who had difficulty enduring the rugged Roros climate. She would have liked her husband to become a bishop so they could move to a better place. Much to his own surprise, Sigismund became firmly attached to this place of harsh life and customs.

Before 1813, all Norwegian clergy were educated in Denmark because Norway didn't have a university. Copenhagen, being a city of culture, retained a strong nostalgia, especially for many first ladies of the parsonage. They felt a superior position over the "natives" who had not travelled beyond their valleys.

Just before leaving Copenhagen, a gypsy woman warned Sigismund against having anything to do with a woman dressed in red that he'd meet in the churchyard early one morning. His first reaction was to discount as fiction what a dirty old hag told him. Afterall, he was an educated man with a university degree and would certainly not compromise his professional ethics. Fatefully it happened early one morning, while answering a pastoral request for help, the young woman in red passed him. He momentarily became white with fear.

The woman, Gunhild, was the niece of the klokker and about to be married to a man she loathed. But since he had a good job and money, her mother pressured her to accept the offer. The old uncle got the pastor's ear about her dilemma. This set the trap to fulfill the gypsy woman's prophecy.

Sigismund was not a willing victim of temptation. He had, however, a rigid streak of predestination and fate, and had a big heart which responded to every need for pastoral care, no matter how difficult. He once braved the fiercest blizzard to minister to a Lapp family. Gunhild's wedding was performed and this began the spinning of the web that was to finally enmesh his conscience and reputation.

Following a series of tragedies in which Gunhild's husband committed suicide and his own wife died, Sigismund's health broke and he came down with consumption. He conducted his last service while hardly able to stand erect. He put forth a powerful effort and entranced the congregation who suddenly saw him to be a prophet of God whom they had not understood or appreciated. The old blacksmith had been his only loyal friend through his time of depression. In the final pages, both pastor and klokker died, and Gunhild remained to mourn them both.

Falkberget was a powerful writer and deserves more American readers. Even if you have not been to Norway, you will be quickly drawn into his stories and will lay the book down reluctantly only because you are finished. His writings hold an additional fascination for me since my second cousin, Kaare Rogstad of Orkdal, was once the pastor of the Roros church which King Olav V honored with his presence on its 200th anniversary.

CHAPTER

35

EDVARD GRIEG REVISITED

No one has done more to popularize the folk music of Norway than Edvard Hagerup Grieg (1843-1907). No one has written a better book on Grieg than Finn Benestad and Dag Schjelderup-Ebbe. It was translated by William H. Halverson and Leland B. Sateren, and published by the University of Nebraska Press (1988). The book itself is a work of art with 441 large pages on high quality paper. There are 404 illustrations and many interesting notes printed on the outside columns. Also included are many musical scores. For anyone who would take music history seriously, or would know all there is know about the composer and his times, this is the book: *Edvard Grieg: The Man and the Artist.*

The name Grieg comes from the MacGregor clan in Scotland. Originally Grig, from MacGregor, it was changed to Grieg. Edvard's great-grandfather, Alexander Grieg, immigrated with his wife to Bergen, where some of the family had settled as early as 1600. There are some claims that he was a fugitive from the gallows. Edvard's paternal grandmother was Danish, the daughter of a violinist from Aalborg.

Edvard's maternal grandfather, Edvard Hagerup, was deeply involved in Norwegian politics and was one of the 112 representatives who signed the Constitution at Eidsvoll on May 17, 1814. Edvard Grieg was also a relative of Ole Bull, the great violinist. His mother was a highly talented singer and considered to be the best piano teacher in Bergen.

If you've ever been to Bergen on a clear day and seen the city from the adjoining mountains, you can't help but be impressed with its beauty. It was the home of the Hanseatic League, German merchants who dominated Norway's west coast fishing industry for hundreds of years during the late Middle Ages. Grieg loved the old houses, narrow streets, the harbor and the surrounding mountains, but he vigorously disliked its middle-class business mentality. He was hungering for more of the artistic and spiritual values.

The 19th century saw the awakening of Norway to become a part of the modern world. The change of government from the ruling class in Denmark to Sweden and the new Constitution called forth an unusual amount of energy and talent in such persons as Henrik Ibsen and Bjornstjerne Bjornson in literature, Iver Aasen in the revival of the Norwegian language (nynorsk), M. B. Landstad and Ludvig Lindeman in music, Jorgen Moe and P. C. Asbjornsen in folklore, the Sverdrups in politics and theology, and many more. Ole Bull became famous in America, but Grieg said he wouldn't cross the ocean for a million dollars. He got sea-sick easily.

Edvard - small of stature - was not known as an especially good student. The rote-learning method of education did not take with his creativity. He used a special trick to get out of school. Getting to class late brought punishment by making the student stand outside until the end of the period. One day he stood under a rainspout (it rains often in Bergen) and got soaked. When the teacher saw him all wet, he sent him home for dry clothes. Since it was a long walk, he had the day off. This trick work well for a time, but one day he tried it when it was hardly raining at all. The suspicious teacher had someone spy on him and that was the end of that. He also repeated third grade.

But Edvard did have an unmistakable musical talent. So did several of the other children in the family. His mother recognized his special giftedness at the piano. While hating lifeless scales and exercises (so did I), he loved to daydream at the keyboard to create new melodies. He began piano lessons from his mother at age six. It was Ole Bull who took hold of him and said: "You are going to Leipzig to become an artist!" And so began the career of Norway's greatest musician.

In the course of his career and travels he met most of the great musicians of the time. He loved French and Russian music most of all, though he refused to perform in Russia because he detested the Czar's government. He said, "They are the worst criminals of our time." He had a special love affair with Copenhagen. It became his "artistic and spiritual home" rather than Oslo or Bergen. While the piano was the center of his musical studies, he also conducted symphony orchestras. In 1880 he became director of the Bergen Symphony. He saw his task as being to turn them into a first class organization. When several members failed to show up for a dress rehearsal in order to attend a large public dance, he dismissed them.

Grieg was a very private person. He couldn't tolerate having any-one near when he composed, so he built a private hut away from his house for this work. His famous summer home in "Troldhaugen," just outside of Bergen, has become a major tourist attraction. When there, you can peak in at the hut where he worked near the water's edge, as well as walk through the house where he and his wife, Nina, lived. The Bergen residence, however, was too hard on his health and they lived in it only during the summer months.

While Grieg was famous for his music, he was equally serious about politics and religion. He held radical political views, even favoring a republic over a monarchy. However, he soundly approved the new monarchy of 1905 with a Danish prince and an English princess for the new royalty. He reacted strongly against social injustice, lust for power and the snobbery that he saw in the ruling classes. Meeting royalty was a painful ordeal to Grieg. He felt that the required protocol was too full of vanity.

In religion, Grieg was a maverick. Though brought up under the influence "orthodox" Lutheranism, he found that it was too confining for his doubts. On a trip to England, he became a Unitarian, which he remained for the rest of his life. His creed was summed up in "love" and the Sermon on the Mount. Yet he kept on good terms with a cousin who was a state church pastor. When buried, his ashes were put in a grotto where visitors may view the site today.

Marta Sandal Rortvedt (1878-1930) sang solos under Grieg's direction. Unlike Grieg, she crossed the ocean thirteen times and apparently never got seasick. She appeared as a soloist with Grieg in his last concert on October 17, 1906, in Oslo, before the new royal family. Grieg wrote a unique introduction for her singing in America. She introduced his music at Carnegie Hall in New York City. She was also presented at the royal court in Russia, but did not sing there. Grieg wrote: "I have no doubt that she will succeed in winning the hearts of the New World as she did in her own country." She was the only authorized "Grieg singer" before the public and received high praise in London, Berlin and Chicago.

In her last years during the 1920s, she lived with her husband, Gudmund Rortvedt, of Heimdal, North Dakota. While her husband farmed, she organized young talent from surrounding communities into a choir. Her daughter, Sylvia, writing of her mother said: "She was always a 'lady'. I might say she was not the kind of a woman that was expected to 'help with the dishes', though, if necessary, she could do menial tasks with her usual aplomb'."

So Grieg did get to America and I get excited every time I hear one of his piano or orchestral compositions. The additional story of Marta brings it a little closer home. If you visit Troldhaugen in Bergen, look for her picture on a table in Grieg's home. And if your curiosity wants to find out the full story of Norway's musical genius, read the book: *Edvard Grieg: The Man and the Artist.*

Edvard Hagerup Grieg

CHAPTER

36

"SKIS AGAINST THE ATOM"

The world has known many heroes, each of them important to their times. The twentieth century, however, has reason to regard Knut Haukelid of Norway as a hero to be singled out for our time. The story of his heroic efforts to keep Hitler from getting the atomic bomb has been told many times by writers and movie producers. The most fascinating of these accounts is his own book, *Skis Against the Atom*, published originally in 1954. A second revised edition was published in 1989 by the North American Heritage Press of Minot, North Dakota.

Skis Against the Atom is an "exciting, first-hand account of heroism and daring sabotage during the Nazi occupation of Norway." A movie, "Heroes of Telemark," starring Kirk Douglas, has also been produced.

In 1985 Haukelid was inducted into the Norsk Høstfest's Scandinavian-American Hall of Fame in Minot, North Dakota. My wife and I had the privilege of being his hosts. Haukelid holds dual citizenship in both the United States and Norway, his parents having lived in America when he was a youth. His father, Bjorgulf Haukelid, a graduate of Oslo's Technical College, was an engineer who designed subways in New York City. He was associated with an engineering firm owned by another Norwegian, Sverre Dahm, known as the "father of New York's subway network." His sister, was an actress with the film name Sigrid Guri.

Haukelid discussed what motivates people to such heroism. Is it patriotism or a desire for adventure? He answered, "only in very few cases was it a desire for adventure that impelled them to take up arms against the foreign invaders. There is little that is adventurous about war, and the boys had small chance of satisfying a desire for adventure in a war in which toil and hunger, and the idea of death at the hands of a firing squad, were our companions. We lost many of our best comrades, not only in battle but also as helpless victims in the hands of the Gestapo."

When the invasion of Norway took place on April 9, 1940, Haukelid was in Trondheim. He woke up in the morning to discover that the city was already occupied. Collecting his ski equipment, he sneaked out into the countryside together with a friend and hoped to find a Norwegian military detachment. They travelled thirty miles south to Storen where they boarded a train. All went well until they got to Lillehammer where all traffic stopped. The German forces were only ten miles to the south. They witnessed the bombing of Elverum where King Haakon and Crown Prince Olav were seeking shelter under the trees. The Nazis intended to kill the Royal Family and then set up a puppet government.

Despite the fact that the Norwegians defeated the Germans at Narvik, they were forced to surrender when the British and French withdrew their armed forces for the defense of France in June 1940. Haukelid expressed deep disappointment to me that they took all their guns and ammunition along. After escaping from arrest and playing hide and seek with the Nazis, he fled to Stockholm, which he said was full of spies from every country in Europe.

Knut went to England to be trained for a return to Norway and fight behind the lines. Their task was to destroy the "heavy water" operation at the Norsk Hydro plant at Vemork, a village about a mile west of Rjukan, about 50 miles west of Oslo. The town is situated so deeply into the valley that during the winter no sunshine reaches the streets. The first attempt to accomplish this mission by the British using gliders failed and all the soldiers were killed, most of them executed by the Nazis, in violation of international rules of war.

Heavy water (deuterium oxide), was produced in large quantities only at the hydro plant at Vemork. Before the war, the German government had tried to buy the heavy water from the Norwegians but were refused. One of the goals of their invasion appears to have been to confiscate the plant and bring the heavy water to Germany for building an atomic bomb.

A curious fortune of war which favored the Allies happened on June 2, 1942. Hitler asked his scientists how long it would take to develop the bomb. They told him two years. "By that time," he said, "we will have won the war," and so he cut the budget for its development. In early 1943, when the Russian front had come to a standstill and the Nazis had sustained heavy losses, he ordered its resumption, but by that time over a half a year had been lost.

Fortunately, the English were kept advised through Norwegian informants about everything happening at the hydro plant. They also were informed about the design of the plant so that the saboteurs might enter the building even if blindfolded and know where to find the heavy water.

It was a cold night in January 1943 when the Norwegians parachuted over the Hardanger Vidda, "the largest, loneliest and wildest mountain area in northern Europe." Haukelid wrote that "no human beings live on these desolate expanses, only the creatures of the wild," including large herds of reindeer. The drop was successful. Luckily they found a hut for shelter, because the next day one of the worst storms that Haukelid had ever experienced struck the mountains.

Each of the men were issued a cyanide pill to be bitten if captured. Death would follow in three seconds. The alternative was torture and execution, and possibly revealing the secret of their mission. The Nazis never found Haukelid. Five of his company, however, did bite the pill during the war.

The strike on the Norsk Hydro plant took place on February 28. Nine men entered the plant undetected by the Germans and destroyed the heavy water. Then they escaped to Sweden, though a massive search combed the area. The plant, however, was back in operation in two months. Then Allied bombers struck the plant, still not putting it out of commission totally, but Norwegian lives were lost.

The Nazis decided to move all the heavy water to Germany. Haukelid was assigned the task of making certain that it would not leave Norway. On Sunday morning, February 20, 1944, the ferry carrying the cargo in steel drums sank in the deepest part of Lake Tinnsjo on the way to Notodden. Knut had gone on board disguised as a laborer and planted explosives. This was a very difficult task for Haukelid because there were Norwegians on board who also lost their lives. Because of Allied insistence, the Norwegian government in London gave its approval. That ended Hitler's hopes of building the bomb.

Informers were a constant threat to the Norwegian Resistance Movement. The Nazis paid well in money and supplied scarce goods to those who collaborated. According to Haukelid, sixty-two Norwegians paid with their lives for being traitors. There were undoubtedly many more. John Steinbeck's book, *The Moon is Down* (1942), tells us more about the struggle for Norway's freedom.

After the destruction of the heavy water, Knut's job was to train Norwegians to take control of the country after Hitler's defeat. They were also to make certain that the Nazi forces in Norway did not return for the defense of Germany. Only 20,000 of the 380,000 Germans in Norway made it back for the defense of their homeland.

The Allies feared that the Germans might make a "last stand" in Norway or would destroy Norwegian industry before leaving. Restraint was exercised so the home guard did not have an open battle with the Germans. This would provoke reprisals and the executions of many innocent civilians. They all remembered Lidice, Czechoslovakia, from the early days of the war.

Fortunately, the German forces obeyed the command to lay down their arms and the war ended without further destruction. The home forces were joined by the "Viking Battalion" from America in taking charge of their nation.

The whole world owes a debt to those brave men who frustrated Hitler's plans for the bomb. They also paid a price. Forty of the 110 men in Haukelid's company died. Without the training on skis during their youth, this sabotage operation could not have been possible.

Haukelid returned several times to America to autograph the new edition of his book, *Skis Against the Atom*. It's one of the most exciting stories of World War II. Be sure to read it.

The world had its last look at Haukelid on television during the Winter Olympics at Lillehammer. He died March 8, 1994, at the age of eighty-two. The world has been a safer place in which to live because of Haukelid's heroism, and of the brave men who accompanied him on his dangerous journeys.

CHAPTER
37

THE PRIME MINISTER WHO SAVED THE KING

After World War II, the Prime Minister of Norway, Carl J. Hambro, was welcomed to America as a hero of the Resistance. When he visited the Buck Ellingson farm near Hillsboro, North Dakota, the newspapers carried front page stories with a picture of him holding one their children. It was touching. Hambro was regarded as next in importance to the king.

An air raid alarm went off in Oslo at 1:00 a.m. on April 9, 1940. Most people thought it was a routine drill, but Hambro, then President of the Storting (Parliament), immediately checked and found out that foreign men-of-war were steaming up the Oslofjord. He instantly understood the implications and advised King Haakon VII that the Royal Family and Storting members should take the next train to Hamar, 100 miles north. It was imperative that the King and his family should not fall into Nazi hands, as well as the royal gold reserves.

The Storting assembled and passed the necessary emergency legislation for the government to function outside of Oslo. Spies followed their every move. Barely had this been done when enemy war planes began to bomb their locations. They moved 20 miles east to Elverum, where at one point, both the King and Crown Prince Olav took shelter under a large tree during the bombing. If they had been killed, Prince Harald, just three years old, would have had a care-taker appointed for him by the Supreme Court. The Nazis planned to control that appointment and the country would be captive. Deep snow hampered travel through the mountains.

Back in Oslo, Vidkun Quisling, a former army officer, proclaimed himself "Chief of State" and appointed a "government" of virtually unknown people who were horrified when told of their new jobs. Quisling had just returned from seeing Hitler in Berlin two days earlier. Dr. Brauer, the German Minister in Norway, presented a list of demands between 4:30 and 5:00 a.m. which amounted to a complete surrender. Delaying tactics were used before responding so the Royal Family would have time to travel further away from Oslo. The demands were then rejected.

After two months of heroic defense, the fighting was over in Norway and the government was relocated to London. Crown Prince Martha and her children, Ragnhild, Astrid and Harald, went to the USA where they were the personal guests of President and Mrs. Roosevelt for the duration of the war.

Who was Carl J. Hambro? The Hambros had moved to Norway from England during the Swedish period and became loyal citizens and significant servants of the nation. But there is an irony in the story. When the famous constitution of May 17 ("Syttende Mai"), 1814, was signed, it excluded Jews from Norway (also Jesuits). Only after this was changed in 1851, was it possible for the Hambros to become "Norwegians." The total number of Jews never exceeded 1500 before the war. But for this reason, Quisling and the Nazis had made a point of attacking Hambro. Throughout the war, he worked tirelessly for Norway's freedom as a leader for the government in exile.

In the early days of the war, Hambro wrote *I Saw It Happen In Norway*, in which described the narrow escape of the royal family. It's a lucky thing that the original constitution was amended, or the Royal Family may have become hostage to Hitler on that fateful morning of April 9, 1940. Norway and Norwegians everywhere continue to honor the name of the Prime Minister who saved the King.

CHAPTER

38

KING HAAKON'S "VAMPIRES"

When Hitler ordered the attack on Norway, code-named "Weseruebung," on April 9, 1940, the Norwegian government was following a strict policy of neutrality. After a harrowing experience of close brushes with death, King Haakon VII and his staff arrived in England where they directed Norway's participation in the war. There is much written about the role of the Resistance Movement within Norway which has an excellent museum at Akershus Castle in Oslo.

Less is known, however, about Norway's active participation as one of the Allies. In a surprisingly short time, Norwegians brought an army, navy and air force into the Allied effort to free their homeland and to destroy Hitler's war machine.

Norway's biggest contribution to the fight against the Nazis was its merchant marine of almost five million tons. Even though one of the world's smallest nations in population, Norway ranked fourth in the size of its fleet. Twenty percent of the world's tankers were Norwegian. One of Vidkun Quisling's first acts as the Nazi approved head of civilian government in Norway was to order all Norwegian merchant ships to head for home, or to German or neutral ports and to await further command. None of the captains complied and eighty-five percent of the merchant fleet escaped enemy control.

The Norwegian government in exile was eager to have Norway be an active military ally in opposing Hitler. They also wanted to have a significant part in spearheading the invasion to liberate Norway. By mid-summer 1940, the Norwegian navy was operating in the Atlantic from Iceland to Great Britain. In June 1944, sixty Norwegian ships took part in the landings at Normandy, together with fighter squadrons and naval ships. About fifty Norwegian officers served with a division from Scotland in the invasion.

Norway had only a small air force when the war began, but Norwegian flyers moved quickly to England and then to "Little Norway" in Toronto, Canada, to begin training. The first squadron of the Royal Norwegian Air Force became operational on April 25, 1941, just a year after the invasion of its homeland. They were equipped with Northrop seaplanes ordered from America before the war. They operated under the British Royal Air Force Coastal Command which was doing anti-submarine patrols and convoy duty. In 1943 they were equipped with Sunderland flying boats stationed in the Shetland Islands. They patrolled from the north coast of Norway to the Azores and to Iceland.

The first fighter squadron, known as 331, was put into action by the Royal Norwegian Air Force in 1941. A second, known as 332 Squadron joined them in 1942. They flew relentlessly in the defense of England and in establishing air superiority over the English Channel. In 1943, 331 Squadron led all the Allied air units in the destruction of enemy planes. The 333 Squadron was organized in 1943, using Catalina flying boats and Mosquito fighter-bombers. They were stationed in Scotland and flew operations over Norway. No occupied country had as many pilots in the British Royal Air Force as did Norway during the war. They were also in staff positions.

A problem for the Norwegian military force in exile was lack of recruits. Yet many Norwegians escaped to England in fishing boats, or into Sweden and were flown to England, where they volunteered for duty. The British navy offered as many ships as the Norwegians could staff. The forces were scattered from Scotland to Iceland and even in the Arctic and Antarctic regions. Many also trained in Sweden to be ready either for the invasion of Norway, or to take charge when the Nazis were defeated. That was a slim hope in 1940 as the German military were mopping up western Europe.

One of the fascinating and little known planes flown by the Norwegian flyers was a De Havilland built "Vampire" jet. In an article written in *Aerospace Historian*, General Bryce Poe II (retired Air Force) tells of his experience with this plane. General Poe's wife, Kari, is Norwegian-born. He has also been stationed in Norway.

Designing the Vampire began in May 1942. Production began in September 1943. Its prototype was the first plane built in either the United States or England which flew over 500 miles per hour. This was attained in the spring of 1944. Contracts were let for 300 Vampires. Besides combat missions, it became a test plane for more jet research.

Until new technologies were developed, the early military planes had to choose between speed and fire power, or protective armor. Limited fuel capacity was also a problem. So drop-off and bag fuel tanks were installed. The Vampire range, however, was just a little over an hour of flight time because of its appetite for fuel. It could carry two 1000 pound bombs, but for only seventy miles. The original fuel tanks held about 240 gallons. In its early stages, the Vampire was designed as an air-defense fighter. Later it was tested for ground attack.

The Vampire had only a forty foot wingspan and was barely over thirty feet long. It weighed only 7000 pounds empty and a little over 12,000 pounds loaded and was powered by a 3300 pound Goblin 3 engine. In 1948 the Vampire set an altitude record of 59,446 feet. The specifications claimed that it could fly 531 miles per hour at sea level. One feature that every flyer noted was that it did not have an ejection seat. Because of its twin fuselages, there were risks in bailing out.

Norway wasn't the only country to purchase the Vampires. Thirteen nations had them. It was being built in Australia, Switzerland, Italy and France, as well as in England after the war. When NATO was organized, many countries were using American built planes, but the Royal Norwegian Air Force was primarily equipped with Vampires and the Royal Danish Air Force with Meteors, both British built.

After logging 1600 hours of flying in Korea and in South East Asia, General Poe got his first look at the Vampire Mk. 52 at Gardermoen AFB north of Oslo in 1952. He hadn't flown anything like it before. The first question he asked the Squadron Commander was "How do you start the engine?" It turned out to be quite simple: "Push the button on the dash." It started smoothly with a little rumble. The close fitting leather helmet kept out much of the engine noise. They warned him about one thing, however. "Keep your thumb off the bloody button, the guns are hot!" The plane had two weapon/tank hard points, one on each wing. It also had four 20mm cannons under the cockpit. The brake system drew no praise from General Poe, but he did write favorably about its quick take-off capability. No daily engine run-up was required.

General Poe seems to have almost forgotten this plane when he ran across an advertisement for one in the "Trade-a-Plane" paper. That prompted his reminiscing and writing an article on it. He described the Vampire as "an airman's airplane" with combat potential in World War II. It's greatest contribution, however, may have been to advance jet aircraft. The Norwegian flyers enjoyed the plane. They used to sing about it: "She's not so very, very big, but she's just as big as the Russian MiG!"

There's a lot more than meets the eye in the winning of a war. Each part is crucial. King Haakon's Vampires, as they were called, played their part in the Allied victory, especially in the development of jet aircraft which is taken for granted today.

❦

C H A P T E R

39

THOR HEYERDAHL AND THE "MALDIVE MYSTERY"

Thor Heyerdahl is the most exciting archaeologist of our century. His adventure, *The Maldive Mystery*, is the most fascinating of all.

I first learned of this scientific expedition in the Maldive Islands while visiting with Knut Haugland, Director of the Kon Tiki Museum in Oslo in October 1983. Haugland was with Heyerdahl on the Kon Tiki expedition in 1947. Heyerdahl refers to him as "my closest collaborator ever since we waded ashore together in Polynesia." He told me about the Maldive explorations then in progress and indicated that the results would require a lot of history books to be re-written.

The *Maldive Mystery* began for Heyerdahl with an air-mail letter in 1982 from Sri Lanka (formerly called Ceylon) south of India. Enclosed was a photograph of a Buddha statue that the President of the Maldives wanted Heyerdahl to examine. They had hoped that his "Tigris Expedition" raft would have landed in the Maldives instead of in Djibouti on the east coast of Africa. The Maldives are a string of islands running 600 miles north and south, to the southwest of India and west of Sri Lanka. There are an estimated 1200 islands of which only 202 are inhabited by 160,000 people. None of the islands rise more than six feet above sea level. They are protected from the sea by coral reefs and sand bars. Navigation is treacherous.

The Maldivians have been Moslems since 1153 and were ruled by a sultan until 1968 when the islands became a democracy. Many archaeological artifacts had been uncovered, but Moslem intolerance of idols (statues) caused most of them to be destroyed upon discovery.

The Maldivians have been reluctant to admit that they had a history before the arrival of Islam. The new government wanted a professional archaeologist of Heyerdahl's stature to visit them.

The famous Norwegian arrived in 1982 to examine the statue. Unfortunately, fanatical Moslems had already destroyed it. All that remained of value was the head. There was no denying that there had been a pre-Moslem culture, in fact several successive cultures. Who had they been? From where had they come? The photographs in Heyerdahl's book show a variety of physical types. This indicates that they had come from no single place. One of the interesting features on the statues was that they had large suspended ear lobes. This was a practice of Hindu royalty who perforated their ears and hung large plugs on them (the original earring).

The earliest level of civilization had been sun worshippers. Their probable origin was in the Indus River Valley, one of the three great places to which the earliest civilizations have been traced. The others are Mesopotamia at the confluence of the Tigris and Euphrates rivers, and the Nile river valley in Egypt.

Large man-made earth mounds, called "hawittas," are the usual source of treasure hunting in the Maldives. Temples for sun worship were built on them. The succeeding civilizations, believed to have been Hindus from northwest India and Buddhists from Sri Lanka, destroyed these temples and re-used the stones to build their own. The sun-worship temples bear striking similarities to those found in Peru, the Easter Islands, the north coast of Africa, Asia Minor and in Bahrain on the Persian Gulf. Archaeology is an exacting science. Excavation is often done with spoons, brushes and sieves, not bulldozers or spades. Heyerdahl believes that there was sea traffic between these places 2000 years before Columbus. He believes that those ancient mariners learned how to follow the sea currents and may have used reed boats.

One of Heyerdahl's quests was to identify a people called the "Redins." They were white with brown hair, had big hooked noses and blue eyes, and were tall with long faces. They were among the earliest settlers.

The Maldivians were the money suppliers for many people of the ancient world with their cowrie shells. These reached the Arctic coasts of Norway by 600 A. D. This was prior to the Viking voyages. It is believed that they were carried there by Arab and Finnish merchants.

Heyerdahl's work will keep historians re-examining their theories about the history of world population movements. He has shown us that those early travellers included some highly cultured people who had great talent in art and building. He concludes that "civilized man suddenly appeared 5000 years ago, when he began to build cities. He was already a seafarer too, building ports along the riverbanks and along the coasts of the Indian Ocean."

It's strange that this famous scientist, who was afraid of water and could not swim as a boy, has spent so much of his life on the sea in daring adventures. Born in Larvik, southwest of Oslo along the sea, he became fascinated with collecting sea shells, butterflies, insects and sea creatures. Before he finished high school, he had his own museum to which teachers would bring their students. Spending a summer in the mountains with a well-educated hermit helped Heyerdahl to learn self-reliance. Since then he has pioneered new adventures which have startled the world.

CHAPTER

40

NORWAY HONORS GENERAL JONES

In the Student Union Building of Minot State University, there is a room dedicated to the honor of General David C. Jones, United States Air Force. He was Chairman of the Joint Chiefs of Staff from 1978-1982, the highest military position of the United States. Ken Robertson, retired Air Force and Curator of the room's memorabilia, called my attention to Norway's recognition of the University's famous alumnus.

On November 24, 1981, Gen. Jones was awarded the Grand Cross of the Royal Order of St. Olav, Norway's highest decoration for non-Norwegians in peacetime. The ceremony took place at the Norwegian Ambassador's residence in Washington, D. C. The presentation was made by Ambassador Knut Hedemann and Gen. Sverre Hamre, Norwegian Chief of Defense.

King Olav V of Norway honored Gen. Jones "in recognition of his outstanding military service as Chief of Staff for the United States Air Force, 1974-1978, and as Chairman of the Joint Chiefs of Staff since 1978."

The "Order of St. Olav" was established on August 21, 1847, by King Oscar I, who was king of both Norway and Sweden. This recognition is an honor that Norway gives to a non-Norwegian. (The reader should understand that even ethnic Norwegians living in America are considered "non-Norwegians" in Norway). The Order has three ranks: Grand Cross, Commander and Knight. The insignia has a golden cross with white enamel and a golden lion on a globe of red enamel in the center. On the reverse side is the motto: "Ret og Sandhed" ("Justice and Truth"). The King of Norway is the Order's Grand Master and all insignia are to be returned to him after the death of the recipient.

The award is given for "outstanding merit for the country or for humanity." Gen. Jones qualified for this recognition because Norway is a loyal and appreciative member of NATO. Sharing a common border with the Soviet Union, Norway could have been a target for political blackmail without American support. The huge Soviet naval base at Murmansk was close to the northern tip of Norway.

General Jones was born in Aberdeen, South Dakota, in 1921, and moved to Minot in 1930. After graduating from Minot high school in 1939, he attended both the University of North Dakota in Grand Forks and Minot State University. He had his first flying lessons in Minot in 1941 under the tutelage of Bill Gunn. Right after Pearl Harbor, in January 1942, he married Lois Tarbell, of Rugby, North Dakota, who was teaching in a nearby rural school. Then he volunteered for the United States Army Air Force and reported to the Roswell, New Mexico, cadet school.

One of Lois' former pupils told me that the future Air Force General was a occasional visitor to the rural school. At recess time he played ball with the students. One day, he took a homerun swing and shattered their new Louisville Slugger bat. They have forgiven him, however, in the light of his later achievements. Besides that they thought it was special that he'd play ball with them.

If you visit the Minot State University campus, be sure to look at the many recognitions which have been bestowed on North Dakota's famed general.

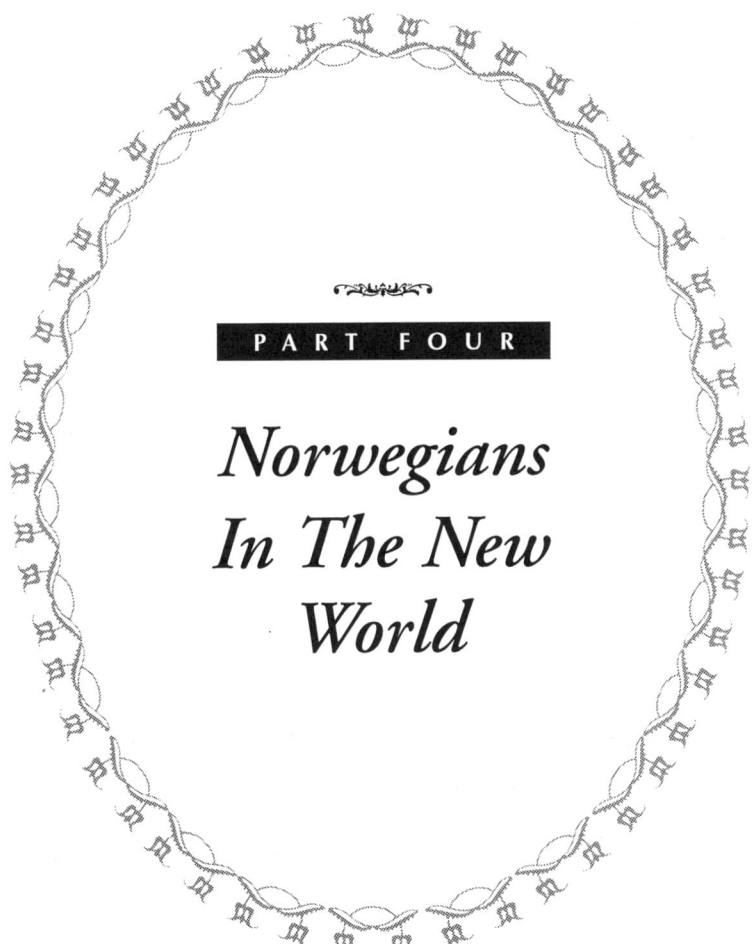

PART FOUR

Norwegians In The New World

CHAPTER

41

CLENG PEERSON,
NORWEGIAN "PATHFINDER"
TO AMERICA

He is remembered as Cleng Peerson, the man who began the migration of 800,000 Norwegians to America. His real name was Kleng Pedersen Hesthammer, born May 17, 1782, in Tysvaer, not far from Stavanger on Norway's southwest coast.

I always like to know what went into the child who becomes a famous person. Cleng came from Rogaland, the part of Norway where Viking expeditions were launched. These were the men who discovered Greenland and Vinland. They were born to be pathfinders.

Peersons's first forty years were spent close to his home. Daily meals usually consisted of flatbread, herring and a bowl of sour milk. I remember how this was standard fare for many Norwegian immigrants when I was a young boy.

Cleng displayed Viking courage and stubborness while still a child. One day his father ordered him to go out into the woods to fetch his lamb so it could be butchered. Instead, Cleng went into the woodshed, placed his hand on the chopping block, and cut off the little finger of his left hand. Then he carried it to his father and placing it on a piece of flatbread, said "here's a piece of meat for you, Father." The lamb was spared.

The Hesthammer farm was a part of the "prestegaard" (pastor's farm). When Cleng was twelve, the pastor's farmhand came to claim the rent that was due. It was to be paid in flatbread. Since that year had seen a poor harvest, it meant that nearly all the food stored in their attic would have to be surrendered. His father burned with bitter anger as he cursed both the bread and the pastor. Cleng was ordered to hold the flatbread as it was delivered to the parsonage. As they crossed a bridge, he hurled it into the river below. The penalty was an extra year of confirmation instruction.

Cleng's mother was the daughter of a former pastor in the parish and she had married his father against the will of her family. His father became melancholy and spent the last years of his life in mental depression. She bore her burden with stately dignity.

Some of the religious practices of the Middle Ages remained in the valleys of Norway in those days despite the reforms of the 16th century. There was an old legend that a blind man had been healed by touching a crucifix in one of the country churches. Cleng brought a young girl who was dumb to the church so she could regain her speech. It was to no avail.

Cleng had a questioning mind, especially about religion. He found the restrictions of the state church to be painful and later became a "dissenter." During the Napoleonic wars, he was imprisoned on board ship by the British and came in contact with Quaker missionaries. He never became one of them, but this contact provided the background for his decision to leave Norway for the freedom of the New World. Before leaving home, his mother cautioned: "There are two things that I must ask of you now that you are going away: That you guard against excessive drinking and that you shun frivolous women." She was not the only mother who has given that advice.

When the wars of Napoleon ended in 1814, Norway adopted a constitution and came under the rule of Karl Johan, king of Sweden. Times were hard due to the British blockade and there was much hunger and starvation. It was even worse for the "dissenters" who had run afoul of the State Church. Among these were some prisoners of war who had returned from England with Quaker sympathies and the followers of Hans Nielsen Hauge who preached a religious awakening in the land.

Peerson became neither Quaker nor Haugean, but he shared their dissatisfaction with the state control over religious practices, including baptisms, confirmations, marriages and funerals. He made his first visit to America in the fall of 1821 and found land for a future home for his countrymen on the shores of Lake Ontario.

Having returned to Norway, Cleng campaigned to get people interested in the New World. Many people called him a liar. But he persisted. Together with Johannes Stene, he bought a twenty-three year old sloop which had been used for hauling herring to Denmark and bringing grain back to Norway. Originally named "Emanuel" after the builder's son, it was later changed to "Haabet," which means "The Hope."

Before the boat, a sloop, was purchased, it had been renamed the "Restauration," because it had been remodeled. The sloop was fifty-four feet long, sixteen feet wide and registered to carry thirty-seven tons. Despite the smallness of the deck, dances were held on board.

There were two ways to America. The northern route was the most common but ran the danger of icebergs and severe storms. The longer route was via Madiera and the Bahamas. Peerson chose the latter, despite the risks of pirates and Turkish slave traders. Setting sail on July 4th or 5th, 1825, with 6300 pounds of rod iron, there were fifty-four passengers, including twenty children.

As they approached Madiera, the pilgrims suffered from lack of drinking water. And as luck would have it, a cask of the famed Madiera wine came floating on the ocean. Though they were temperate people, in their thirst they consumed the whole barrel and as the ship sailed into the harbor, they were all asleep on the deck. At a later reception in their honor, they were the only teetotalers at the party. They learned their lesson well. Pirates were eluded by painting their hands and faces as though they had bubonic plague. While stretching out their hands and crying for help, the pirate ships quickly fled.

The "Sloopers" arrived in New York, a city of 15,000, on October 9, only to discover they were overloaded and fined $4500. Authorities impounded the ship and imprisoned the captain. It took the help of

Quaker friends and an acquittal signed by President John Quincy Adams to get them out of that scrape. The ship was sold to raise money for the colony.

In October 1975, Norwegians gathered all over America to celebrate the Sesquicentennial (150 years) of that famous voyage which began their emigration. As a result of this celebration, several annual "fests" were begun which still meet. Among these are the Nordland Fest in Sioux Falls, South Dakota, and the Høstfest in Minot, North Dakota. A scale model of the Restauration is on display in Christ Lutheran Church in Minot. It's worth seeing.

What made people so restless that they set out to discover new worlds? Sometimes they just don't fit into the world where they were born. This seems to have been the case with Cleng Peerson when he orchestrated the Restauration expedition at age forty-three.

He had been married twice, but neither wife was a partner in his pioneering work. He was "tricked" into his first marriage in Norway by a much older woman of unscrupulous morals and wealth. As soon as the vows were pronounced, he fled from the scene and received no financial benefit from it. His second marriage, to a girl much younger than himself, took place in the Bishop Hill Colony of Illinois. It was a mass ceremony performed by Erik Janson from Sweden, a self proclaimed prophet, priest and king. Like Jim Jones, he came to a bad end, shot by a posse while celebrating the eucharist. The marriage ended tragically in a cholera epidemic.

Peerson's adventures in America covered three states: New York, Illinois and Texas. The first settlement in 1825 was at Kendall, on the shores of Lake Ontario, in New York. It did not turn out to be the "promised land" as they had hoped. In 1833, Cleng led an expedition to the Fox River near LaSalle, Illinois. This grew into a permanent colony of Norwegians which still exists. He is remembered as the founder of the settlement.

Of all the places in which Peerson settled, he liked Texas the best. At age 74, Cleng sold his farm in the Fox River Valley and moved to Bosque County west of Clifton in 1856. There Norwegians founded

Clifton College which is now merged with Texas Lutheran College in Seguin. He loved the warmer climate of the Lone Star State. The Texas legislature awarded him 320 acres for bringing new settlers. The community is still known as Norway and was visited by King Olav V in 1981.

The war between the states was a strain on Norwegian immigrants, especially those who lived in the South. Texas was a slave-holding state. Most Norsemen were violently opposed to slavery, though it is known that a few joined the practice. His countrymen fought on both sides and some of them ended up at Andersonville, a notorious prison camp in Georgia, a place of almost certain death. Peerson also came to know the Indians well, especially Chief Shabonna who was something of a "medicine man."

In his last years, Peerson lived in a small house on the farm which he had sold to a nephew. He used to go visiting a lot. When he arrived at a farm, people stopped working to hear him tell stories, just as if it were a Sunday afternoon. His favorite food on these visits was flatbread and sour milk. He died December 16, 1865, at the age of eighty-three. The inscription on his tombstone reads: "Cleng Peerson, the first Norwegian immigrant to America." It concludes: "Grateful countrymen in Texas erected this monument to his memory." They are not the only ones who are grateful. I join the children of 800,000 more immigrants who say, "thanks" to Cleng Peerson, the "Father of Norwegian Immigration" to America.

CHAPTER

42

EARLY NORSE SETTLERS IN THE NEW WORLD

I've had an awareness of my Scandinavian heritage since earliest childhood and was probably five years old before realizing that I lived in America. That was when my father told me that Franklin Roosevelt, a Democrat, was going to be president of the United States. Since the picture of the Norwegian royalty hung in our living room, I wondered, "What will happen to the king?" That was the beginning of my education as an American. After that, I decided Norway must be the same thing as heaven, from the way everybody talked about it, and was sure that's where I'd go when I died.

Since that time I've been curious about every Scandinavian who settled in America. Some time ago, there came into my possession a book entitled *Normaendene i Amerika* (Norsemen in America). It was published by Martin Ulvestad in 1907. It's printed in Gothic script and has no statistics after 1900.

Of special interest is Ulvestad's map, "Norge i Amerika" ("Norway in America"). The solidest concentration of Norwegians at the time was in Wisconsin, Minnesota, northeast Iowa, northeast Illinois, eastern South Dakota, eastern and northern North Dakota. If his research had been a little later, he would have colored in most of North Dakota plus eastern Montana. He does, however, include western Washington, parts of Oregon, Utah, Boston, New York and Philadelphia as having heavy concentrations.

Norwegians who fought in the Civil War are listed. Special recognition was given to Colonel Hans Heg (1829-1863), commander of the 15th Wisconsin Regiment (made up of Scandinavians), who died at the Battle of Chickamauga. He listed three colonels, twenty-seven majors, fifty-two captains, seventy-six lieutenants, 154 sergeants, 219 corporals, and 4042 enlisted men. Their places of birth and where they lived after the war are given.

I was surprised to learn that Pembina County was the home of the first Norwegian settler in North Dakota. R. E. Nelson was the first homesteader in the state, according to Ulvestad. He noted that Burlington was the earliest site of Norse settlers in Ward County. Among these were Ole Ingesen from Skien, Ole Spokkeli from Telemark, John Jacobsen from Kongsberg, Sivert Anderson from Sogn and H. Gasmann from Gjerpen. They had come from Wisconsin. Among the next earliest, he listed the Ramstads from Sigdal, Watnes from Sogn, and Johnsons from Nordland.

Kendall, in New York state, founded by Cleng Peerson and the "Sloopers" in 1825, was the earliest Norwegian settlement in America. The first colony to have continuity was the Fox River settlement in LaSalle County Illinois (1834). The main center of Norwegian immigrants in Illinois was Chicago. The first settler in Cook County was Halstein Torrisen who arrived in September 1836. There were some outstanding community leaders among these immigrants.

Jefferson Prairie was the first Norwegian settlement in Wisconsin. Ole Nattestad arrived from Nummedal in 1838. Muskego, about twenty-five miles southwest of Milwaukee, was settled in 1839. Racine was the first city in the state to attract Norwegian settlers. The Johnsons (a famous family in that city) were the first Norwegians to set foot on Wisconsin soil. Racine later became the favorite city of Danish immigrants. Koshkonong, near Madison, was settled in 1839-40. Being on the Great Lakes, Milwaukee had an early settlement of Norse.

Keokok, in southeast Iowa, became that state's first Norse settlement (1840). Winneshiek County, however, in northeast Iowa, became the main settlement of Norwegians in the state. Decorah is still the center for Iowa Norwegians, having been settled in 1852. The first settler was Erik Anderson Rude from Voss.

Minnesota's earliest Norwegian settlement was in Fillmore County ("Little House on the Prairie" country) in 1851. The Minneapolis area began to attract Norwegians about 1855 and it developed into the most Norwegian metropolis in America. The St. Anthony Park community of St. Paul (near the Minnesota State Fair Grounds) became a favorite place for these immigrants. It's the location where Norwegians built Luther Seminary for training pastors. It's the largest Lutheran seminary in the New World.

South Dakota's first Norwegian settlement was in the Yankton area in 1859. Settlers came from Hallingdal, Ulvik, Voss and the Sogn area while it was still "Indian Territory." The South Dakota settlements in the Canton and Sioux Falls area were made famous by Ole Rolvaag's writings.

Not enough is known in the Midwest about the large number of Norwegians who settled on the West Coast, the largest concentration being in Washington. The earliest known "hvide Mand" ("white man") to settle in the state, according to Ulvestad, was Martin Zakarias Tosteson who landed at Dak Harbor in 1847. Seattle still has a very active Norwegian community. The fishing and lumber industries were a natural attraction to them. Besides that, there were mountains. What could be a more natural habitat for a Norseman?

It's easy for many of us to assume that all Norse settlements in America are in the Upper Midwest. Martin Ulvestad's map of "Norway in America" shows that by 1900 Norse settlements were in every U. S. state except Arkansas and Nevada, and were in the Canadian provinces of Quebec, British Columbia, Ontario, Alberta, Manitoba, Saskatchewan and "Assiniboia" (Indian territory north of Montana). Free land from Wisconsin to Montana after the Civil War is the reason this region became the Scandinavian "heartland" of America. The New World wanted settlers and Scandinavians have always been looking for land.

The seacoast cities were the natural places for Scandinavians to settle. The first Norwegian settler in Massachusetts was Ole Haugen, who came to Lowell County from Bergen in 1815. New England was considered to be "Leif Erikson" land. Since New York City was a port of immigration, a large number settled there. Brooklyn still has a distinct Norwegian population with its own newspaper - *Norsk Tidende*. In 1970, while attending a national youth convention in the Big Apple, I was interviewed by one of their reporters. My North Dakota background interested them, even though I was living in Chicago at the time. The first Norwegian congregation founded in New York was in Brooklyn (1860).

Some of the most interesting Norse settlements were in Texas. John Nordboe from Ringebo in Gudbrandsdal was the first Norwegian to settle in the state. He took land in Dallas County in 1838. Cleng Person, who started the Norwegian immigration to America in 1825, founded the best known Norse colony in Bosque County (1854). King Olav V visited the community on one of his recent trips to America.

A look at the Salt Lake City phone book shows that many Scandinavians settled in Utah, largely recruited by Mormon missionaries. My mother-in-law remembered their activity in Denmark when she was a little girl. The first Norwegian in Utah was Augusta Sondrason Bakke from Tinn in Telemark, who joined the Mormon trek to Utah from Nauvoo, Illinois, in 1847.

It has surprised me to learn how many Norwegians settled in Michigan. There is a strong Scandinavian center in Detroit with its own Symphony Orchestra. The first Norwegian settlement in the state was at Muskegon County in 1848.

Nebraska had its first Norwegian settlement in 1857 at Newman Grove. A strong Hauge Synod congregation was started there in 1873. The first Norwegian settlement in Kansas was also in 1857.

California had an early attraction to Norwegians (and still does). Sailors and gold seekers were the first to arrive. The "I Remember Mama" television series featured these immigrants in San Francisco. Portland, Oregon, had its first Norwegian congregation in 1876.

The story of Norwegians in Montana deserves special attention. Chris Boe of Billings has gathered this material and has shared some information with me about such men as Martin Grande, pioneer of the sheep industry in the state; Anton Holter, a leader in the lumber industry; and J. Hugo Aronson of Sweden, who was governor from 1952-1960. I hope his research is published. It's an exciting story.

We could count many more settlements: New Hampshire (1854), Oklahoma (1869), Idaho (1876), Colorado (1878), Tennessee (1887) and Georgia (1898). Individual Norwegians found their way to all the states, but because they were often a small segment of society, they did not form ethnic groups as in the Upper Midwest.

One of the colorful, though ill-fated, Norwegian colonizing attempts was by Ole Bull (1810-1880), who bought 120,000 acres of infertile, title-flawed land in Pennsylvania. The world famous violinist set up the "Oleana" colony in Potter County in 1852. About 1000 people tied their hopes to his community, but it turned out to be a money-losing disaster. If music could have maintained a settlement, "Oleana" would have become the paradise of which he dreamed, now it's only a song at which people laugh and choke back a tear.

British Columbia in Canada had a Norse settlement by 1860. Quebec, a point of entry for many immigrants, had Norwegians by 1857. The Norwegian settlements in Canada are in Alberta, Saskatchewan, Manitoba and British Columbia. Travelling with the Concordia College Choir by boat from Seattle to Vancouver in 1946, I visited with a man from Saskatchewan who told me about the "Norwegians" north of Saskatoon. In typical English style, he spoke of them as "foreigners." The first Norse settlement in Alberta was in Calgary (1886). Manitoba followed in 1887 and Saskatchewan in the 1890s. Saskatoon is a Norwegian center. Another significant location of Norsemen is in the Peace River country, the home of the Ronning family which has given distinguished service in Canada, China and the United States.

It continues to amaze me that 100 years after emigrating, Norsemen continue to cherish their ethnic roots while being strongly committed to their new lands. It's inevitable, I suppose, that some day, like the Scandinavians in England and Ireland, the New World Norse will just be called Americans and Canadians.

CHAPTER

43

THE NORWEGIANS IN TEXAS

Texas is a big state. You'd hardly expect that a handful of Norwegian immigrants would even be noticed. But they were. The first Norwegian settler in the Lone Star state was Johan Nordboe from Ringebo in Gudbrandsdal. Deeply in debt at age sixty-four, and with four children, he went to America as his only hope. Nordboe was also one of the founders of the Fox River settlement of Norwegians in northern Illinois. He bought land in Dallas County in 1838.

The first Norwegian community in the state was at Brownsboro,Henderson County, in 1845. The leader was Johan Reinert Reiersen who is considered to be the "Father of Norwegian Immigration to Texas." Reierson spent two years in Texas before meeting his family in New Orleans and bringing them to Kaufman County. He represented a liberal political view which was common to Norwegian immigrants (the conservatives stayed in the Old Country). Reierson became a personal acquaintance of General Sam Houston, the president of the Republic of Texas.

The best known writer among early Norwegians in Texas was Elise Waerenskjold who arrived at Brownsboro in 1847. She was the daughter of a Lutheran pastor in Norway and who at age nineteen became a schoolteacher. This was unusual for a woman in those days. Elise and her husband, Wilhelm, were skilled writers and became staunch defenders of their new home. She wrote: "I believe Texas is the best of the States to migrate to, partly because the climate is milder and more pleasant than in the Northern States and partly because the land is cheaper."

The first real Texan that I ever met was a classmate at seminary, Bernt I. Dahl, Jr. After graduation, he became a pastor in Vashon Island, Washington. Today he lives in retirement on the family farm near Waco.

At the 1987 Norsk Høstfest, I became acquainted with Wayne A. Rohne, an attorney from Arlington, home of the Texas Rangers baseball team. He had read my book, *The Scandinavian Heritage*, on a trip to China. The chapter about the Norsk Høstfest attracted him to Minot. Returning to America, he received a letter from Vesterheim, the prestigious Norwegian-American museum in Decorah, Iowa, announcing that its 1987 Annual Meeting was to be held in conjunction with the Høstfest. That's how we first met. We visited again at the 1988 Nordic Fest in Decorah. In the meantime, he'd sent me a large packet of information about the Norwegians in Texas.

Included in the packet was the Centennial Gathering booklet of the Dahl family which left Romedal, Hedemarken, Norway in 1850 for Bosque County in eastern Texas. Rohne's deceased wife's great-grandparents were prominent among the Norwegian in Texas. Their picture appears on the cover of "The Norwegian Texans," a pamphlet published by the Institute of Texan Cultures, The University of Texas at San Antonio (1985).

The name "Dahl" shows a Danish influence on the spelling of the Norwegian "Dal," which means a valley. Since Norway has so many valleys, it's not an uncommon name, but it frequently suggests a family which had lived on better than average farm land. Travelling through the port of New Orleans, the Dahls settled down to become loyal Texans. The oldest son of Hendrik Dahl, Ole, served in the Texas Cavalry in the Civil War. He returned safely after the conflict ended.

There's an interesting story about Indians coming to the Dahl home and wanting a swordlike knife that was placed between the ceiling and the shingles. Mrs. Dahl stomped her foot so forcefully and told them they could not have it that they left peacefully. The Dahls lived in frontier country where the Kiowas and Comanches were still raiding settlements. Sentries had to be posted to keep a lookout for raiding parties. It was not unusual for farm houses to be looted and children to be kidnapped for a ransom of groceries and other merchandise.

Later when Henrik returned to Norway to visit his aged mother, forty new immigrants joined him on the return to America. Crossing the Atlantic, they encountered a fierce winter storm. Dahl became ill on the return trip and died shortly after arriving home. His reputation as a horse trader is still remembered.

Mrs. Dahl took up the responsibility of rearing nine children. With their help, she became an expert farmer and continued to increase the land holdings, the cattle and horses. She also took time to help the church, even attending all the business meetings. Because of her strong interest, she was given the right to speak and vote at the meetings, a rare courtesy extended to women in those days. She was also one of the boosters of Clifton Lutheran College, which later merged with Texas Lutheran College in Seguin. The Dahl farm has never been sold out of the original family. In 1954, their descendants held a centennial celebration with about 240 people at the homestead. B. I. Dahl, Sr., was named President of the family association to plan the next gathering.

The most famous of the Texas settlers was Cleng Peerson (1782-1865) who sailed from Stavanger in a converted herring boat called the "Restauration" in 1825. His biographies by Alfred Hauge give an interesting account of this famous Norsemen who is credited with starting the Norwegian immigration to America. Even though Peerson was sixty-seven years old when he moved to Texas in 1850, he was influential in bringing many new settlers. The Texas legislature created Bosque County in 1854 and offered 320 acres of free land to anyone who would settle there. In recognition of his services to Texas, Peerson also received an allotment. Peerson made his home with Ovee Colwick, a cousin of Mrs. Rohne on her father's side. The southwest part of the county is the most thoroughly Norwegian community in Texas. It is the only place in the state where the Old Country customs still are observed.

As the Civil War clouds overshadowed Texas, Elise Waerenskjold expressed the sentiments of Norwegians in the state when she wrote:

"I believe that slavery is absolutely contrary to the law of God. ...People have asked me if I would tolerate having a Negro woman as a daughter-in-law. I must admit that it would not please me very much to have grandchildren who are slaves. ...We immigrants, to be sure, can do nothing to abolish slavery; we are too few to accomplish anything for this cause and would merely bring on ourselves hatred and persecution. All we can do is to keep ourselves free of the whole slavery system." About 50 Norwegian-Texans, however, did serve in the Confederate armies. Distasteful as slavery had been, the Reconstruction period was not kind to the former slaves either. Extreme poverty was to be their lot for many years.

The first pastor to become a resident in Texas was Ole Olsen Estrem (1869-1877). He was followed at Norse, Texas, by John Knudsen Rystad who served Our Savior's Lutheran Church for 58 years. He also served as the first president of Clifton Academy in 1896 which was later to become a college.

Norwegians kept coming to Texas, but not in such large numbers as came to the Middle West or Far West. By 1880 there were 880 Norwegians who were born citizens in the state. By 1900 the number had reached 1356.

One of the best known Norwegian-Texans was Mildred Didriksen (Babe Zaharias). She became one of the greatest women athletes of her day, dominating the 1932 women's events at the Olympics and named "Woman Athlete of the First Half of the 20th Century in 1950." She is usually pictured swinging a golf club.

These folks are exciting people. They have an enthusiastic dancing group that performs in colorful "Texas bunads" which blends rosemaling and original Texas motifs. Those wishing to learn more about the Norwegians in Texas should write to the Norwegian Society of Texas, c/o Dr. Alfhild Akselsen, Rt. 2, Box J-13, Beaumont, TX 77705.

CHAPTER

44

EARLY NORWEGIANS IN CHICAGO

Minot, North Dakota, founded in 1887, is called the "Magic City" because of its rapid growth when the Great Northern Railroad came through in 1884. What then shall we call Chicago, founded just forty years earlier on a swampy river mouth at the southwestern tip of Lake Michigan? First seen by the French explorers Louis Joliet and Jacques Marquette in 1673, it began as a minor trading post with the building of Ft. Dearborn in 1803. The fort, destroyed in 1812 by an Indian raid as a part of the war with England that same year, was rebuilt in 1816, but was still unnoticed when Illinois became a state in 1818.

Before the Civil War was over, Chicago had emerged as the leading city of the Midwest, even exceeding St. Louis. It's population increased seventeen times between 1850 and 1870. Immigrants from northern Europe came in droves to work in construction, in the meat packing plants and factories. Carl Sandburg (1878-1967) characterized the city well in his poem, "Chicago," in 1914. Then came the fire of October 8-10, 1871, which virtually destroyed it. Today it's the hub of travel and business for all mid-America. It continues to grow and nothing seems to stop it.

This is the city which became the Norwegian center of the New World from 1840 to the early 1900s. Only then was it replaced by Minneapolis as the center of "New Norway." The opening of the Erie Canal in 1825 coincided with the beginning of the Norse migration to America prodded by Cleng Peerson and the arrival of the "Restauration" into the New York harbor. Soon newcomers to America were ferried across the Great Lakes to the unoccupied lands of the West.

But Norwegians had arrived ahead of Cleng Peerson's "refugees" from Stavanger. Fredrik Peterson was among the soldiers killed during the massacre of 1812. There were others too who travelled without fanfare to America. After the defeat of Chief Black Hawk in 1832, Illinois was considered safe for settling. The first Norwegian to take up permanent residence in the city was a sailor named David Johnson from Voss in 1834. Having been trained in operating a printing press, he quickly found work and influenced other Norwegians to join him. By 1844, Norwegians were the third largest ethnic group in this new city after the Germans and the Irish. It's interesting that early census records counted the Germans and the Norwegians together as one ethnic group called "Dutch."

The "Vossings" were the most numerous of the Norwegians in Chicago. I've met many people in the "Windy City" who claim their heritage from Voss. That's what attracted Knute Rockne's family to Chicago. The most prominent of these early immigrants was Iver Lawson, whose name had originally been Ivar Larson Boe, who arrived in 1844. Trained in Norway as a tailor, he worked as a day laborer in the beginning and ended up as the publisher of the *Chicago Daily News*. He was also a member of the city council and was appointed marshall of the city. As marshall, he was in command of the police force when Abraham Lincoln was nominated for president in 1860.

Lawson was active in organizing the first Norwegian Lutheran Church in 1848. Today it's known as Lake View Lutheran Church near Wrigley Field, the home of the Chicago Cubs.

Many of the Norwegians preferred to move on to Wisconsin. The triangle between Chicago, LaCrosse and Milwaukee became the early center of Norwegians in those days. The early Norse settlers preferred the Democratic party. They switched to the Republicans, however, during the heat of the slavery issue which preceded the Civil War. The Norwegians became active in the "Underground Railroad" and were ardent supporters of Lincoln and the Union during that fratricidal war. The Fifteenth Wisconsin Regiment with 890 men was made up of mostly Norwegians under the command of Col. Hans Heg, who was killed at the Battle of Chickamauga in Georgia. When they travelled through Chicago, they were given a rousing patriotic welcome by the

Norwegians living there. This demonstrated proof of their patriotism to America.

Health conditions of the new metropolis were deplorable, as they were in most large cities of the time. The streets were filthy, drinking water was polluted, drainage was inadequate and the wet swamps were breeding grounds for mosquitoes. Malaria and cholera combined to bring a plague on the people. Nutrition was also poor. The new settlers rarely took baths or kept themselves clean. In the epidemic of 1850, forty-five of the 332 Norwegians living in one area died. When speaking about the plague, it was commented by the Yankees that it was fortunate that the deaths happened mainly "among our foreign citizens."

As the flood of immigrants from Norway swelled, the Norwegian government became alarmed. The clergy were the spokesmen to warn people away from America. The Vossings in Chicago took up the challenge to defend their new land and organized the Vossing Correspondence Society to enlighten their friends back home about the virtues of America. The Norwegian Debating Society was organized to stimulate awareness of life in America, especially slavery. Annual social events were also sponsored by the society. The Vossing Emigration Society, founded in 1856, gave assistance to Norwegian immigrants that needed financial assistance.

Except for the "free-thinkers," the Norwegians adopted Yankee "puritanism" in their opposition to liquor and were advocates of sabbath observance. Their clergy also opposed dancing and theatre. There were a few dissenters among them, especially Dr. Gerhard Paoli from Trondheim, a physician who became president of the Chicago Medical Society. Another noted free-thinker was Marcus Thrane, a socialist reformer. Both of these men, like Bjornstierne Bjornson, opposed the Norwegian clergy and the conservative theology of most immigrants.

The Lutherans weren't alone in doing soul care among the Scandinavians. The Baptists, Episcopalians and Methodists were also active to evangelize the immigrants. Gustaf Unonius, an Episcopalian, is quoted extensively in Page Smith's volumes of American history. Revivalism hit Chicago in the 1860s. Dwight L. Moody, one of the leaders helped organize the Chicago YMCA in 1858.

An early Swedish Lutheran pastor from Sweden was Erland Carlsson who arrived in 1853 and built a strong congregation. They did much to assist immigrants, meeting them at the train station, finding places for them to live, buying money orders, helping them with language and finding jobs. One Norwegian congregation, Our Savior's Lutheran (named after the cathedral in Oslo), built a brick church that seated 1200 people.

The new settlement attracted celebrities too. Ole Bull, the famous Norwegian violinist, came to Chicago in March 1854 and gave concerts. He was highly praised by the Chicago Tribune's critics. Early ethnic organizations for the Scandinavians included the Swedish Svea Society in 1857, the Norwegian Nora Society in 1860, and the Danish Dania Society in 1862. These secular organizations were often in conflict with the immigrant church on social issues.

The Great Fire of 1871 destroyed almost four square miles of the new frontier city. The wooden sidewalks and dry weather moved the flames along swiftly. Both Swedes and Norwegians suffered heavily from the fire.

By the turn of the century, Humboldt Park, Milwaukee Avenue and Logan Square to the northwest of the original city had become the center of the Norwegian community. I came to know that area after World War II when quite a few Scandinavians still lived there. Today it has become mainly an Hispanic community. English is again a foreign language there, as it is in many parts of the city. The Norwegians have moved mainly to the northwest suburbs of the city. But they are still there as I learned when living in Chicago a second time from 1967 to 1973. And they still love their ethnic foods served at Sons of Norway lodges and at their Constitution Day celebrations on May 17.

An excellent resource for learning the story of these early Norwegians in Chicago is *A Century of Urban Life: The Norwegians in Chicago before 1930* by Prof. Odd S. Lovoll. Dr. Lovoll spent two years leave of absence from St. Olaf College to write his findings. The book was published by the Norwegian-American Historical Association (1988) headquartered at St. Olaf College in Northfield, Minnesota.

CHAPTER

45

LAKE VIEW CHURCH
OF CHICAGO

Ole Munch Raeder was a Norwegian scholar who visited America during 1847-48. He was sent by the king to study the American jury system. The letters he sent back to Norway were lost for almost eighty years in the University of Oslo's Library until found by a Norwegian-American researcher. As a result we have a better understanding of what life was like when the early Scandinavian settlers came to America.

Munch was quite impressed with the good reputation that Norwegians had in America, except for Chicago. He wrote in 1850 that "there are many bad characters among the more than 600 Norwegians in Chicago. I have not been there and consequently cannot speak from personal experience." Among the vices to which some Norwegians had fallen were drinking, gambling and fighting. He was impressed with the fact that in Illinois a Norwegian had been elected to be a justice of the peace.

They were not all rowdies, of course, perhaps only a small minority. Among the new immigrants from Norway were the people who organized Lake View Lutheran Church in 1848, the first Scandinavian congregation in Chicago. It's still a viable community of faith.

The beginnings of Lake View Church go back to 1834 when it was a mission station and Sunday School. A building fund was started in 1847. They received $600 from Trinity German Lutheran Church in St. Louis, which is the best known of the early Missouri Synod congregations. The pastor, Dr. C. F. W. Walther took a strong interest in the ministry among Norwegians. He is remembered as the "grand daddy" of the Missouri Synod and a founder of Concordia Seminary in St. Louis. The gift from Trinity was put together with a local fund drive and a building was begun.

Then tragedy struck. The leader of the fund drive absconded with the building fund money and a wind storm badly damaged the building under construction. Discouraged but not defeated, they contacted Paul Andersen, a student at Beloit College in Wisconsin who had come from Norway in 1843. He accepted the challenge on condition that Norwegian and English would be used on an equal basis. The congregation was officially organized on February 14, 1848, as "The Scandinavian Evangelical Lutheran Church of Chicago." Andersen was ordained the following year. One of the charter members was Iver Lawson, the father of Victor F. Lawson, the founder and publisher of the *Chicago Daily News*.

When a boatload of Swedes arrived in 1852, they were struck with a cholera epidemic and had no money. The Norwegians responded to their needs and nursed them back to health. Jenny Lind, the great Swedish singer, heard about this kind treatment to her countrymen and in appreciation gave the congregation a silver communion set. The communion set is now on display at the Vesterheim museum in Decorah, Iowa. The Swedes and Norwegians worshiped together for a while, until it became apparent that they would do their work better separately. The Norwegians sold their building to the Swedes and in 1854 built a large brick building for $18,000 which seated over 900 people. It was called the "cathedral church" of Norwegian Lutheranism in Chicago.

Then another crisis came. Pastor Andersen had not worn the traditional vestments, including the "krag," the ruffed collar worn by clergy of the Norwegian state church. Pastor Peterson who came in 1861 liked the traditional vestments. Unfortunately, a church fight occurred and even though Peterson's side won, it split the congregation, with many people quitting church altogether. The unhappy affair was put to rest in the great Chicago fire of 1871, just a month after the split resulting from a court case in favor of Peterson's side. It wasn't only the church building that burned, but also the homes of many members.

Still they didn't give up. In November 1874, they erected another building also seating 900. Special offerings were taken to erase the debt with its 10% interest. Times were difficult and in 1891 a small group of this original congregation moved into the Lake View area, north of downtown near Lake Michigan. This is how the name "Lake View" became attached to the congregation. Their first pastor in this neighborhood was Rev. Olaf Brandt, who later became a professor of theology at Luther Seminary in St. Paul.

I first became acquainted with Lake View Church in 1950-1951 during my internship in Chicago. When I returned to the metropolitan area in 1967-73, Lake View was beginning a new direction. My son, Mark, attended worship at Lake View Church from 1981-84 while attending DeVry Institute of Technology. By this time it was no longer a Norwegian congregation. In 1972 a new Spanish ministry began together with the English. Pastor Julio A. Loza of La Paz, Bolivia, arrived to minister to the people of the community. While many of the north European background people have moved to the suburbs, Lake View has stayed in their building constructed in 1961. Now they are back to two languages again, but this time Spanish has replaced the Norwegian.

Lake View Church has opened up its facilities to four Alcoholics Anonymous groups, a Narcotics Anonymous group, Girl Scouts and other community agencies. They started a "Ministry Center" in January 1988. This has formed networks with community agencies to avoid duplication in needed services to the hungry, sick, poor, homeless and oppressed of all ethnic backgrounds. They also work with other congregations to develop the resources necessary to plan and underwrite the needed programs.

One of these services is the Volunteer Resources which provides bulk and mass mailing services to small not-for-profit organizations in the community together with giving support to needy individuals. They also give professional services such as financial and computer services to organizations and congregations, with oversight from a qualified accountant and staff trained in computer systems.

I'm impressed that Lake View Church has entered into a joint venture with the Lutheran General Medical Center in suburban Park Ridge to have a "Parish Nurse Program." A registered nurse on the staff helps provide health education and support services to a network of eight congregations and social service agencies of the community. This program was pioneered by Dr. Granger Westberg, author of the bestseller *Good Grief.* There is now a national parish nurse program affiliated with Lutheran General which trains nurses and congregations to do this kind of work. I became acquainted with Dr. Westberg in 1950 when he was the chaplain at the Augustana Hospital in Chicago.

Lake View Church is involved in the "Northside Ecumenical Night Ministry" which goes out on the streets at night to minister to people in need. Among these are the homeless and those involved in drugs, alcohol, prostitution and abuse. They have a "Youth Street Outreach" which concentrates on reaching youth who have no homes. They provide AIDS education to many of them. They cooperate with a "Genesis House" which provides hospitality for women, offers job counseling and health education. The "Exodus Homes" is a demonstration project which provides foster home care and support services for homeless and high risk youth.

They are also involved in the Street Volunteer Program and the Lake View Community Shelter. About twenty-five people sleep in their building every night between October and April, supervised by volunteers. They also have a day time drop-in center where people can get warm, have coffee and receive counseling. The Lake View Emergency Relief Project, which provides both shelters and food pantries, is also headquartered at the church. Lake View Church belongs to a network called Volunteer Attorneys for the Homeless and the Center for Sibling Loss of the Southern School.

I find it especially interesting that the "Church of South India Congregation" uses the building every Sunday evening. Most of these people are new immigrants to the United States.

They do all this work for a budget of less than $100,000. But that's pretty good for a congregation with less than 100 adult members. $17,700 of their 1988 budget was income expected from renting out their parking lot for Chicago Cub baseball games. With the Cubs now playing night games, they'll be busier than ever.

Who would ever have dreamed back in the 1848 that this congregation started by Norwegian immigrants to Chicago would have ventured into such an innovative ministry almost 150 years later. I take my hat off to the people of Lake View Church for resisting flight to the suburbs and doing ministry where they are. May they continue to prosper.

CHAPTER

46

THE CHALLENGE
OF THE PRAIRIE WINDS

There's nothing like an old fashioned three-day snow storm. The early pioneers were soon to discover this special feature of prairie life. Evelyn Dale Iverson of Canton, South Dakota., has written a delightful book about these wintery storms. The story centers on her grandfather, Nils A. Dale, who immigrated to America from western Norway in 1868.

The book, entitled *Prairie Wind, Blow Me Back*, is the story about one immigrant, but it's typical of thousands more. The book had a special interest for me since some of Nils' grandchildren attended Concordia College when I did in the 1940s. Their father, Hans (Nils' son), was on the college administration staff.

The immigrants were surprised how hard the wind blew across the prairies of the New World. Once when we were visiting with a cousin of my wife in northern Jutland (Denmark), he asked, "Does the wind blow in North Dakota?" We assured him that it did. Then he asked, "But how can it when you're so far from the ocean?" But blow it does, and anyone who lives on the prairies can attest.

Nils came from Breimsvatn, in the Westlands of Norway, about twelve miles northwest of Skei in Jolster. That's an area where some very beautiful folk music has been preserved. Not far to the east are snow-capped mountains. Living on small farms along the fjords was challenge. Fishing, farming, and often carpentry were all needed to keep families alive.

It was a time of "America Fever." Letters from the New World inflamed the imaginations of those Norse folk in whom the spirit of adventure had been latent since time immemorial When Nils turned twenty-five in October 1867, it was apparent to all the family that he had set his mind on America. Those emigrating from western Norway usually left from Bergen and sailed to Quebec, which is what Nils did. Before leaving, he signed the Church Book as Nils Amundsen Stokke. the name was taken from his mother's parents farm. He was born while she was visiting there. Later, however, he took the name "Dale" from his father's farm.

Nils travelled to America with a friend named Arne. During the first winter, they worked at a lumber camp in Wisconsin, where they experienced a classic midwestern snow storm. Out in the woods when it started, they had no idea how frightening such a storm can become. With the help of more experienced woodsmen, they made it to shelter and safety. Arne's right foot became white and was frostbitten. The foot was saved, but it left him with a limp.

One winter in the woods was enough for Nils and Arne. They went off farming near LaCrosse. Like many other bachelor immigrants, Nils and Arne kept their eyes open for new arrivals from the Old Country, they were lonesome and hoped to meet the girls. When Nils met Rakel, it was love at first sight. To his proposal, she answered: "Oh, I'm only sixteen, my father wouldn't let me marry so young." "Well, Nils replied, "How old would you have to be?" She answered, "At least seventeen." They were married four months later, four days after her birthday.

The immigrants were eager for news of the outside world. The great Chicago fire of 1871 shocked them, especially since a Norwegian community burned out. There had also been fires in Brown and Manitowac counties in which 3000 homes were destroyed and thousands of people killed. This raised the concern for fire protection. After that, Nils always plowed a wide strip around his buildings.

1872 was a good year for farming. But 1873, a hailstorm took Nils' largest wheat field. In 1874 grasshoppers darkened the sky. They tried everything they could to protect their garden. Nothing helped. The hoppers came back in 1875, but were not so bad. While all these things were going on, they were also rearing a family. Times were tough, but there was still a little money squeezed out to give to St. Olaf College begun in Northfield, Minnesota, in 1874, and for Luther Seminary in St. Paul in 1879. It turned out to be a good investment since two of his sons attended St. Olaf.

The great "Dakota Land Boom" was on by 1879. Nils was now 37 years old. With a group of seven other land seekers, he rode the train to Sioux Falls, South Dakota, and ended up in Volga. They got a room in a hotel (barracks style) and then set out looking for homestead land. It was out in these Dakota prairies that they discovered the full fury of the west winds. Its force was so hard that it nearly blew their coats off while prospecting for land.

It was a long trek to Dakota Territory travelling in covered wagons and leading their cattle. Oxen are slow, but they can face any wind. Not too many years before, earlier settlers had encountered hostile Indians. The Native Americans could not always understand the peaceful intent of these newcomers. Many of their earlier encounters with the white people had been traders, soldiers and shysters. How could they know the intentions of these aliens who had come to settle on their ancient homeland? And the newcomers had not been informed about the trail of broken treaties. But as luck would have it, they didn't meet any of the "hostiles."

A 10' x 12' building was required to "prove" a claim. Nils, however, built a 14' x 16' sod house. The strips were one foot wide, three feet long and about four inches thick. The flat prairie land was so different from what they had known in both Norway and Wisconsin. They told their children, "Mr. Wind has blown away the hills, and leveled the land all the way to the edge of the sky." There was also good fishing and hunting.

On October 15, 1880, a fierce blizzard caught the small colony of Norwegian settlers unprepared for winter. Nils' house was the only one completed and some of the men were gone to find work elsewhere. So everyone crowded into Nils' sod house. There wasn't much room for anyone. The air can get pretty stuffy at a time like that. To keep their up courage, they sang songs about Norway, its trees, waterfalls, lakes, fjords, mountains, fields and oceans. They recited Psalms, learned by heart in the Old Country Schools. They prayed, and they prevailed. This storm went beyond the three long days we've heard about. Then followed bitter cold and more wind. Heavy snowfalls continued until spring and many animals starved or froze to death.

By 1882, a Ladies Aid Society had been formed and by 1885 they had put aside $450 towards building a new church. These women met twice a month in their homes and it always included coffee and Norwegian pastries. Some walked for many miles carrying a baby while knitting all the way. The church was built on six acres of donated land. Included was land for a fenced cemetery and a buggy shed.

Nils returned to Norway in 1883. His father was still living, but his mother had died twelve years earlier. Such reunions were happy ones but they also had some sadness. Not only were things changed in the homeland, but the new ideas garnered in America had changed the Norse immigrant.

Some years were good. 1886 was one of them. But 1887 was the beginning of many disasters. Drought dried up the streams. Dry winds ripened the grain prematurely. Prairie fires were a constant threat. Then came the famous blizzard of 1888. Snowdrifts were so high that farmers had to make tunnels from house to barn. Those winters seem to last forever. And in the midst of it all citizenship papers had to be filed.

Nils returned to Norway again in 1892. Rakel went along this time. Less than two years later, his father died. It was a bitter cold day in January 1894 when the grave had to be dug for the funeral. The church choir sang "Den Store Hvide Flok," a favorite hymn of Norse folk to this day, also in America.

Back home in Howard, South Dakota, disasters hit. The town had burned down. A recently built flour mill exploded from combustible grain dust. A diphtheria epidemic broke out. Nils and Rakel lost an eight-year old daughter. Nils built the pine coffin himself. The next year they lost another child shortly after birth. Still they had eight healthy children for which they were grateful. That year on Christmas eve, Nils suddenly died of internal bleeding from falling out of a tree while looking for lost cattle. Rakel was left a widow at forty-three, yet that same evening she read the Christmas story from St. Luke to her children.

The winds blew hard on the prairies. They still do, but we have better shelters now, including better communications, medical care, all-weather highways and heated automobiles. Our homes, schools and churches are more comfortable, too. But, we must never forget those courageous people who bucked the west winds to build communities that have become good homes for us.

CHAPTER

47

"UNDER THE OAKS," NORWEGIANS AT WEST KOSHKONONG

Among the oak trees, about twenty miles to the southeast of Madison, Wisconsin, one of America's earliest Norwegian settlements was established in 1839. It was called West Koshkonong, named after a lake. The people had left their homeland despite the pleas and warnings of the clergy, who spoke in the name of the king. They warned of great sea-monsters in the Atlantic and of Indians lined up in New York harbor ready to scalp them. Leaders of the Norwegian government didn't want to lose people, but they left anyway. The old wanderlust of the ancient Vikings came alive as they looked for a better life. When the pastors saw that they could not keep the people from emigrating, they fervently admonished the confirmands on how to live in that land of "Barbarians."

It was not an easy life to which they journeyed. There were no roads or schools. According to Erling Ylvisaker, author of *Eminent Pioneers*, "every home was self-governed, self-educated, and self-provided - as far as their provisions reached." He cited the story of a farmer's wife who pulled a sledge loaded with cheese and butter for twenty miles to market in Madison.

Homesickness hit them hard. Some lost small children and other family on the boat en route to the New World. Fever and cholera epidemics made death a familiar visitor to every cabin in the woods. More than one young bride died of a broken heart or in childbirth, leaving a distraught young husband to build a coffin and lower her body into the earth. The stronger ones survived, and they were many. Through tears and brawn they eked out a life that has left a healthy heritage for their children's children. It was common to press a rose between the pages of a book after a funeral to save some remembrance of one who died. This was still being done when I was a child.

Back in Norway, the church was the center of social life. In America they had no houses of worship or pastors. The Norwegian State Church did not provide pastors for the departing emigrants. Religious quacks took advantage of the trusting immigrants. It was not until five years later, in 1844, that Rev. Claus Clausen of the Muskego community southwest of Milwaukee spent a few weeks among them to organize a congregation. Later that year, Rev. J. W. C. Dietrichson, trained for the ministry in the Church of Norway, arrived. He had been promised $150 a year. He gathered 60 people under the oaks for the first service. A new log church was dedicated on December 19. It was the first Norwegian Lutheran church to be dedicated in America.

The Counsel General from Norway was not very flattering about the building. He said it looked like a barn, but was "neat and tasteful inside." There was not much support from the old country for those who settled in the new land. They left Norway at their own risk.

The new pastor was used to having people tip their hats to him and salute with their hands. In Norway, he was the king's appointee. The story is told that when the pastor and his young wife came to spend a few days at a certain home that Mrs. Dietrichson "wanted to know if there was fresh bread in the house." Upon learning that the bread was two days old, she said, "My husband must have fresh bread." Dutifully, the hostess baked fresh bread for them. They had travelled first-class across the ocean so they wouldn't have to associate with "ordinary passengers."

When it came to baptisms, if the name chosen by the parents sounded too Yankee, Dietrichson would give the child a Norwegian name. One mother wanted her daughter baptized "Thea Alice." Dietrichson named her Torbjor Aslon. However, after Dietrichson returned to Norway in 1850, the mother enrolled her daughter in confirmation class as Thea Alice.

There was no postal system to deliver mail in those days in Wisconsin, so when the pastors travelled from place to place to organize congregations and conduct services, they also carried the mail. Pastors had to be robust in those days as they were often the ones who shoveled the paths through the drifts after a snowstorm. Despite his arrogance, Dietrichson was no loafer. He worked hard to serve the people's spiritual needs, and they were many in a strange land.

The lay people took their religion seriously. It's told that one farmer never permitted his family or hired man to begin breakfast without first singing a hymn to give praise to the Giver.

In 1852, Rev. A. C. Preus and his wife walked more than 20 miles to Koshkonong to begin their new work. He organized the building of a new church which would seat 1000. It was the Norwegian custom to build churches on a hill. It had eight walls. Bjornstjerne Bjornson wrote that this signified their high regard for the church.

The "Klokker" was a familiar person in the church service. He was a layman. We might call him a "deacon." He prayed the opening and closing prayers, led the singing and was often the catechism teacher, going from house to house to teach the children. The klokker was usually well educated and was the one who would write letters for the people back to Norway. They wouldn't ask the pastor as they thought he was "far removed from farm thoughts."

By 1860, the West Koshkonong church had 800 members. Central Church in nearby Edgerton has about 2000 members today.

Not everything was peaceful and quiet under the oaks of Koshkonong. There were some whose affection for liquor got them regularly into fist-fights. This did not end with the past century. When the pastor preached about things they didn't like, they'd mock him in public by hitching up the horses and plowing on Sundays, or pulling a bottle from their coats when he was near.

There were those who had imaginative excuses for staying away from worship in those days too. One man said he didn't hear well. Another said he had to tend his traps as there were always more muskrats in them on Sunday than any other day.

There was also strife in the congregations. The doctrine of "pre-destination" became a hot topic in the 1880s. Most of the people knew practically nothing about the subject, but they'd bring in all kinds of Norwegian "heathens" to the church meetings to vote. They even went to court with their disputes. Civil judges had to warn them not "to make public fools of themselves."

But most of the people attended church faithfully and they gave generously of their time and means to support the church. They hauled the water to mix mortar for the building, others hauled bricks and sand. There was no thought of being paid for these services. There were no trucks or pavements and they often lived in humble houses themselves, but they wanted the best for the church. Today the attitude is often that people want the best for themselves and that anything left over ought to be good enough for the church.

A later generation thought the octagonal church was too out of style. In 1892 they destroyed it with dynamite and built a new Gothic style building. There were many tears among the faithful that night.

Many of the original settlers at West Koshkonong moved to Iowa and Minnesota. As land became more scarce, many of their descendants moved still further west into the Dakotas, Montana and Canada. A large number continued moving west across the Rockies to the West Coast during the 1930s. But wherever they moved, many of those original Koshkonongers remained faithful to the values of their heritage, while struggling to survive and live useful lives in the New World.

First East Koshkonong Lutheran Church, Cambridge, Wisconsin. First Norwegian Lutheran Congregation in America. Present building erected in 1893.

CHAPTER

48

STOUGHTON'S "SYTTENDE MAI" CELEBRATION

Wherever there are Norwegians, there will also be a "Syttende Mai" (pronounced SIT-tende MY) celebration. This simply means "May 17th" and it's the day which commemorates Norway's constitution of 1814.

Some people refer to it as "Independence Day," but this was short-lived wishful thinking by some signers of the constitution. No nation recognized their self-proclaimed independence and before the year was over, Norway was forced by its neighbors to elect Sweden's king as their ruler. In return, he promised to respect the new constitution, with a few changes. This gave Norway considerably more self-determination than it had under the rule of Danish kings. Denmark didn't get a constitution until 1849.

The Norwegians clung to their constitution, modeled after the French constitution of 1791 and the American constitution of 1787 with some additional ideas from English law. They made some revisions along the way to their full independence of 1905. However, they did have more freedom under Swedish rule than they'd had under Denmark, for the Danish kings had no constitution at the time and made laws as they pleased.

Stoughton, Wisconsin, was founded in 1847 by a Vermont Yankee named Luke Stoughton who built a dam and sawmill on Catfish River. I'm indebted to Eugene and Beatrice Kalland of Stoughton for much of my information on the community. They're active at the Stoughton

Historical Museum. Beatrice is also the president of the Wisconsin State Rosemaling Association.

Stoughton is located just fifteen miles southeast of Madison and has a population of 7600. The first Norwegians arrived in Dane County in 1839 in the Koshkonong community a few miles to the northeast of where the city was established. In his book *Normaendene i Amerika* (Norsemen in America), Martin Ulvestad referred to this as the "first and best known Norsk settlement in America."

The Koshkonong community attracted a large number of Norwegian settlers. One of the first things they did was to build churches. Among the well known pastors who ministered there were J. W. C. Dietrichson and Herman Amberg Preus. The Norwegian Synod and Luther College in Decorah had much of their early support and leadership from these congregations. They also had the distinction of electing one of their people as the first Norwegian in the Wisconsin legislature, Gunnulf Tollefsen in 1868. Knut Nelson, the first Norwegian to be elected a governor in America, also grew up in the community. Besides serving as Minnesota's chief executive, he also was elected to both the US House of Representatives and Senate.

At the turn of the century, Stoughton was the home of the famous Mandt wagon factory, where up to 35,000 wagons a year were made. They also had ten passenger trains daily, with hourly connections to Madison and the nearby resorts. They advertised that "labor troubles are unknown, rents and living expenses reasonable and surroundings healthy and wholesome."

It's no wonder then that these Stoughton Norwegians are proud of their heritage and celebrate with colorful pageantry and emotional fervor. The celebration is held on the closest weekend to "Syttende Mai." They have a king and queen for the celebration, as well as junior royalty. They claim that Norse ancestry is not required for being chosen as royalty, but my guess is that most of them are.

The Stoughton Hall of Fame also inducts new members at the Syttende Mai event. In 1987, the 140th anniversary of the city's founding, Dr. Michael Iversen (1861-1929) was chosen. A native of Norway,

Iversen was the founder of the Stoughton Hospital. Before coming to America in 1891, he'd studied medicine in both Norway and Germany. His fame as a highly skilled surgeon spread far from Stoughton. Way back in 1896, he operated on a six year old boy who was born blind. The newspaper story reported that he could "now see perfectly with both eyes."

The Chamber of Commerce sponsors a trip to Norway for two as the "grand prize" of the festival. Of course there is food. Not only the restaurants, but special food stands are set up in the streets. You wouldn't need to ask if they have lutefisk, lefse and lots of coffee. Rosemaling is also a favorite event.

Besides these they have folk dancing, arts and crafts, a quilt show, a canoe race, a "Syttende Mai Run" of twenty miles beginning at the state capitol and ending at downtown Stoughton. The people of Stoughton love parades and even have a youth parade. Over one hundred entries participate, including the local chapter of SADD (Students Against Drunk Driving). Representatives of their sister city in Norway, Gjovik, also ride in the parade.

Concerts, worship services with Norwegian music and liturgy (the sermon, however, is in English), and a costume show are part of the program. Stoughton High School even has a Norwegian Dancer's group which entertains with up to five performances. The high school Madrigal Singers also sing a concert of Norwegian music, as well as the Grieg Chorus. They have some extra fun with their "Ugliest Troll Contest." The "village theatre" which puts on several performances of a play with a Norwegian theme. They hold the raffle drawing on the trip to Norway at the very end of the last day. That keeps the crowd. The local Sons of Norway gets into the act too with food services, besides helping out all over town.

My earliest acquaintance with Stoughton came in the late 1950s, through the Skaalen Sunset Home, a highly rated nursing home. Two friends from North Dakota, Arne Bjorke of Rugby and Keith Anderson of New Rockford, have been administrators. The Skaalen Home chooses their own king and queen for the event.

The whole state recognizes Syttende Mai. The Governor makes an annual proclamation recognizing all Norwegian communities in Wisconsin and the constitution of 1814. The proclamation reads: "We are pleased to salute all Wisconsin citizens of Norwegian heritage and join them in celebration of their honored traditions during this rich, colorful, cultural festival weekend."

For those who can't be in Stoughton for this event, you'd find the Historical Museum an interesting stop at any time. Stoughton is easy to find if you should be driving to Chicago from the north. It's just off Interstate 90 south of Madison. Stoughton is an example of a community that loves the New World but still carries a torch in their heart for their heritage in the Old World.

Luke Stoughton, founder of Stoughton, Wisconsin.

CHAPTER

49

THE NORWEGIAN-AMERICAN PRESS TODAY

Out of the 400 Norwegian language newspapers that once were published in America, there are only two left today. They are the Western Viking in Seattle and Nordisk Tidende (Norway Times) in Brooklyn. They have stories in both Norwegian and English.

During pioneer days in the Dakotas and Minnesota, the *Decorah-Posten* was standard reading in every Norwegian home. The comic strip, "Han Ola og Han Per," (He's Ole and He's Per) was awaited every week. But in 1972, the Iowa paper's subscription list was sold to the Western Viking. It's a weekly Norwegian-American newspaper with a nation-wide coverage. Stories are written in both Norwegian and English. They still carry "Han Ola og han Per."

Henning C. Boe, a native of Oslo, gave tireless energy to the *Western Viking* for many years. His is not a desk job by any means. Born in 1914, each week finds Boe putting together the pages of the newspaper. He started in the printing business at age fifteen to support his family. Boe came to the New World in 1951. Not caring for the Big Apple, he went to the Middle West to set type for the *Decorah-Posten*, then the largest Norwegian language newspaper in America. He returned to Norway the next year.

Boe went to Seattle to work for the *Washington Posten* in 1954. In 1958 he purchased the newspaper and changed its name to Western Viking. Even though Boe knew the printing business well, he enrolled at the University of Washington's School of Journalism to study writing for two years. In his office he proudly displays the certificate show-ing that he was decorated by King Olav V, receiving the Order of St. Olav. He has also been recognized by St. Olaf College and the Sons of Norway.

A big day for the Norwegian language papers is when they carry the stories about the upcoming "Syttende Mai" (17th of May) which celebrates the Norwegian constitution of 1814. Norwegians love to re-tell the story of Eidsvoll and how they hoped for a while that they might even have independence. It was not to be for another 91 years as the British forced the king of Denmark to give Norway to the king of Sweden. But they kept their constitution! For the first time they'd have a national parliament in their own country. Norwegians in the New World have not forgotten the meaning of this event.

Nordisk Tidende is published in Brooklyn. On a trip to New York City in 1970, I was interviewed by a reporter of the paper and also ran my picture. I was living in Chicago at the time and they wanted to get some reflections on Norwegian heritage from someone whose roots were in North Dakota. Articles are published in both English and Nor-wegian. Brooklyn has a strong Norwegian community. The Brooklyn Norwegians are more apt to go to Norway for a vacation than to visit Yellowstone Park or the Grand Canyon.

Like the *Western Viking*, the *Nordisk Tidende* has an eye for the events going on among Norwegians in the Middle West. The Brook-lyn paper had a big story in September 1988 when the Bismarck, North Dakota, City Auditorium was renamed in honor of the late Belle Mehus, a Norwegian-American music teacher and cultural leader. She had died the previous January at age 91. The dedication tribute called her "Bismarck's First Lady of Music."

Many people read the paper as much for its advertising as for the news. If there is anything Norwegian to be found, these papers are likely to tell you how and where to find it.

The *Nordisk Tidende* is quick to report news that shows Norwegian genius. One of the stories that broke in 1988 was the charge that the American polar explorer Robert Peary (1856-1920) did not really reach the North Pole in 1909 as reported. According to Perry's own notes, it was claimed, he had not gotten closer than 115 miles from the pole. The National Geographic, however, has since affirmed Peary's claim to discovery. If Peary had not discovered the North Pole, Norway's Roald Amundson would get credit for this achievement. In 1911, Amundson crossed over in a dirigible. The first person to set foot on the spot, however, was an American, Joseph Fletcher, in 1952. The *Nordisk Tidende* put this story on front page.

One of the interesting stories reported in the Brooklyn paper was how Norwegian sailors after World War II gathered intelligence information for the CIA and for the British M16. They took photographs and made sketches in Communist bloc countries of warships and defense installations. Though illegal for Norwegians to do, it was kept up for about thirty years.

When I've visited in Norway, people have always asked me questions about politics in America. They follow the presidential elections as though they were their very own. They watched the candidacies of Humphrey and Mondale with great interest because of their Norwegian heritage. It happened again in 1988. Though there were no Norwegian candidates, Sen. Lloyd Bentsen, the Democratic candidate for Vice President, was of Danish rootage. They generally favored Dukakis. They were, however, quick to express their congratulations to President Bush and some of their press called him "America's most underestimated politician."

The Chicago based *SCAN USAMERICA*, a successor to the *Viking*, was short-lived. It was even-handed in its reporting for the five Scandinavian countries: Denmark, Finland, Iceland, Norway and Sweden. They gave an excellent report on the Norwegian pavilion at Epcot Center when it opened at Walt Disney World in Florida. They also gave Art Lee, history professor at Bemidji State University, a good review of his books with Lutefisk titles. A full page ad invited the public to attend a concert which featured seven outstanding Scandinavian stars, including Victor Borge and Arve Tellefsen. In 1988 there was an abundance of Swedish-American stories in celebration of 350 years of Swedish settlers in America along the Delaware River.

One ad caught my special attention in the Chicago paper. The Norwegian Lutheran Memorial Church (Mindekirke) in Logan Square advertised its church services stating that there is "English translation of Norwegian sermon available," and "Security guard outside the church." The old neighborhoods aren't like they used to be. Street gangs have taken over in some of the sections where Scandinavians once lived without fear of personal safety. Despite having their memorial church where it used to be, most Norwegians in Chicago have moved to the suburbs. So have many other people.

I'm glad that there are still at least two of these Norse ethnic newspapers being published. They help keep the heritage alive and give us some understanding that we'd otherwise miss.

CHAPTER

50

EARLY NORWEGIAN IMMIGRANT VIEWS ON AMERICA

Organized immigration of Norwegians to the New World began with Cleng Peerson who brought the first group on the "Restauration" in 1825. This set in motion an exodus of about 800,000 people from Norway to America. The English, French and Spanish were the original European colonists who established kingdoms in North America. It wasn't long before large numbers of Germans arrived, particularly in Pennsylvania. But Germany had not yet become united and there never was an imperial German colony in America. But even so, German almost became the language of Pennsylvania alongside English in court cases.

Three well-educated Norwegians came to America in the 1840s and have left a written record of what they thought about this new land. They were Hans Brandt, a physician; J. W. C. Dietrichson, a pastor; and Ole Raeder, a lawyer.

Most Norwegians came directly from their homeland and entered by way of New York. Some, however, sailed from Gothenburg in Sweden, Hamburg in Germany, and Le Havre in France. Those sailing from France entered America in New Orleans and settled in Texas. Between 1950 and 1970 a large number of Norwegians also came to America through Quebec.

Brandt embarked May 18, 1840, from Hamburg to New York on a voyage of 67 days, which he described as "difficult and unpleasant." He was not impressed with his fellow passengers whom he wrote "revealed a great deal of ignorance of the states to which they were going." Their goal was to pick the gold up off the streets in New York, then return home and live like kings. He noted that shortly after arriving, disillusionment set in because they couldn't find work to match their skills and didn't have money for return passage. There was no gold to be found on the streets.

After staying in New York where he concentrated on learning English, Brandt went in search of his fellow countrymen in Wisconsin and Illinois to give them medical care, going first to Milwaukee, a city of just 1,800 inhabitants. Though trained as a physician, he served as lawyer, doctor, minister, mediator and police officer in some of these communities.

The first Norwegian colony in Wisconsin was at Muskego, about twenty miles southwest of Milwaukee in Racine County, the home of the Hegs from Lier near Drammen in Telemark. Hans Heg, a Colonel in the Union Army, was killed at Chickamauga in Georgia during the Civil War. His statue stands in front of the Wisconsin State Capitol in Madison.

Brandt walked 150 miles through uncleared forests and prairies from Wisconsin to visit the Norwegians in Illinois, located about 150 miles southwest of Chicago near Ottawa. He found conditions depressing, with more disease than in Wisconsin. It wasn't profitable to be a physician there, Brandt wrote, because the people wouldn't pay him even for medicine. He noted that there were a "couple of so-called holy men from Stavanger" who added to the confusion of the community by their interpretations of the Bible. He also mentioned that the drinking water in Wisconsin was better than in Illinois.

The only people in Norway that Brandt advised to come to America were farmers, and then only if they had enough money to pay for their passage and to buy forty acres of land. He thought that tanners, shoemakers, tailors and carpenters "might find it easier to make a living here than in Norway, especially in the Western states." He advised against the seaport towns and larger cities as they were overcrowded and had no decent jobs for immigrants. He warned of corrupt politics, materialism, lack of educational opportunities and medical quackery. Brandt settled in Missouri.

Dietrichson, one of the pioneer pastors of the Norwegian Synod, made two trips to America to "bring order and stability to the religious life of his countrymen." He visited the colony at Muskego in 1844 and conducted a service. He was deeply moved by the response of the people to hearing the liturgy and sermon in Norwegian, and seeing the Norwegian clerical robes again. It made them feel "at home."

One of Dietrichson's encounters in Chicago was with Gustaf Unonius who had led a colony of Swedes to the New World. Unonius left the Swedish Lutheran ministry to become Episcopalian. Dietrichson regarded this as indifference to the Gospel. T. F. Gullixson, former president of Luther Seminary in St. Paul also made such comments about Unonius in some of his writings. The State Church of Sweden, however, often urged Swedes immigrating to America to join the Episcopalian Church rather than the Augustana Synod made up of Swedish immigrants. Dietrichson was instrumental in having Herman Amberg Preus, called to Wisconsin as a pastor. Dietrichson wrote of the hard times the immigrants were having in America.

Ole Raeder, a distinguished lawyer, was sent over by the Norwegian government in 1847 to study the American jury system. His letters were published in Norwegian newspapers.

Raeder was more optimistic about America than Brandt. He wrote that America would undoubtedly some day become the leader of the world. So he urged Norwegian immigrants to become Americans "as is the duty of holders of American soil." But, he noted, "this need not prevent them from remaining Norwegian for a long time to come."

Politics has always been an important part of American life, because this is a nation in which the people have political self-determination. In the 1840s, Jefferson was still popular. The Whigs (precursors of the Lincoln's Republican Party) were battling a radical wing of the Democratic Party called "Locofocos." They attacked the American banking system and wanted to keep the government out of banking. They were afraid that it would encourage setting up an aristocracy. The Locofocos appear to have had some things in common with the Populist movement of the late nineteenth century.

Raeder credits the Norwegians with defeating a referendum that would have given Wisconsin a constitution. As a result, Wisconsin didn't become a state until 1848. One of the issues was whether married women could own property separately from their husbands. Raeder favored this. When the issue of a constitution came up in Illinois, copies were circulated in English, German and Norwegian.

A number of other splinter movements from Democratic Party were also making their appeals for support of the people, especially the "Barnburners" and "Hunkers." The Barnburners were accused of wanting to burn down the barn to get rid of the rats (in the government). The Hunkers were accused of remaining loyal to the party because they were "hankering" for political jobs.

This was the America that met the early Norwegian immigrants. It was by no means a place for the innocent and naive. It was a tough world just to survive. Contrary to what is popularly thought, however, it was not just the impoverished that came to America. There were people that had money enough to buy land, construct buildings and make loans to their friends. With hard work, inventive minds and frugal living, they built up some excellent farms and businesses.

Recent immigrants are still doing this. I visited with a young Palestinian man some years ago. He told me, "Anyone can make it in America." He earned a Ph. D. in psychology and holds a responsible position in health care today. There are many others. Every generation would benefit if the people would think of themselves as "immigrants." Inherited wealth has some inherent dangers, even though it may be everybody's dream. America is still the land of opportunity to those who will risk the challenge.

CHAPTER

51

THE POLITICAL VIEWS OF NORWEGIAN IMMIGRANTS

Few immigrants were so prepared to participate in the democratic process as those from Norway. Since 1814, Norwegians had come alive to their right to be free people. That was the year when Denmark was forced to sign Norway over to the King of Sweden in the Treaty of Kiel because it had reluctantly entered the continental wars on the side of Napoleon.

The Norwegians immediately called a constitutional convention at Eidsvoll on April 10 and had a document ready to sign on May 17 ("syttende Mai"), modeled on the new American and French constitutions. Napoleon's Marshall Bernadotte, who had recently become Crown Prince Karl Johan of Sweden, invaded Norway and put a stop to secession.

Having gotten that close to independence, the ancient spirit of the Norse free assemblies ("Things") came to life. While it took another 91 years (three generations) to gain their full freedom, these immigrants to America were dedicated to democracy. Even in the darkest days of the Middle Ages, the farmers of Norway and Sweden never lost their freedom, though they had to battle kings, nobles and bishops to retain it.

While conservative in their personal economy, the Norse immigrants were usually to the left of center in their political views. An excellent book on this subject is *Voice of Protest*, by Dr. Jon Wefald, based on his doctoral dissertation at the University of Michigan, published by the Norwegian-American Historical Association (1971).

The Norwegians were different from many of their Yankee neighbors or most of the other European immigrants, who were politically conservative. The Norwegians brought with them a deep feeling of community and challenged the capitalistic exploitations which they experienced when entering the job market in America. They didn't buy into the myths of Horatio Alger's success story, social Darwinism and laissez faire ("hands-off") economic theories. They favored government regulations to curb the unbridled greed of capitalism and wanted the producer and consumer in closer contact, eliminating middlemen.

While the dream of establishing a "Little Norway" was not to be, they were highly successful in politics. They broke with the Democrats over the slavery issue in the Civil War and generally voted with progressive Republicans who promised free soil, free speech and free men. Norwegian immigrants liked Teddy Roosevelt, Populism and cooperatives. Their definition of a "Yankee" was someone who'd cheat you out of your last cent and refuse a night of lodging when you were broke.

As foreigners, the Norwegian immigrants faced discrimination in the job market and in elections. But it wasn't long before they banded together and a Norwegian name became a political asset. They were used to political debates from their homeland. One of their heroes was Johan Sverdrup (1816-1892), leader of Norway's Liberal Party in its campaign for freedom during the Swedish period (1814-1905). His grandfather had been president of the Constitutional Convention. It was natural for Scandinavian immigrants to participate in local civic affairs, unlike most other Europeans.

By 1889, the year that North Dakota became a state, Norwegian immigrants won the majority of the best offices in Trail County. By 1905, they occupied 2000 county offices in America. State and national positions were not long in coming. Knute Nelson of Minnesota attacked the American industrialists, including big banks, corporations and labor unions. He was the first Norse immigrant to become a governor and served in both the U. S. House and Senate. Andrew Lee was a Norwegian Populist governor in South Dakota. Karl Rolvaag wrote about Populism in *Their Father's God.* I get the feeling that he admired the idealism of Populism but didn't think it would work.

Resentment rose against the Norwegians for their aggressive pursuit of public office. The Mayville Tribune attacked the Scandinavian Republican league, saying it was "entirely foreign to Americanism." It complained that "the Scandinavian element all over North Dakota today (1889) has three-fourths of the best offices in nearly every county." The Minneapolis and St. Paul papers joined in the protest. In 1907, thirty Norwegian-born Americans were in the North Dakota House of Representatives. The state capitol buzzed with the Norse language. Five Norwegians served on the railroad commission between 1900 and 1907. In Wisconsin, the Norwegians found Robert M. La Follette to their liking, but elected one of their own, James Davidson, to succeed him as governor.

The Norwegians brought with them a "socialism" based on rural values imbued with Christian ideals which favored equitable distribution of wealth. It was not to be compared with Marxist socialism and determinism. They were oriented to protest and reform, especially in North Dakota where they brought radicalism, according to historian Elwyn B. Robinson. The Nonpartisan League would not have happened without the Norwegian immigrants. They were passionately loyal to America. It was well expressed by Congressman Gilbert Haugen of Iowa: "Every man's duty...is to strive to benefit this country, protect the weak, relieve the distressed, uplift humanity." This was their dream for the New World, and the dream lives on.

CHAPTER

52

MARCUS THRANE, RADICAL NORWEGIAN SOCIAL REFORMER

Norwegians around the world celebrate "syttende Mai" as the greatest day in their modern history. There's a lot of truth in this, but the constitution signed on May 17, 1814, didn't automatically bring freedom and equality. It took many years to make these things happen.

One of the people who became impatient with the constitution was Marcus Thrane (THRAH-neh), born in Oslo on October 14, 1817, just three years after the great document was signed. Prof. Terje Leiren, University of Washington, has written an excellent biography on him entitled *Marcus Thrane: A Norwegian Radical in America* published by the Norwegian American Historical Association, 1987.

The constitution was technically illegal as Norway had been signed over to the king of Sweden at the treaty of Kiel four months earlier on January 14. The men who drew up the document at Eidsvold did a good job of expressing the ideals of the Norwegian people at the time, but they had no power to enforce it. In fact, the signers ran the danger of being treated as revolutionaries. The fact that they had borrowed many ideas from the American and French revolutionary constitutions did not endear them to a Europe where monarchies were becoming nervous about holding on to their power.

There were thirty-seven farmers on the committee which wrote the constitution, but after the delegates went home it was the aristocrats who took charge. The first step was to get the Swedish king to honor it, which he did with a few changes. That wasn't good enough, how-ever, for Marcus Thrane. He had been born into a family of wealth but it had been lost by his father when Marcus was just three years old. His father, a member of the Board of Directors of the Bank of Norway, had "borrowed" some funds to cover a risky investment. He repaid his debt but was broken both financially and socially.

Marcus grew up on a slim budget but was a determined young man. He travelled on the Continent and learned French in Paris. Then he returned to Norway and entered the University at Oslo to study theology. He developed an intense antagonism against the upper class-es and started to crusade for more power to the workers, including a labor voice in running the government.

Thrane's first position of influence was being editor of a newspa-per in Drammen. He wrote openly about the need for government support of industry to guarantee wages, he opposed the practice of the wealthy to buy their way out of military service. He also advocated loans to working people to buy inexpensive housing. He took the social teachings of Christianity seriously and wanted Norway to be reformed according to them. As as result, he was fired in 1848 because the privileged classes were alarmed at his ideas.

This didn't deter Thrane. He became a champion of the labor movement and established his own newspaper in 1849. He claimed that Christ was a revolutionary and a "true socialist." He gathered over 12,000 signatures and sent a list of grievances to the king in Stock-holm. Among these requests were help for the cotters (share-crop farmers) to own their own land, no exemptions for universal military training, reforms in the judicial system and better schools. The king rejected all the requests, but the movement grew.

To silence Thrane, the government offered him a position in the bureaucracy which he rejected. Then he was arrested early on the morning of July 7, 1851, and imprisoned for seven years. His wife's health was broken from the ordeal. Frustrated in his attempts to be a social reformer, Thrane went to Germany to learn photography and returned to be one of Norway's first professionals in the business.

After his wife died, he took his four daughters and sailed to America on February 2, 1864. His son, Arthur, remained in Norway to complete his studies at the University. The Civil War was raging, but this did not keep him from emigrating, even though he intended to go to Brazil. His first job was to found a Norwegian language newspaper in Chicago. His goal was to raise the Norwegian immigrants to a level where they would not be looked down on with contempt by other nationalities in the America.

Thrane attacked slavery, supported the common (public) schools and the needs of workers. He severely criticized the Norwegian clergy in America, calling them a "stumbling block to civilization" for the immigrants who ought to be becoming "Americans." He saw the immigrants being indoctrinated with the oppressive social ideas of the Old World. There was one exception. He liked Paul Anderson who founded the first Norwegian Lutheran Church in Chicago today known as "Lakeview." M. Falk Gjertsen, a prominent Minneapolis clergyman, opposed Thrane, but he was praised by Kristofer Janson, a pastor who had converted to Unitarianism.

Social reform on behalf of Norwegian immigrants was Thrane's passion, and he advocated the eight hour working day. Having to fend for himself, he turned to the theatre. He wrote and produced several socially oriented plays, some of them successful but none of them making him much money.

His most ambitious publishing venture was to publish a philosophical-religious journal named "Daglyset" (Daylight). Influenced by French philosophers, he advocated elimination of prejudice, superstition, ignorance, stupidity and called for "free thinking." Though he called himself a socialist (pre-Marxist), Thrane continued to support private ownership of property. He often quoted Thomas Paine who said, "The world is my country and my religion is to do good." Thrane was an idealist who believed in the perfectibility of human society.

Until 1872 when a worker's rally was crushed in Paris, Thrane had not been a revolutionary. But after this he helped organized a rally in Chicago where the red flag was displayed and the slogan "Workers of the World Unite" was on a banner.

Thrane lost confidence in constitutions and thought the American office of president was an aristocracy which kept the working people in bondage. He saw America through his reflections and disappointment of Norway. In the great Chicago fire of October 8, 1871, half the city burned. It destroyed all the Scandinavian printing presses, so the journal ceased and brought loss of financial support. He moved temporarily to St. Louis. He also visited Norway but discovered he had been forgotten.

Son Arthur was a physician in Eau Claire, Wisconsin. Thrane went to live with him, having concluded that reform was impossible. When he died on April 30, 1890, he left instructions that his funeral was to be conducted without clergyman, sermon or other religious ceremonies. There was a memorial service for him in Chicago at which 500 people attended. A band played the "Marseille," music of the French Revolution, and everyone sang Norway's national anthem," Ja, Vi Elsker Dette Landet."

I find a lot to admire in Thrane, even though I would have disagreed with him on many issues. His concern for the poor and politically oppressed was way ahead of its time. Much of what he advocated we take for granted today. Norway rejected Thrane in his lifetime, but has now adopted many of his reforms. While theologically a "heretic," Thrane understood the social issues of the day better than those who condemned him.

"Prophets" are a strange breed of people. Their calling is to be "gadflies." First we reject them and then we praise them. It's a risky business.

CHAPTER

53

GEORG SVERDRUP, "APOSTLE OF FREEDOM"

The name Sverdrup was synonymous with freedom in nineteenth century Norway. The Sverdrups had come from Slesvig (south Denmark) in the seventeenth century and supplied a long line of able leaders. It's not surprising that when Georg Sverdrup (1848-1907) came to America in 1874 that he took with him the family passion for human rights. His great-uncle, another Georg Sverdrup, was president of the Constitutional Convention at Eidsvoll in 1814. An uncle, Johan Sverdrup, whose statue stands by the parliament building, was leader of the People's Party and prime minister. His father, Harald U. Sverdrup, was a pastor at Balestrand and a member of parliament for twenty-two years.

Norway has a history of concern for the rights of people. Even in pre-Christian times, no man could legally be king without popular consent and kings were subject to the law of the land. The pastors in the state church, being royal officials, were often aristocratic, proud and domineering. The blame for this, according to Sverdrup, lay in the educational system which alienated theological students from the people they were supposed to serve.

After studying in Oslo and Paris, Sverdrup spent time in Germany, Italy and England before coming to America to become a professor and later president of Augsburg College and Seminary in Minneapolis. His two main concerns for the immigrant congregations were to have clergy who were educated for service in the New World (not Norway!) and to have "living congregations" that were geared for mission work. He wanted pastors and lay members to share in the administration of the church's work, neither dominating the other. This was a new vision for the immigrants.

Sverdrup was a champion of the public schools and believed firmly in the separation of church and state. He held that education should integrate life's experiences with academic learning. Concerned for the health of congregations in America, he wrote: "The king does not have the right to appoint pastors in a foreign country...only the congregation has the right to call pastors."

Zeal for freedom, unfortunately, took Sverdrup out of the mainstream of Norwegian congregations. In 1897, he and a group called the "Friends of Augsburg" organized the Lutheran Free Church. They feared that denominational ownership of Augsburg would threaten the freedom of congregations by preparing pastors who were not properly trained for work in America. Prof. Warren Quanbeck lamented this schism, stating that allied with such men as J. N. Kildahl, Sverdrup's insight and eloquence could have produced "a healthier evangelism and a more ecumenical and open churchmanship." He claimed Sverdrup to be "almost a century ahead of his time."

I discovered a connection between Sverdrup and Bethany Lutheran Church in Minot where was pastor from 1974-1989. One of Sverdrup's Augsburg professors, John Blegen, gathered a group of Norwegian immigrants in July 1886 to form Bethany.

To my further surprise, I learned that Jacob Sverdrup, brother of Georg and Norwegian cabinet minister for Church and Education, married into my wife's family in 1860 back in Denmark. It's a small world.

CHAPTER

54

M. FALK GJERTSEN,
A PASTOR UNDER FIRE

Things are not always what they seem, and frequently not as claimed. But it's often difficult to know the difference.

The story of Melchior Falk Gjertsen (YAIRT-sen) is a case in point. He was born at Kaupanger, near Bergen, Norway, on February 19, 1847. His father, Johan, educated in theology, was a teacher. The family moved to Chicago in 1864. The next year, Johan became a pastor in Racine, Wisconsin, and young Falk went to Augustana Seminary in Paxton, Illinois. After graduating in 1868, he spent the next thirteen years as a pastor in Illinois and Wisconsin. I'm indebted to Nina Draxten's book *The Testing of M. Falk Gjertsen* (Norwegian-American Historical Association, 1988) for much of my information.

Then came the big move that occupied the rest of his life. In 1881, Gjertsen went to Minneapolis to be pastor of Trinity, the oldest Norwegian Lutheran Church in the city, founded in 1866. It wasn't long before he was a leading citizen. He was active in organizing a Temperance Society, the Associated Charities of Minneapolis, the United Norwegian Lutheran Church (1890), and the Lutheran Free Church (1897). He was best known for his role on the School Board. Elected in 1887, he introduced many reforms and improvements: Free text books, manual training (woodworking), elimination of basement classrooms, and establishing four high schools so that all children were in walking distance. He served as both secretary and president of the board.

All was going well when Gjertsen at age fifty-three made a trip to Norway in the spring of 1900. He arrived in time to speak for the seventeenth of May (syttende Mai) Constitution Day celebration at a prayer-meeting house (bedehus) in Bergen. Gjertsen was recognized as one of the outstanding preachers among Norwegians in America. People were profuse in their praise. Besides, he was a local hero who came back from America as a success.

Little did he realize, however, that this day would lead to trouble which would cloud his life as long as he lived. Attending the service was a licensed lay preacher and his young wife, Michael and Esther Biernakowsky Paulsen. Mrs. Paulsen had been deeply "touched" by the message, according to her husband and wished to discuss the needs of her soul more fully with him.

Gjertsen was unaware that Mrs. Paulsen was a woman with a hidden past. She seemed so sincere. She even persuaded her husband to request Gjertsen take her back to America with him. The request was declined. This didn't her stop attempts to get the attention of Gjertsen. Wherever he went on his speaking tour and visits, there was Mrs. Paulsen, at the railway stations, stopping by the homes where he was a guest and even seeking entrance to his hotel room. He treated her politely and expressed kindness as towards a daughter.

Gjertsen returned to America in September and resumed his work at Trinity Church. All was going well when just before Christmas a letter arrived from two pastors in Norway denouncing Gjertsen as unfit for the ministry and charging him with "impropriety" towards Mrs. Paulsen. They claimed that Mrs. Paulsen had shown them a sensuous letter. It was unsigned and undated. She claimed that Gjertsen had written it and that it had caused great damage to her marriage.

Needless to say, Gjertsen was shocked and immediately wrote to Mrs. Paulsen expressing sorrow that she would make such unfounded charges. Despite being convinced that the charges were false, Trinity's pastor recognized his position of high trust in the city and decided that he could not ignore the charges. A similar letter was sent to Prof. Georg Sverdrup, President of nearby Augsburg Seminary, a leading member of Trinity church. It meant going back to Norway to clear his name. A leave of absence was granted to him and money was raised for his legal costs.

Once back in Norway, Gjertsen learned that Mrs. Paulsen had quite a reputation. A Bergen bank employee claimed his family life was ruined by her. He offered to sign a deposition of his illicit encounters with Mrs. Paulsen. Unfortunately, the bank pressured him to withdraw the statement because the publicity would be harmful to them.

The civil authorities were also none too cooperative. They didn't want to embarrass the state controlled church. After several frustrating attempts to clear his name, Gjertsen returned to Minneapolis, a troubled man.

The issue centered on the anonymous letter. It seems that Gjertsen's correspondence with Mrs. Paulsen was misinterpreted. His religious language was capable of a double meaning. Since Gjertsen had destroyed the letters sent by Mrs. Paulsen, there was no way to prove if there was a case for reading between the lines. Mrs. Paulsen produced other letters also, but these were guessed to be forgeries. It turned out that she had an accomplice who had copied Gjertsen's penmanship. This woman also turned out to have a shady reputation and went by two different names. Those letters made Gjertsen out to be a philanderer and a cad. She did not charge him with adultery but with being "amorous."

Even after another trip to Norway, Gjertsen never did get his name properly cleared. The Paulsens disappeared after 1901 and were never heard of again. Gjertsen returned to Trinity Church. Things didn't go well, however, as the *Minneapolis Tribune* and some of the Scandinavian newspapers carried headlines on the scandal every week. He resigned from Trinity and founded Bethany Church on Franklin Avenue in 1902. In 1908, leading citizens of the city persuaded him to be a candidate for the School Board again and he was easily elected. He had Norwegian and Swedish language study introduced as electives in the high schools.

In addition to his work as a churchman, Gjertsen became active in the Sons of Norway. When the noted Norwegian writer, Bjornstjerne

Bjornson, died in April 1910, Gjertsen delivered the funeral eulogy to an overflow crowd at the City Auditorium. This is noteworthy as Bjornson was known for his anti-clericalism. He also became an advocate of peace and of the working classes which is where most of the Scandinavians found themselves.

After retirement in 1911, the Gjertsens moved to San Diego for a short time but then returned to Minneapolis. In the summer of 1912, he addressed a crowd of 2000 people at Hillsboro, North Dakota, for a mid-summer festival. He also took part in laying the cornerstone of the Lyngblomsten Home for the Elderly in Minneapolis. In the spring of 1913 he became suddenly ill and died of a pleurisy attack on April 22. His funeral was the largest funeral ever held in south Minneapolis. The Tribune lavished praise on Gjertsen as a most worthy citizen. Mrs. Gjertsen lived in Minneapolis until her death in 1939. The anonymous letter was never discussed in family.

Men of the cloth, like other people in the public's eye, have often been targets of slander. While people must bear responsibility for their own actions, people like Gjertsen rise again, even though they have been deeply wounded. Whatever went on between Gjertsen and Mrs.Paulson (if anything), he believed enough in himself to live again, instead of dwelling in self-pity. He survived under fire.

There's a lesson in this story. If you want to rebuke someone, say it to their face. If you want to praise someone, put it in writing. It's a lot safer that way.

CHAPTER

55

THE ADVENTURES OF A NORWEGIAN "CHEECHAKO" IN ALASKA

The story of Harold Eide is one of the most fascinating tales I've ever read. His book, *The Norwegian: A Rollicking Tale of Wild Trails and the Lure of Gold*, was given to me by my son, John. He discovered it while stationed with the Army at Ft. Wainwright in Fairbanks.

Eide was born in 1896, 300 miles north of the Arctic Circle in Norway, had spent a year with an Arctic expedition in Spitzbergen Island, the northernmost inhabited place in the world while only seventeen years old. In the spring of 1914 at age eighteen, Eide got off the boat in New York City without knowing a word of English. He was dazzled beyond imagination by what he saw in the New World.

The newcomer's thoughts had been to go to Minnesota or North Dakota, even though he had no relatives anywhere in America. But after one day in the Big Apple, he decided that it would be too boring to be a farmer. Having seen a picture of San Francisco in his hotel room, Eide bought a train ticket to the city of the Golden Gate to seek his fortune. San Francisco was not too bad a place for a Norwegian in those days, as many of his fellow countrymen had settled there.

While switching trains in Chicago, Eide stopped into a clothing store to buy a new suit for fifteen dollars. In a hurry to catch his train, he had the clerk wrap it rather than put it on. Imagine his surprise when opening the box in the men's room on board the train and discovering a rumpled up old tramp's suit. He'd learned his first lesson on survival in America. No one would ever make a sucker of him again.

San Francisco was a fun place for a young Norwegian and Eide thought seriously about staying there permanently. But then he met another Norwegian just back from Alaska who told him about the wonders of that vast land and all the gold to be had just for picking it out of the streams.

Eide was on the next train to Seattle and found the first boat to Alaska. When he arrived in Nome, he bought a hundred pounds of equipment, including a Krager rifle and ammunition. He left for the wilds, having spent his last eight dollars on a supply of Union Leader tobacco. As he left Nome, the last words he heard were: "Good luck, kid, but I know you will never come back alive." The prediction nearly proved to be true.

Mosquitoes, bears, rivers, snow, frigid temperatures and lonesomeness tested his courage and physical strength. On September 15, Eide was caught in a snowstorm while crossing a plain. It took all his effort to reach the forest for which was heading. Once in the shelter of the trees, he used his axe to cut logs and build a 10 x 16 foot cabin with a fireplace. He used wooden pegs in pace of nails. Skins of a bear and several caribou covered the earthen floor, and mud filled the cracks in the walls. The hardest part of the construction was cutting shakes for the roof and making it waterproof. Moss was packed into the cracks.

When Christmas came, Eide cut a tree and decorated it with the tinsel formed from empty tobacco pouches. The winter was a long one. So he sang hymns which he'd learned in Norway and read large sections of the Bible to keep his sanity. This gave him consolation, for he'd not found a fleck of gold dust yet.

Spring finally came and the search for gold began in earnest. After many failures, he finally found the coveted metal. There was more gold in the streams than he'd ever imagined. Unfortunately, he threw away a lot of platinum because he didn't know what it was. It was worth even more than gold. So with his pockets and rucksack loaded with gold, Eide headed back to San Francisco looking like an impoverished hobo. He didn't dare to tell anyone about his gold and other passengers insisted on giving him charity. It had been over a year since he's had a haircut, and a beard was beginning to show.

For three months Harald Eide lived like a rich king. But being inexperienced with money management, he was taken advantage of by "freeloaders," especially a troupe of twenty theatre actors who moved in on him. He rented a whole floor of the Palace Hotel for them. Then one day, after paying the hotel bill, he discovered that he had only twenty-five cents in his pocket. So he told the actors that the party was over. They'd have to move out. He'd also bought a Cadillac and had a hired chauffeur who was outfitted with the proper clothes for the job. Eide gave these to his driver and set off on foot for Seattle to find more gold. Passing through Oregon, he worked in a lumber camp long enough to buy a steamship ticket and had enough money left over to get outfitted for another expedition.

While waiting in Seattle, Eide saw a drunk sailor being robbed by a couple of hoods. He jumped into the fray and with his fists knocked one of them flat, while the other fled. A fight promoter, watching his skills with fisticuffs, offered him a hundred dollars, win, lose or draw, to get into a ring with a prize fighter. Eide accepted, even though he'd never seen boxing gloves before.

The unexpected boxing match meant a week's delay on returning to Alaska. So Eide got a job and trained at night in a nearby gym. When the night of the fight came, he had to borrow trunks and shoes before entering the ring. Having no experience in such matters, Eide decided he'd regard his opponent as if he were an Alaskan bear. He wouldn't get close unless he saw his chance to score. Even though he floored his opponent in the first round, Eide did not respond to the cries of the crowd which screamed, "Finish him off." After a few rounds the veteran became careless and came out swinging wildly for the kill. Quick as a flash, Eide caught him with a solid right to the jaw and then a flurry of body blows. The referee declared him a winner and he collected the money, but declined a contract for more fights. He wanted more of Alaska's gold.

Returning to his former panning site, Eide found the sluice box which he'd left behind. This time he hit it bigger than before. He'd also learned how to be careful with his money.

Back in San Francisco, he was amazed to learn that his chauffeur had set up a taxi business and had banked his profits. This was an unexpected surprise. He was richer than he thought.

After spending several weeks in the Palace Hotel, Eide became restless and made plans to travel north again. On the way, however, he decided to visit with an acquaintance who lived in Oregon that he'd met in Alaska. Carlson was glad to see him again and invited him to stay as long he liked. Mrs. Carlson was a "take-charge" person and decided to play the role of "matchmaker." She tried to fix him up with a local beauty who seemed quite cooperative. The Carlsons also pointed out that there were 80 acres for sale across the road from their farm.

Eide suddenly remembered that he had some business to attend to in Seattle the following morning. He took the next afternoon train. Two days later he was on a boat en route to Alaska - still a free man.

After finding his fortune in the streams of Alaska, Eide turned writer and lecturer and has since regaled thousands with his tales of the Northlands. He described himself as a "Cheechako" when arriving in America. That's an Eskimo word for "greenhorn." But one year in the wilds had changed all that. It did for many others too.

C H A P T E R

56

THE VEBLENS, AN EMINENT IMMIGRANT FAMILY

The creative activity of parents does not end with the birthing of children. That's where it really begins. What can parents give their children that will make them a blessing to the world? The story of Thomas and Kari Veblen excites our imaginations and helps us to think of greater horizons for human potential.

The name "Veblen" was not unknown to me as a young person, it was a town in northeastern South Dakota, not far from where I grew up in southeastern North Dakota. Only later did I learn that it originally referred to a Norwegian immigrant family.

The best known of this family was Thorstein Bunde Veblen (1857-1929), born in Manitowac County, Wisconsin, who wrote *The Theory of the Leisure Class* in 1899. It was a critical discussion of the new industrial society. Historian T. K. Derry of Oslo wrote: "Thus Scandinavia was identified in American eyes as ranking very high among the European sources from which the new nation had been recruited." Thorstein won fame throughout the world for his writings.

Like many other young children growing up in an immigrant home, he did not learn English until he started school. Yet he was able to graduate from Carleton College in Northfield, Minnesota, in just three years, proving himself to be a brilliant scholar. From there he studied at Johns Hopkins and Yale universities, receiving a Ph. D. from the latter in 1884.

When Thorstein could not find employment, he returned to his father's farm at Nerstrand, Minnesota, where he spent the next seven years reading. Then he enrolled at Cornell University as a graduate student where he impressed his economics professor, J. Laurence Laughlin, so much that when Laughlin moved to the new University of Chicago as head of the economics department in 1892, Veblen went along. Though brilliant, he did not advance to the professorial level at Chicago.

Veblen was appointed to an associate professorship at Stanford University in 1906 Three years later he went to the University of Missouri. In 1923, he gave up teaching and moved to California where he died in 1929. Though brilliant in academic work, Veblen's personal life tended to be disorganized. Still the academic world highly respected him for his insights in economics and the effects of the economy on society, and he became even more famous after his death than when he was alive.

My interest in this famous economist was his parents. What kind of people were they? What influence did they have on his life? His mother, Kari Bunde, was the first woman to emigrate from Valdres to America. Thomas and Kari packed up for America in 1847. Just the day before leaving, a son died and they had to bury him immediately. The trip across to America was difficult. Every child under six died en route and had to be buried at sea.

Crossing the Atlantic in 1847 was not without incident. Leaving from Drammen, the ship went to Hamburg where the captain told the passengers that he had changed his plans and wasn't going to America. Fortunately, they met a captain of a whaling vessel who had just returned from the Arctic with a load of blubber. To show their appreciation for his offer of passage, the immigrants helped unload the cargo and cleaned up the boat for its trip to America. It was no simple task to rid the ship of the whale oil smell. They scrubbed furiously for days to get rid of the oil and its odor.

The captain turned out to be a very caring person. He conducted religious services, administered medical care and gave courage to the people as the ship heaved and tossed on the stormy seas. The ocean was unusually rough that summer. They arrived in Milwaukee, via Quebec, four and a half months later on September 16. They had only three dollars upon arrival. The day after getting to Milwaukee,

Thomas walked 25 miles to Port Washington for a job with another Norwegian, even though he was very weak from the trip.

The struggle made the Veblens more determined not only to survive but to succeed in the New World. A son, Andrew (Anders), was born in 1849. He went on to become a professor of physics at Iowa State University and is known as the "Father of the Bygdelags," organizations which provided for the fellowship of the immigrants in the new land. A daughter, Betsy, was born in 1850.

Their encounters with Indians was a new challenge. They hadn't known "Redskins" in the Old World. The Indians often came to visit them, asking for food. On one bitterly cold morning, a young boy was along who was shivering without shoes and had only a blanket wrapped around him. Kari gave her own shoes to the grateful lad. This generosity left its mark on the children.

Christmas was a special celebration, regardless of how poor they happened to be. They scrubbed their house clean. The men chopped wood and everybody took a bath in wooden tubs that were so large that children could splash in water up to their necks. At the dinner table, Kari led in hymn singing and Thomas read the Christmas Gospel with as much emphasis as if he had been the pastor. Then gifts were distributed and there was candy too. The calm and quiet of the evening turned into a a noisy party. The Veblen's Christmas celebration lasted for two weeks.

Sunday was a day of solemnity. They didn't do field work, only necessary chores. One Sunday, one of the boys found his father's carving knife and whittled on a piece of wood. When his sister saw it, she scolded him saying, "Oh, now what have you done? The preacher will surely come and cut out your tongue because you whittled on Sunday." During the thirteen-day Christmas holiday, Mrs. Veblen put her knitting aside and the spinning wheel didn't make a turn. Knitting was usually done during conversation. Talking made the knitting go faster. It was a scandal of some magnitude when it was learned that some newly arrived young women from Oslo knitted on a Sunday afternoon. Those "city girls" were not highly regarded for their irreverence to things held to be sacred.

Building barns and houses became a necessary skill. They built with rugged construction. Some of the buildings are still standing after more than 100 years. They used hardwood which they cut and hewed, not even sparing the decorations expected on a barn.

These folks loved to read. Kari subscribed to the *Skandinaven*, a Norwegian newspaper from Chicago. They also worked hard at learning English, so well that Thomas could correct errors when they appeared in documents.

But most important of all was the education of their children. The pastor was usually the one who kept urging that this be done. No good mind must be wasted. Teachers, "huslaerers," came to the home and the living room was turned into a schoolroom. They were strict about learning. Yet the children developed deep affection as well as respect for them. An incentive to learn the catechism was that if a child could recite well on Monday morning, he would be excused from recitation for the rest of the week. In just a few months, Anders learned subtraction, multiplication and division. Their daughter, Emily, was said to be the first Norwegian girl to be graduated from a college in America.

It's true that their children studied under prestigious professors, but it was their mother who was remembered as their best teacher. She taught them the "A, B, C's" and about life, including instruction for their religious faith and hymns. But she also helped to shear sheep, spin yarn, wove cloth, and made clothes for both men and women. She made linen from the flax they grew and remembered the poor. During the Civil War, times were hard. Mrs. Veblen helped a destitute widow who lived alone. She also cared for the sick of the community, visiting them and bringing them food. The neighbors regarded her as highly as a trained physician. And she had a good success record. When she didn't have medicine, she gave advice which worked as well as medicine. Using poultices and massage, she cared for a little boy who had shot himself in the arm. He was well within a week.

The Veblens were successful. When they later moved to Minnesota, they had cleared their land, paid all their bills, and had a fine team of horses which had cost six hundred dollars. But their greatest achievement was the family that they left behind. Can any of us do more?

CHAPTER

57

ANDREAS UELAND, "RECOLLECTIONS OF AN IMMIGRANT LAWYER"

The name Ueland, pronounced "UU-eh-lund", was well known in Norway during the 19th century. Ole Gabriel Ueland (1799-1870) was a travelling rural school-teacher from 1827-1852. He was elected to the Storting (parliament) in 1833 and remained there until 1869. Ueland, though conservative in outlook, demanded "ruthless economies at the expense of the official class," according to historian T. K. Derry. In the parliament he became a powerful leader for the farmers and called for the jury system in the courts.

Ole's son, Andreas, had the same dogged determination as his father. In his memoirs written in 1929, he told of his beginning education. It was from listening to his father talk with neighbors during the long winter nights by the light of flickering candles. He told of watching the travelling tailors and shoemakers work at their farm between Egersund and Flekkefjord.

Despite the strong influence of Hans Nielsen Hauge in the Ueland home, Andreas remembered that there was still some remembrance of the old Asa religion. This became most apparent at Christmas time when nights were the longest. Many people were sure they had seen the devil along the lonely mountain roads at night. Judgment day was their greatest fear.

Growing up as a young boy in those days meant certain duties. Most important was to memorize the catechism explanation by Bishop Pontoppidan, Bible verses and hymns for confirmation. There was also farm work to do. It was common for ten year old boys to herd sheep up in the mountain pastures (seters) during the summer.

One of Andreas' delights was travelling to Oslo with his father when he went to Storting meetings. There young Andreas met many famous people who took a liking to him. He might have had a political career in Norway had he wished, but Andreas set out for America after his father died in 1870. The following year, at age eighteen, he travelled on an English steamer from the Stavanger harbor. His destination was Rushford in southeastern Minnesota, home for many other Norwegians.

The young men from Norway looked for farm work as soon as they arrived at their destination. Andreas might have become a farmer if someone hadn't told him about Minneapolis. Ueland moved to the Minneapolis and set about learning English. After three years of hard manual labor, he started studying to become a lawyer (advocate). In those days, it was common to be apprenticed to another lawyer and take the bar examinations when ready. Of the five who passed, Ueland had the highest marks.

Starting out to be a lawyer often provides an income near the poverty line. Ueland was no exception. As a law-clerk he earned only three and a half dollars a week, if he got paid. As a full fledged lawyer, he started at seven dollars a day and earned a thousand dollars his first year. That was considered pretty good.

One of the most controversial Norwegians to visit America was Bjornstjerne Bjornson (1832-1910). Bjornson was thoroughly disliked by most of the Norwegian Lutheran clergy for his criticisms of the church. Most of it was directed against the state church clergy of Norway. However, this criticism spilled over against almost all the Norwegian pastors and theologians in America. His religious expressions often mixed Christian aspirations with the pagan mythology of Old Norway. Bjornson, however, had high praise for Andreas' father, regarding him as a champion of the common people.

In June 1885, Ueland married Clara Hampson whom he had first met ten years earlier when she was only fifteen. It was love at first sight.

She was beautiful, highly talented and had a strong community consciousness.

Ueland told of holding court at Medora, North Dakota, in 1906. Minneapolis lawyers were often invited to travel to the frontier. That was real cowboy country in those days. He described the town as having about a half dozen houses and half a dozen "blind pigs." According to Ueland, prohibition didn't dry up this Bad Lands community. He commented that the lawyers and jurors looked sleepy during the trials, but were wide awake at night when playing poker in the bars.

He told of a blacksmith, who, while under the influence, had insulted a storekeeper with an unusually rich vocabulary of scorn. Some local lawyers advised him that he would be justified in shooting the blacksmith. But because he was running for the legislature, he didn't want to give his opponent a chance to distort the facts during the campaign. He had to settle for seeing his adversary spend fifty days in jail instead.

Ueland used to write his letters while riding the trains. In 1907 he wrote his daughter while riding on the North Coast Limited past Dickinson about the beauty of the North Dakota prairie in late March.

The theological struggles in the Norwegian Lutheran Church in the New World involved Ueland. He criticized the church for holding on to Norwegian, charging that this blocked progress among the immigrants in becoming Americanized. This meant that they wouldn't get good paying jobs and that their children would be hindered in the New World.

During the controversy for control of Augsburg College and Seminary in the late 1890s, Ueland represented the United Church (Forennede kirke) against the "Friends of Augsburg." In 1917, he did the legal work for organizing the Norwegian Lutheran Church of America, which united most of the Norwegian Lutherans in this country.

On a trip to his homeland in 1909, he wrote that in Norway all the women voted. American women had not yet been granted suffrage. During the 38 years since he emigrated, Norway became independent and was learning how to be a free nation of the world.

In 1913, Ueland returned again to Norway, this time on the same ship as the St. Olaf College Choir. A highlight of the trip was an audience with King Haakon VII. For the visit he bought a silk hat and a pair of brown gloves, and wore his Prince Albert suit. The king acknowledged Andreas' father and engaged in small talk. A royal concern was that too many Norwegians were leaving their homeland. Ueland assured him that this would diminish since the free land was all gone.

During World War I, Ueland went to Cooperstown, ND, to visit his uncle's farm. The farmers in those days were challenged to raise enough wheat to feed the soldiers. It took two days for the war news to reach Cooperstown from Minneapolis. He pointed out that the American-born Germans were highly patriotic Americans.

Ueland was a highly regarded lawyer and citizen of Minneapolis. When the Federal Reserve Bank was organized in the city in 1914, he became its general counsel. In 1926, Ueland came to Minot to defend the Federal Reserve Bank against a decision by the Supreme Court of North Dakota.

Many people in Minneapolis still perk up their ears when the name of Ueland is mentioned. Two sons, continuing in the law profession, were also highly regarded in the community.

In North Dakota, another Ueland, Lars, a farmer from Edgeley, was a member of the state's first House of Representatives. He championed the citizen's right of initiative and referendum. The "Ueland Bill" finally became law in 1914. Lars was accepted into the Norsk Høstfest's Scandinavian-American Hall of Fame in 1986.

I was fortunate to get a copy of Andreas Ueland's *Recollections of An Immigrant* when it was being discarded by a library. Ueland was an interesting person, someone I'd like to have known.

CHAPTER

58

A TRIBUTE TO "BESTA"

"Besta" is short for "Besta Mor," meaning "Grandma." It means the "best mamma" in Norwegian. Norwegians and Danes also use the terms "MOR-mor" (mother's mother) and "FAR-mor" (father's mother). I suppose that "Besta" could also refer to a grandfather, "Besta Far," but in this story it's about a grandmother.

Elsie Heiberg Hjellen (pronounced "YEL-len") wrote a story about her grandmother, Johanna Marie Slettebak (1830-1924). I'm indebted to Leona Olson Fund of Ada, Minnesota, for my information about this noble lady of pioneer days.

Family names were often changed in Old Norway. Besta's grandfather, born Rodseth, took the name Slettebak from the farm of his wife's family when he married. It was located near Lake Brusdalsvatne in the area of Aalesund. The land was given to them by Besta's parents.

Norway was highly class conscious in those days. Elsie Hjellen mentions in her book that the "fornemme" (the elite people) of the city used to visit the farm during the summer. They brought along delicacies such as "kaffe brod" (coffee bread), "sukker kavring" (sweet rusks), kringle and white bread for the visit. This insured their welcome.

Grandpa Slettebak was remembered as a strict man with his one surviving son and seven daughters, as well as having a red beard. The children all learned to milk cows, tend sheep and cattle, and work in the fields. In the winter they brought wood across the lake to heat their house. As a result, the daughters who married farmers were well prepared for life.

Their youngest child met with tragedy while still a toddler. They were by a sand pit getting sand for scrubbing and polishing an unpainted floor. The little child came too near the pit and was accidently buried alive when a cave-in took place. Even though Besta dug in the sand until her fingers bled, it was too late. In her grief, she wore only black and white clothes for the rest of her life.

Shortly after this tragedy, in 1882, the Slettebaks immigrated to a farm near Twin Valley, Minnesota. Besta's husband died in March 1887. By 1893 she had disposed of all her property. Together with her youngest daughter, Ludvikka, she came to make her home for a number of years at the Jorgen Heibergs. That's why Elsie came to have such vivid memories of her grandmother. Probably because of her generosity, she didn't realize much money from the sale of her property. One of her prized possessions was her bridal outfit, including a silver crown, which was lost in the trunk coming over from Norway.

Once in retirement, Besta busied herself with kitchen work, including doing the dishes and making lefse. Elsie wrote that she was a "whiz" at that. She added both white and dark flour to the mashed potatoes and rolled them out with a grooved rolling pin. She had her "spa," a spatula made of wood, to flip the lefse as soon as it started to bubble. I remember helping my father make lefse over our wood burning cook stove on the farm exactly the same way.

People of today would be surprised to see how dressed up the women of a hundred years ago were for special occasions. They wouldn't have been caught dead in blue jeans. This included going to church, and especially to funerals. It was a common site to see Besta dressed up with gloves, hymnal and purse. She often walked the two miles along the railroad track and always arrived early, never after the bell rang.

Like lots of people who were serious about their piety, the church was important to Besta. She belonged to the "Hauge Synod," named after Hans Nielsen Hauge (1771-1824), a farmer who led a religious revival in Norway. The Haugeans had a deep faith and placed a lot of stress on the outward behavior of Christians. One of her hopes was that a grandson would become a pastor.

Prayers at meal time and at bed time were a regular part of life for immigrant families. Many Norwegian-Americans still use the meal time prayer in the language of there homelands: "I Jesu navn gaar vi til bord, at spise or drikke paa dit ord. Dig Gud til aere, os til gavn, saa faa vi mat i Jesu navn. Amen."

It was a custom in Besta's home to eat fruit before going to bed. Apples, pears, oranges, bananas and grapes were shipped in regularly to her home. The one thing that Besta refused to eat was bologna. She had heard a story that a sausage maker had disposed of his wife by grinding her up for sausage. That completely spoiled it for her.

Children would usually eat what their parents ate, but Mrs. Hjellen told that they would not eat "gammelost" and didn't care for sour milk. Some of the original old timers thrived on such fare. I concur with her that the smell of gammelost is enough to make you want to leave the room. They all liked fish. Living by a river, they had a diet of pickerel, bass, pike, perch, red horse and suckers. They also ate lutefisk, of course, and soaked the dried cod to prepare it. This was an every winter event on the farm where I was reared. My father would order 100 pounds of frozen Lake Superior herring from Fradet's Fish Company. I looked forward to every meal it. Occasionally, we'd order some of the more expensive fish too.

Besta went visiting her children in the summer. One of her daughters, Emelie Trandum, lived on a farm near Bottineau, North Dakota and there was also an Uncle Ramus who lived in Bottineau. When she visited another daughter near Oslo, Minnesota. She used to take the steam boat from Grand Forks. The common way to travel over land in those days was by wagon, sitting on a spring seat. This is how milk and cream were transported to market.

The Heiberg home was a regular stopping off point for newcomers from Norway. Among those who came was a nephew, Leif Sverdrup, who later became a famous architect in St. Louis and a Major General as an engineer in World War II. I knew him and have written of him a story about him. He became one of the best known citizens of Missouri.

Besta had clear views on marriage. Her slogan was: "When the right one comes along, you'll know" ("naar den rette kommer saa vil du vite det"). Maybe that's why there were so few divorces in those days. If it was the "right one," it would work out despite difficult times.

Almost every Scandinavian mother spent a lot of time knitting, especially stockings, mittens and scarfs. Babies in those days were almost always breast fed. This gave mothers time to think and resolve their problems. It was also a time for reading to the other children. The modern mother who has to go back to work a few weeks after giving birth is denied this luxury.

Christmas was a special time in Besta's time. No child was allowed to see the decorated tree until Christmas Eve, after the supper was eaten. Those were great days. It hadn't changed in my childhood either. Today most people are tired of Christmas before it comes because we start celebrating so far in advance.

Besta lived to be ninety-four years old, passing away on July 1, 1924. Her grandson, Martinus Stenseth, a World War I ace and later a brigadier general, circled over her grave and dropped a wreath on it at the time of her burial. She was a small lady, according to her biography, but left a powerful legacy of courage and determination to her family. The world needs more of her kind.

CHAPTER

59

ANNA THE IMMIGRANT GIRL

Much has been written about the men of Scandinavia who came to toil in the New World. But what about the women? The record leaves no doubt that they were just as heroic and hardworking as the men, and often outlived them.

Anna Hedalen was a typical frontier woman. Born in 1841, her parents emigrated the week after she was confirmed at age fifteen. She had taken care of some neighbor's children and the neighbor lady wanted to keep her behind in Norway. Her mother, however, could not bear the thought of such a separation. As a token of appreciation, the neighbor gave her a lace dress for confirmation.

The first day out of Bergen, every passenger was sick except Anna and two men. She worked night and day to bring water and food to the other passengers.

The Hedalens went to a farm eight miles east of Madison, Wisconsin. In the winter of 1856-57, Anna worked as a servant in the governor's mansion. She spoke to the First Lady in "sign language" until she acquired English. Many nights she cried herself to sleep and lit a candle to read from the hymnal to forget her lonesomeness. She was glad she'd studied her confirmation lessons faithfully, as memorizing hymns was part of the course.

Preferring farms to city life, Anna worked in the fields for five years, doing men's work. She knew how to hitch up the oxen to the "kubberulle" (wagon). She was gentle with them and they responded willingly.

Anna married Nils Ellestad in 1860. Neither of them had money, yet they always had something to give a neighbor in need and the Indians who came for soup and "kaape" (coffee). If a baby was born in the neighborhood, Anna would bring a kettle of "rommegrot" (cream porridge).

Eleven children joined their home. Anna never had so much as a midwife or a doctor, nor had she seen a hospital bed. When the children were small, she'd tie the youngest on her back while milking the cows in the yard. The only problem was that when the flies were bad the cow's tail would start to swish. In the winter, when Nils was busy cutting wood, she did the milking as well as the cooking. Besides this, Anna sheared the sheep, carded the wool and spun the yarn before knitting clothes for the children. They never had store-bought clothing.

The "Yankees" who had settled before the coming of the Scandinavians often felt that they were better than the newcomers, certainly more stylish. That didn't bother Anna. It wasn't long before the natives could see that their new neighbors were cultured people and highly literate. They said: "Them 'ere Norwegians are almost as white as we are, and they kin read too, they kin." They didn't have many books, just the Bible, catechism, and a hymnal. Many homes also had an "Andagtsboker" (daily devotional book). The Ellestad dining room served as the "parochial school." This was how faith was kept alive for the immigrant families.

As they began farming, cinch bugs took their barley, wheat and corn for the first three years. Yet optimism prevailed. The saving feature to Anna's charm was that even on her ninety second birthday, a visitor reported that she had not lost her sense of humor.

CHAPTER

60

THE "VIKINGS" IN BENSON COUNTY

In the summer of 1886, a group of young Norwegian farmers walked from their new land south of Maddock to Devils Lake, North Dakota, to file their homestead claims. August Aanderud, Abraham Faleide, Andrew Gilbertson, Timan Quarve and Rasmus Wisness were among the vanguard of settlers from Spring Grove, Minnesota, who settled in Viking Township of Benson County. In the early days, there was a post office named Viking in their community as well as a country store.

It was a hardy bunch of people who went out in search for land that took them as far west as Burlington. Their records indicate that they also spent a little time in Villard, east of Minot. They stayed with Johannes Kopperdahl, the "Skole Laerer" (parochial school teacher) who had come from Norway. They travelled in prairie schooners and brought their oxen with them for the trip.

Before the 1880s were over, a sizeable migration had taken place to the Maddock community west of New Rockford and southwest of Minnewaukan. The Northern Pacific and Great Northern railroads came through in those same years bringing new Norwegian settlers to this land of promise. At that time, Benson County bore the name of De Smet, named after the famed Belgian Jesuit missionary from St. Louis who travelled vast areas of the trackless prairie.

The 1880s were known as the Great Dakota Boom period. Lumber yards, hotels, banks, general stores, medical doctors, and lawyers, plus lots of shysters appeared in this land that had once been the home of buffalos and Indians. Free land was the reason they risked this adventure with the unknown. The United States law entitled any man over twenty-one to file on two quarter sections of land. One quarter could be a pre-emption and the other either a tree claim or homestead. After proving that he had lived on it for fourteen months and paid the government $1.25 an acre, he could take a third quarter of land. It's no wonder that the Norwegian communities from Minnesota, Wisconsin and Iowa began moving westward. The land further east had all been taken.

The first thing the homesteader had to do was to build a shack, usually with a minimum of lumber, covered with tar paper and built up around with sod. The six young settlers from Spring Grove completed their first shack on July 6, 1886. The record states that July 4 that year fell on Sunday so they rested from their work. Then they averaged a shack a day until completed. Lumber was transported from New Rockford and cost $6.24 per 10 x 12 foot shelter, including windows, and sash. They had to move swiftly in filing their claims and getting some evidence of occupancy or their claims might be "jumped" by other land seekers.

One of the farm implements which they carried with them while travelling was a sod busting plow. Virgin soil was tough soil to break with their kind of equipment being pulled by horses or oxen. Patience was the rule for success.

It often happened that while these folks were travelling to their destinations that their horses ran away while loose for grazing. In one such case they searched for many days until the horses were found. They'd occasionally meet a stray, but well armed, traveller coming across the prairie on horseback. This happened to Timan Quarve while looking for horses. There was always some danger in this, but fortunately the one he met was a Norwegian named Ole Berg. Ole had been roaming the prairies for several years, hunting, trapping and travelling between army posts. He had three outfits gathering up buffalo bones which could be sold for up to $10 a ton. The buffalo had been slaughtered for their hides and the carcasses were left for birds and animals. By the 1880s they were practically extinct.

One of the unusual things to see for the newcomers was the "Minnie H.," a big side-wheeler steamboat that travelled between Devils Lake and Minnewaukan. It made regular trips from spring to fall. In the late 1880s the lake began to dry up and the excursions were limited to Fort Totten and the Chatauqua grounds six miles south of Devils Lake. By 1905 the lake had shrunk so much that the famous old steamboat was abandoned and left to fall apart.

After a number of country post offices and general stores closed, Maddock became the chief trading center and remains so today for people of southern Benson County. It was named after an Irish settler from St. Croix Minnesota, named Michael Maddock (1861-1904), well known for his pioneer success and generosity. An earlier settler named Peter Anderson might have given his name for the city if he had stuck around when he first visited there in 1881. The Maddock family still lives on a farm in the community.

Benson and Bottineau counties have the two largest concentrations of Norwegians in north central North Dakota, according to William C. Sherman in his book, *Prairie Mosaic: An Ethnic Atlas of Rural North Dakota*. In the Maddock area, two townships still carry a Norse preference, North Viking and South Viking. The first settlers from Spring Grove built their farmsteads in South Viking and the community center was the Viking Lutheran Church. They date their history to November 6, 1887, on the Timan Quarve farm. For their centennial in 1887 they published a handsomely bound volume of 414 pages. The history of the church and community are bound together.

The nearest Lutheran pastor to the Viking community was in Devils Lake, over fifty miles away over some rough road. Rev. T. L. Aaberg conducted the first service on the afternoon of July 1887. The second service was not held until October 2. Worship services were first held in the Aanderud School until a building was constructed in 1903. In June 1909, the Viking Church was host to the national convention of the Norwegian Lutheran Synod, at which time the building was dedicated. The cornerstone was opened in 1962.

I've come to know a lot of people from the two Viking townships and they have a deep pride in their community. I first became acquainted with the Norwegians from Maddock when I was a student at Concordia College. Later when I lived in New Rockford I came to meet many more. I had family living in the Maddock community from 1961 to 1981 who still maintain close ties. My father was living there at the time of his death in 1969. If you meet people from Maddock, it's a pretty safe bet to ask if they are Norwegians. And those that are, are proud to admit it.

CHAPTER

61

NELS KLEPPEN, PRAIRIE PATRIARCH

Most of the Scandinavian immigrants who came to America brought few worldly goods with them. Usually there were the clothes they wore plus a wooden trunk. Among the goods were some articles of faith such as the Bible, a hymnal, a devotional book and the catechism. Most of them didn't have much money, just enough for the one-way passage and the twenty-five dollars that the immigration laws required. Often that had to be repaid to a relative in the New World who acted as sponsor.

Nels Kleppen was one of the 800,000 who left Norway for a better life across the sea. Nels was born Nils Jakobsen Birkeland in 1877 on a island northeast of Bergen called Osteroy. I was fortunate to secure a copy of his autobiography which he spoke into a tape recorder in September 1965 at the home of his granddaughter, Helen Silseth of Minot. Even at 88 his memory was sharp and his speech coherent for the two hour narration. He died in April 1968.

When "America Fever" hit those northern lands it had about the same effect as stories of Constantinople in the Viking days. It was pictured as a land of abundance where everybody could get rich quickly. A few eventually did, but not very many and almost none quickly. But the enthusiastic letters written back to the homelands, loaded with a degree of propaganda, had the desired effect. Whole communities sometimes joined the caravan of wagons to the seaport cities. The passage across the Atlantic Ocean was usually in the worst of travelling conditions. All except those who were experienced at sea usually became ill before the voyage was completed.

It was common practice in Norway that if a man moved to the farm where his wife came from he changed his name to hers. That's how Nils Birkeland took a different name. His wife's name was Kleppe. However, when he got to America, he changed it again to Nels Kleppen because there was another Nils Kleppe where he homesteaded. Their mail kept getting mixed up.

When Nels came to America in 1903, he left behind his wife, Katrina, and three children. Two other children had died and Katrina was expecting at the time of his departure. Like so many others, he was enticed by the hope of making a better living. Katrina's brother, John, sent a ticket for Nels to try his luck in the new land. It took another four years before the rest of the family could make the journey. One of his friends said, "I thought when I came to America that I could sweep the money up very easy but I find it different, you have to work for it." A lot of people made that same discovery.

They entered the New World in Quebec and travelled through Sault St. Marie and ended up at Emerado, North Dakota, after two more weeks of travelling. It takes only about eight hours of flying time to make the same journey today. But fifty years earlier it often took up to three months travelling with sail-driven boats. The first thing they noticed was the hot weather. The woolen clothes packed in their trunks weren't suited to the summer climate of North Dakota.

Money was hard to come by but Nels was willing to work to save enough money to bring his family over here. Fortunately, there was plenty of farm work at harvest time. Shocking grain for two dollars a day was the average pay and maybe they could get two and a half dollars during threshing. But when winter came farm workers were lucky to find someone who'd give them room and board to do chores. That hadn't changed during the 1930s when I was growing up. My father never lacked help on our farm during the winter months. It was the surest way to get a job when field work began in the spring. Shoveling grain was another of the jobs that took strong backs and arms. One of the things that Nels discovered during threshing was that one of the other workers had lice. From then on, Nels slept in straw piles. There he heard mice crawling all over. But mice were preferable to lice.

After working at Emerado and Hatton the first year, Nels heard about homestead land available near Columbus, North Dakota. He filed for land twelve miles south of town in December 1905 and built his 10 x 12 foot shack the next summer. It took fourteen months to "prove up" the land before legal ownership took place.

Sometimes it seemed to Nels that he'd never get his family to America. It was so hard to save money. Finally, he decided the only way was to borrow the money to get them here. To his surprise, he got a letter saying that Katrina and the children were arriving at Vassar, Manitoba. Besides taking care of her family, Katrina earned the money to purchase passage to join her husband. When Nels went to meet them, no one showed up. You can imagine his feelings of helplessness. So he went back to Winnipeg to look for them at the railway station. They weren't there. He even checked the register in a Scandinavian hotel. Then he took to walking the streets in search for them. Suddenly he looked up and there they were, heading straight for him! For the first time he saw his little daughter, Nelsie. It was a happy reunion.

Times were hard for the early pioneers. Nels told about the time he had to ask the grocer in Columbus for forty dollars credit. He paid ten percent interest on the loan. Interest was fifteen percent in some places. In the 1930s, Nels had an $840 seed loan. Not until about 1939 did the rains return and were there good crops again.

The flu epidemic of 1918 hit the Kleppen home. They only had a three room house. Eleven people were down sick in seven beds. The flu was complicated by pneumonia and nose bleeds. Fortunately, they all recovered. At one time, Magne, Helen's father, was so ill that Nels feared he was dying for sure. Then Magne raised up his arms and his parents thought "there he goes." But they continued praying for him and Magne lived. He told of seeing three angels at his bedside when he raised up his arms.

Prairie life was often hard on women. Katrina was no exception. In 1939 she became deathly ill and Nels was advised by three different physicians that there was no hope for her. After the others had left, he knelt by her bedside and prayed, "Lord, isn't it possible that we can have her with us yet? She has been so dear and is so dear yet." While still kneeling, he heard a voice saying to him, "not yet." The next morning he touched her face and said, "how are you feeling this morning, Mama?" She was much better and lived for another 31 years. Shortly afterwards, they left the farm and bought a house in Columbus.

After Katrina died, Nels used to visit his family, staying about two weeks at each place. Sometimes he didn't sleep well at night, but he told his family not to worry about him as he had so many people to pray for as he lay in the dark. He used to tell his family "my best advice for you is to raise up your child in the Lord, as your children are the only things that can go to heaven with you."

The Kleppens had 11 children, besides the two that died in Norway, all living within a 15 mile radius of Columbus. Everyone of them sang in the church choir. At the time of Nels' death,, there were 42 grandchildren, 100 great grandchildren and four great-great grandchildren.

During those visits to her home, Helen remembers that "Grandpa Kleppen," as they called him, spent a great deal of time reading the Bible and singing hymns. I listened to Nels' singing on the tape. Even at age eighty-eight, he carried a tune quite well. Those pioneers who claimed this country for future generations were a hardy breed, made of the same tough stuff as the Old Testament patriarchs. "Prairie Patriarch" is a fitting epitaph to mark the memory of Nels Kleppen. Fortunately, there were more like him in those days of land-claiming and community building.

CHAPTER

62

THE NORSE CENTENNIAL CELEBRATION IN AMERICA

The Norwegians in America had their "party of the century" at the Minnesota State Fair Grounds on June 6-9, 1925. Worship services in both English and Norwegian were held on Sunday in the Hippodrome. The grand finale came on Tuesday night in the centennial pageant, with music being furnished by the Luther College Band of Decorah, Iowa, directed by Carlo A. Sperati.

Even Calvin Coolidge, president of the United States, and Mrs. Coolidge were present, as well Lord Byng, Governor-General of Canada, and Lady Byng. The Bishop of Oslo, Johan Lunde, brought greetings from the church in Norway. Greetings were also brought from King Haakon VII, the Storting (parliament), and the University. A medal was struck with a Viking ship on one side and Leif Eriksen on the other to commemorate the event.

They had a lot to celebrate. It had been a hundred years since Cleng Peerson (1782-1865) had set out from the Stavanger harbor with his sloop, the "Restauration," to bring a load of Norwegian immigrants to the New World. It wasn't much of a ship, just fifty-four feet long and sixteen feet wide, registered to carry thirty-seven tons. On board were fifty-four passengers, including twenty children and 6,300 pounds of rod iron. To be sure, Norwegians had come to America before, but never a whole boatload. This marked the beginning of the immigration from Norway to America. Professor Theodore Blegen of the University of Minnesota gave an address about Peerson.

Music and speeches were a prominent part of the celebration. The Centennial Exhibition had twenty-two departments of exhibits. These included pioneer life, church, schools, agriculture, the press, literature, art, men in public service, charity and mutual aid, women's arts and crafts, societies and organizations, music, trade and commerce, Norwegian skiing, Sons of Norway, Daughters of Norway, the medical profession, industries, engineering and architecture, a Minnesota state exhibit and a Norse-Canadian exhibit. They took over the entire Fair Grounds in St. Paul for the celebration. Dr. Knut Gjerset, curator of the Luther College Museum (now Vesterheim), was chairman of the exhibits.

An athletic program of baseball, soccer, bicycle racing, plus a track and field meet provided extra entertainment. Baseball teams from Concordia, Luther and St. Olaf colleges held a tournament. The soccer games were played between the Norwegian-American Athletic Association of Chicago and the Norge Athletic Club of Minneapolis.

Prof. Olaf Norlie, famous for his published statistics on Norwegians in America, wrote an article entitled "Why We Celebrate" in the centennial book. He pointed out that George Washington traced his ancestry back to Norse ancestors in Yorkshire in 1030 and that he was a proud member of the Scandinavian Society in Philadelphia. He also cited William Jennings Bryan's claim that he had descended from Norwegian stock which had settled in Ireland.

Norlie noted that most of the English immigration to America came from Norwegian counties in England. He also claimed that the heaviest Irish immigration came from the Norwegian element in Ireland and that "most of the French stock in America has come from the Norwegian sections of France." The "Pilgrim Fathers" who came to America on the Mayflower were "mainly of Norwegian descent," according to Norlie, the same counties where "William the Conqueror met with most opposition from his kinsmen in the Norwegian counties of England." These are some interesting claims.

A lot of Norwegian pride was shared as the people at the Centennial were reminded that the first white child born in New York City was of Norwegian stock. Norwegians came over with the Dutch settlement in New York and others settled among the Swedes along the Delaware River in 1638. Norwegians were also early land owners in downtown Chicago, the area called the "Loop."

The Norwegians were proud of their patriotism in war. During the Civil War, nine percent of the total Norwegian population in America enlisted to save the Union and to fight against slavery. In World War I, six percent of the Norwegians were in the military while only four percent of the country at large was drafted. All three of my uncles eligible to be in the Army fought in France. Two returned.

More than anything, the Norwegian-Americans celebrated their heritage of freedom. It had begun in the local assemblies called the "Things," before the coming of Christianity. Norlie cites the claim of B. F. De Costa that our freedom of speech is derived from the Northmen.

There's no doubt about it, this was a time for the Norwegians to boast of their success in America. The centennial book states that over 5,000 graduates of Norwegian technical schools had come to America where many of them achieved fame in engineering, shipping, finance, business, commerce, lumbering, fishing and the skilled trades. The list included famous musicians, journalists, writers, publishers, churchmen, educators and schools, painters and sculptors. He cited F. Melius Christiansen, director of the St. Olaf Choir; Ole Rolvaag, author of *Giants in the Earth*; and Col. Hans Heg, who led the 15th Wisconsin Regiment in the Civil War.

Norwegian-Americans in public service were given their due. By 1925, twelve of them had served as governors: Knute Nelson, J. A. O. Preus and Theodore Christianson in Minnesota; Andrew Lee, Charles Herreid, Peter Norbeck and Carl Gunderson in South Dakota; James Davidson and J. J. Blaine in Wisconsin; R. A. Nestos and A. G. Sorlie in North Dakota, and J. E. Erickson in Montana. Senators and congressmen were also recognized, including Asle J. Gronna, Martin Johnson, H. T. Helgeson and Olger Burtness from North Dakota. Considering that the Scandinavians didn't arrive in large numbers to America until after the Civil War, that was an impressive record. Why did they succeed so early in public life? Their high rate of literacy and passion for political freedom, are cited as the reasons.

Knute Nelson, born near Voss, Norway, and Rasmus B. Anderson, born at Albion, WI, were given special attention. Nelson was the first Scandinavian to become a governor in the New World (Minnesota). He later became both a congressman and a senator. Erling Rolfsrud has written a delightful book on Nelson. Governor Preus called him "one of the most illustrious of her sons that Norway has given to the New World." Anderson organized the first department of Scandinavian languages and literature in America at the University of Wisconsin in 1875. He was also the first Norwegian to serve as an ambassador (Denmark) from 1885 to 1889. The Encyclopedia Britannica has called him "Father of Norse literature in America."

Norsemen are fond of statues. The Leif Eriksen statue in Boston and the statue of Ole Bull, the famous violinist, in Minneapolis' Loring Park are pictured in the book. When the 200th celebration will be held in 2025, I hope they'll include the statues in Minot's Centennial Park of two famous skiers, Sondre Norheim and Casper Oimen, both born in Norway. There are only four statues of skiers in the whole world.

I have a feeling that there might have been just a little bit of bragging in all those speeches and perhaps even some interpretations of the tradition which had their heroes walk on water. My guess is that no one minded all the hyperbole about the Norse achievements. But there was also thanksgiving to God for his mercies.

Every ethnic group should celebrate its successes and hold up its values for their future generations and for their neighbors to see. A reason why Norwegian-Americans have had a good success rate is because they've been challenged by American pluralism. It takes people of many backgrounds to build good communities. We can learn a lot from each other.

CHAPTER

63

CONCORDIA COLLEGE, "FOSTERING MOTHER"

Great ideas and projects usually begin in a small room with just a few people. Often the events take a different turn than was envisioned by the original planners. The story of Concordia College in Moorhead, Minnesota, is a case in point. I was reminded of this in 1989 when I returned to my Alma Mater, Concordia College to attend a Homecoming chapel service.

In the 1880s when Norwegian immigrants began pouring into the Red River Valley of North Dakota and Minnesota, there was concern about their children's education. The existing schools didn't meet the needs of these newcomers. Language, culture and religion all played a part in the planning that led to Concordia's founding.

Fortunately, good records were kept. One of these accounts, *Concordia College - Through Fifty Years* (1891-1941), was written by Rasmus Bogstad who was associated with the school for nearly all his professional life and was president from 1902 to 1909. The *Cobber Chronicle* by Erling N. Rolfsrud is an excellent story of the school.

It all started at a meeting in Crookston, Minnesota, on January 6, 1891. The leading Lutherans of that city wanted a Norwegian college. Having heard about the meeting, some Grand Forks and Fargo people also attended. Crookston dropped its plans, but the Grand Forks Norwegians started a school in 1892 which lasted just two years.

There were already several schools in Fargo-Moorhead. The Congregationalists had established Fargo College. The Episcopalians started ed Bishop Whipple School in 1882 in Moorhead and the Swedish Lutherans opened up Hope Academy in 1888, also in Moorhead.

North Dakota Agricultural College (now North Dakota State University) started in rented quarters in the fall of 1891.

Even though relations were strained between Norway and Sweden over the Independence issue, the Norwegians made overtures to the Swedes to join their corporation. The Swedes agreed that the Norwegians could attend their school and have an instructor teaching Norwegian, but could not be on the board of directors.

About that time the Episcopalians were looking for a buyer, their school having closed after five years for lack of students. The Red River Valley had filled up with foreign immigrants, Norwegians being the most numerous. They offered to sell their $30,000 campus to the Norwegians for $10,000.

Moorhead wasn't a paradise. Organized in 1871, it was called the "wickedest city in the world." A newspaper reported that "almost every night there is a shooting." Crooks, gamblers and prostitutes had free run of the city. When North Dakota entered the Union in 1889 as a "dry" state, the saloons moved to Moorhead and provided free rides across the river. More than one unsuspecting farm worker walked into a tavern through the front door, but after being mugged and robbed was carried out the back and dumped into the river. Fargo was no place of innocence either, being called the "divorce capital of the world."

Raising the money to pay the $10,000 wasn't easy. The newly arrived Norwegians didn't have much money and hardly any to spare for a school. Yet they did.

Rasmus Bogstad was a young pastor from Norway who had been educated in America and had barely begun his pastorate at nearby Kindred in North Dakota. He was called by the newly formed "Northwestern Lutheran College Association" to teach religion and Norwegian. Upon arrival, he was told that instead of teaching he would have to raise money.

The school was named "Concordia," Latin for "hearts in harmony." But its founding was marked with derision from the "Yankees." With established schools struggling for existence, they scoffed at the idea that the foreigners from Norway could have any success. What they didn't know was that Norwegians were highly literate and that English would be the language of instruction.

Bogstad traveled with endless energy against all kinds of adversity to raise the $10,000. He succeeded. Tuition was seven dollars and fifty cents for the spring and fall terms, and twenty-five dollars for the winter term. Board was two dollars and twenty-five cents a week and room 50 cents a week. It cost an extra 25 cents a week for heat in winter. Concordia students were not allowed to leave the school after 7:00 p.m. because Moorhead wasn't a safe city.

Bogstad not only gathered money, but recruited students. Concordia opened with just twelve students on October 15, 1891. There were over 200 enrolled for the winter quarter. Bogstad began working for Concordia on November 1. At that time, St. Olaf and Luther colleges had enrollments of about 125. In 1893, the year that financial panic struck the nation, Concordia had 261 students.

The other private schools began to fold due to hard times, but Concordia raised more money for buildings. Professors were active in politics too. Hans Aaker, the principal (later called president) ran for mayor of Moorhead on the Prohibition ticket in 1900 and won. He kept his promise "to clean up the town." Saloons had to close at midnight.

By the time that I arrived on campus as a freshman in September 1944, Fargo-Moorhead was pretty civilized. It was hard to believe the stories which some of the old-timers told. Tuition was still a bargain, only about $100 per semester. When the World War II veterans began to arrive in the fall of 1945, enrollment began to grow and that called for more buildings.

"Alma Mater" is a term referring to the school where one has graduated. It means "fostering mother." That's a good description. I was a farm boy who knew how to pluck a rooster, harness horses, milk cows and operate a tractor. I loved every day of it.

Because of declaring my intention to be a pastor, I enrolled in college. Concordia, just forty miles away, was the most natural place to become qualified for seminary. In the spring of my senior year at Oak Grove Lutheran High School in Fargo, I walked the two and a half miles to Concordia and announced myself to the registrar. As soon as he learned that I would be pre-seminary, he took me into the office of Dr. J. N. Brown, the president. Brown told me that I'd be a student of theology for the rest of my life (I thought I'd be done after eight years) and that I should take a classical course of studies, concentrating on philosophy, Latin, Greek, Hebrew, plus basic sciences, history and psychology. I went back to the farm to cultivate corn and worried all summer, wondering how I'd ever survive.

But I made it and President Brown was right. I have been a student of theology ever since. What happened was a complete transformation of my world view. Singing in Paul J. Christiansen's concert choir, attending concerts of world renowned musicians, associating with serious students of great ability, even putting on a football uniform as a freshman, had a powerful effect on my life. In a very true sense, Concordia became a "fostering mother" to me and I'll ever be grateful. In my associations with friends from the big name and Ivy League colleges, I've never felt that I'd been academically deprived in that school started by Norwegian immigrants one hundred years ago.

Bogstad would not just turn over, but would spin in his grave if he were to learn about Concordia's Centennial Fund Campaign of $46,500,000. He would never have understood how $25,000,000 could already be pledged before the drive was officially announced at Homecoming 1989. At its completion the fund drive raised $55,500,000. It would have also have amazed him to see the excellently equipped campus of nearly forty buildings for the almost three thousand students. Back in the 1890s they couldn't even field a football team to play the Swedes who called them "corn cobs" because the campus was surrounded by corn fields. Today the "Cobbers" have gained national recognition in athletics even though the school offers no "athletic" scholarships. Over ninety-eight percent of those who lettered in four years of sports graduated in four years with a B. A. degree between 1981 and 1988. This compares to the national average of forty-five percent who graduate in five years. Over 22,000 degrees had been awarded by 1995.

And what's it for? The college catalog states: "The purpose of Concordia College is to influence the affairs of the world by sending into society thoughtful and informed men and women dedicated to the Christian life." This is expressed in the Hymn to Concordia - "On Firm Foundation Grounded." The motto of the school is "Soli Deo Gloria" - "To God Alone the Glory." May it ever be so.

C H A P T E R

64

OAK GROVE LUTHERAN HIGH SCHOOL, NORSE "ALMA MATER"

When in February 1943 the Colfax Hi basketball team went to Fargo, North Dakota, for a game with Oak Grove Lutheran High School, I never dreamed that I would be transferring to Oak Grove the next year. As I recall, we lost the basketball game, and that was the last time I thought about the school until the following July at the Red Willow Bible Camp near Binford, North Dakota.

In the meantime I had decided on my career goals. After my last year of high school, I planned to attend Concordia College in nearby Moorhead, and then Luther Seminary in St. Paul to become a pastor. Nine more years of school seemed a long stretch of time to a farm boy who had spent most of his available time driving a tractor.

Rev. Thor Quanbeck (1899-1966), president of the school, visited the Bible Camp and encouraged me to transfer to Oak Grove in the light of my career goals. Those were the days of World War II and class "C" schools like Colfax Hi had a difficult time getting qualified teachers. The high school had only two teachers. Despite the smallness of the school, we still got a pretty good education, but with many of the men teachers off to war and women working in defense plants, it wasn't possible to get all the courses required for college entrance. I wasn't interested in taking high school make-up courses while in college.

When I returned to the farm at the end of the week and told my parents about these plans, there was solid silence. It would mean a sacrifice on their part, both for the costs and because I was needed for farm work. Fortunately, Oak Grove started three weeks late in the fall and got out three weeks early in the spring as a way to help the war effort. We made up the time by going to school for an extra hour each day. Since many of the students lived on campus in the dormitory, that wasn't a problem.

Another advantage of Oak Grove in those days was that classes were held from Tuesday through Saturday noon. This made it easier to get a job on Mondays when there was no competition with students of other schools. Since I was interested in journalism, work was arranged for me with the *Fargo Forum*. My job was re-writing obituaries from the county newspapers to shorter size.

Oak Grove was established by the Lutheran Free Church in 1906 as the "Oak Grove Lutheran Ladies Seminary." It was common in those days for private academies of high school level to call themselves seminaries. Today, we mostly think of seminaries as post-graduate professional schools to study theology and prepare for a career in the church. The school opened on Reformation Day (October 31). Twenty-four young women began their studies in domestic science, Norwegian, music and Bible, with a faculty of six teachers.

In the early 1920s there was a proposal to turn Oak Grove into a women's college. Augsburg was the men's school of the Lutheran Free Church with high school, college and seminary departments. However, Oak Grove became co-educational in 1926 and was renamed "Oak Grove Seminary." Augsburg also made the transition to coeducation. That same year Oak Grove was approved for accreditation by the North Central Association of Colleges and Secondary Schools. This made it easier for its graduates to be accepted into colleges and universities.

The purchase of the Barnes estates "castle" provided the original home for the school. In 1922 the first major building was constructed and is known today as Jackson Hall, named after Ida Jackson, who was a Bible teacher and spiritual leader on the campus for many years. After World War II, a fund drive was held and a gymnasium-boy's dormitory building was erected. It was named after Rev. Jens. E. Fossum (1872-1960) who served Oak Grove from 1907 until 1949. He was president from 1907-1925 and 1930-1937; and Treasurer from 1937-1949. He also served as a teacher.

Another name change took place in 1952 when the school became known as "Oak Grove Lutheran High School." The school originally got its name from the Oak Grove Park which borders the Red River and is adjacent to the campus. A classroom-administration was built in 1960 and a new gym in 1972. In 1977 Oak Grove expanded its curriculum to include Junior Hi. The latest building is the "Center" built in 1985 which houses both the food services and a chapel.

A number of foreign students have traditionally been enrolled at Oak Grove. In some past years, children of missionaries have also be enrolled if there were not adequate educational facilities where their parents worked.

It was quite a change for me to leave the farm at age sixteen to live in a dormitory while finishing high school. It was the life of luxury not to have to go out to the barn and do chores before going to school. We started classes at 8:30 a.m. and finished at 4:30 p.m. After supper in the dining hall, we were free until 7 p.m. Then we had to be in our rooms to study until 9. Between 9 and 10 p.m. was free time, but 10:30 was "lights out." We were allowed one night a week to leave the dorm with permission. The dean of boys checked the rooms to make sure that there was no unnecessary noise or fooling around, and that no students were absent without leave.

To my surprise, I was elected president of the senior class of 1944, though I had been on campus but a few weeks. Attending Oak Grove made it possible for me to get the math and science requirements for college, besides voice lessons and choir. The choir took a tour of northern Minnesota after graduation. War time restrictions made a longer tour impossible. That gave me my first chance to see Bemidji's Paul Bunyan statue.

Since that time, North Dakota schools have been reorganized and offer excellent preparation for college. North Richland High School now stands in the place of the Colfax Hi that I knew. But there were many communities in the state that had no high school in those days. The choice was between renting a room in a town with a high school or not going further in education at all. A lot of good students lost out on education for that reason. Schools like Oak Grove offered the alternative of a home away from home with some degree of supervision and guidance, while getting a high grade education.

Oak Grove has a strong policy on students using alcohol, drugs and tobacco, not just because they are illegal, but because the swift academic pace required students to be at their best. The Student Handbook requests those who can't get along without these things not to apply. Because Oak Grove is a church related academy, some people expect it to have a "behavior modification" program for youth whom neither parents nor the public school can discipline. Oak Grove expects its students to have a high degree of self-discipline and maturity.

Today Oak Grove is a part of the Evangelical Lutheran Church in America and has its own corporation elected from congregations in North Dakota and Minnesota. The Oak Leaves Club, an association of graduates, former students and friends, has worked actively in support of the school in the Fargo-Moorhead area. Oak Grove is the only one of the many high schools established by Scandinavian immigrants which is still operating.

A new alumni directory was published in 1989. It brought back a lot of nostalgia while paging through it. It's a full evening of entertainment just to discover where one's schoolmates and other graduates are living and what they are doing today. High school friendships are held close to the heart and the prestige of an Oak Grove diploma grows with the years.

I suppose that those of us who graduated nearly a half century ago were pretty naive by comparison to the sophistication of today's high school students. Many today have had foreign travel and are taking courses in high school not available in universities in those days. But schools like Oak Grove did a pretty good job to prepare us to take our place in society. Much has changed since I was an Oak Grove student, but it still has a strong spiritual emphasis with a campus pastor to guide young people with seeking minds.

In October 1994, our class had its fiftieth anniversary. It was fun to be there to renew acquaintances. Our looks have changed. Five of the class are no longer among the living. But the spirit of the school lives. It has been a high privilege for me to call myself one of its alumni.

When you're in Fargo, drive over to the campus and see this exciting school founded by Norwegian immigrants.

CHAPTER

65

ATTENDING A
HALLINGLAG "STEVNE"

Growing up on a farm seven miles south of Walcott in southeastern North Dakota, I took it for granted that most people in the world were Norwegian and that at least half of them were Halling. I knew some other kinds of people too, mostly German, but also a few English, Irish, French and Swedish. There were, of course, a few Native Americans (whom we just called Indians), and I'd heard about Danes, Chinese, Africans, Mexicans and Gypsies.

But of Norwegians, I soon learned there were many kinds: Hallings, Tronders, Sognings, Nordlings, people from Numedal, Telemark and some other places. They each had their own different way of speaking Norwegian, but if one listened carefully and they didn't talk too fast, it was possible to understand them.

In 1907, twenty years before I was born, the Hallings held a "stevne" in Walcott to organize their "lag" (lodge). A stevne is a rally where people get together to enjoy each other's company, mostly because they are glad to be Norwegians from the same valley in the Old Country.. In the old days, Walcott, Colfax, Kindred, Abercrombie and the other nearby towns were quite some places. You could buy practically anything you needed without having to go to Fargo or Wahpeton, except when you had to do some business at the court house. The general stores sold everything from food to salt blocks, overalls, shoes and material for the women to sew clothes for the family. These little towns also had banks, farm machinery, lumber yards and blacksmith shops, as well as churches and grain elevators. There were also shoemakers who could make harnesses for the horses. Those were exciting towns, especially on Saturday nights. A lot of the old buildings still stand, but many are boarded up today.

I visited my home community for a few days in the summer of 1989 to attend a Hallinglag stevne in Wahpeton, being invited to give the keynote address. All of the above recollections passed through my mind as I looked over the changes that have taken place in the past generation. Good highways and fast automobiles are called progress, but they've made the small towns unnecessary. And there aren't many young people left.

The Hallings have changed too, according to what I remember about them from the days of my youth. They've tamed down quite a bit, if what I was told about them is true. They used to have some peppy parties, with spirits provided privately during the days of prohibition. The Hallings were also noted for wearing their knives, as a part of their dress-up bunads. Back in Norway, those knives were more than decorations at some of the week-long wedding parties. It's said that women used to pack their husbands' burial clothes when attending these events.

My earliest ancestry in America is Halling and I was proud to "stand tall" at the stevne. The Hallings may have slowed down with age and the civilizing process, but I like those good friends and hope to attend more stevnes.

My wife and I visited Hallingdal in 1985. It's a beautiful area northwest of Oslo. I didn't find any trace of relatives. It may be that they all went to America. My great-grandparents, Ole and Kari Bakken ("Holle" in Norway), immigrated from Hemsedal in Hallingdal to Blooming Prairie, Minnesota, in 1867. Twelve years later, they obtained land west of Walcott. Their descendants still live on the land.

I was impressed with the friendliness of the people I met. About forty Hallings came from Norway. Some come every year. While travelling with SAS (Scandinavian Air System) on a trip to Europe a few years ago, I visited with the pilot who was a Halling. He'd been to Seattle to attend a stevne that summer. Many Hallings come every year to the Høstfest in Minot.

The stevne was called into sessions by the sound of a lur played by a twelve year old boy. The lur today is a long wooden instrument used in the mountains of Norway. Originally it was a bronze-age S-shaped trumpet developed by early Scandinavians - the oldest metal musical instrument. It's tones carry far into the valleys. Distance seems to enhance their beauty.

The sessions were held at the North Dakota State College of Science in Wahpeton. Besides the formal business sessions, there was a lot of music. A trip was arranged to visit historic Ft. Abercrombie, about twelve miles north along the Red River.

One of the very interesting events at the stevne, apart from just having a good time visiting with old friends and making new ones, was listening to songs played on a "stonophone." The only one in the world, it was built and played by Rolf C. Johnson, formerly of Carpio, North Dakota, who is now retired from teaching music at Montana State University in Bozeman.

What is a "stonophone?" You have to see it and hear it to believe it. Prof. Johnson had found some musical stones in Confederate Gulch to the northeast of Canyon Ferry Lake in Montana. He's rigged up six stones whose notes range from G through D. He thinks that the varying density of the stones is what gives them their tones and that the size of the stone has nothing to do with it. Johnson strikes the rock with a steel bar, while accompanied by guitar.

The first time the instrument was played in public was on April Fools Day, 1976, at the University. When Johnson and the guitarist joked around a while before hitting a note, the people in the audience were sure it was all an April Fool joke. But when they started to play, amazement overtook them as it did us at the Halling stevne. A picture of the Stonophone with a recording was sent to a musician in Norway. It ended up being played on the Norwegian National Radio System. Johnson, who has spent a whole career in teaching music and directing both bands and choirs, spent seventeen years at Montana State University and sixteen years before that in public school music, besides being City Music Supervisor for the city of Bozeman for seven years.

Johnson told me that he got his first real band experience under Prof. Arturo Pettruci at Minot State University.

The 1989 Stevne was the 150th anniversary of emigration from Hallingdal to America. In 1839, two people from Aal made the journey. One was Knud Gjermundson Gullstein, a bachelor, thirty-five years old. Ordinarily, he should have inherited the farm and would have stayed in the Old Country. But his father was fined heavily for taking part in a political demonstration in 1818. Since the fine could not be paid, the government foreclosed and Knud had to find a new place to live.

The other Halling was Svein Torgeirson Tufto. He left Norway because his parents died when he was an infant (1814). The farm was sold at an auction and he was reared by an aunt. The boat on which Svein travelled transported 16 unmarried girls emigrating to America. Though there were quite a few newly married couples, and some couples with small children, there were no "senior citizens."

They sailed from Drammen, southwest of Oslo, and settled near Jefferson Prairie, Wisconsin. Why did they leave Hallingdal? Overpopulation is the reason mostly given. Emigration kept the people from starvation. Most of the immigrants were young, between fifteen and thirty years old. Many immigrants sent money back to Norway to help others emigrate. Occasionally an inheritance returned to Norway and that was a happy day.

How long will the stevnes keep going? I don't know, but my observation of the Hallings is that they're having too good a time to stop. Peter Gandrud of Bemidji, Minnesota, is president of the Hallinglag. If you are "Norwegian" and any part of your ancestry is from Hallingdal, it's not too late to join up. If you want more information, write to "Hallingen," Box 2263, Fargo, ND 58102

C H A P T E R

66

WALDEMAR AGER, PIONEER OF NORWEGIAN-AMERICAN LITERATURE

Many nations and races of people have had their day of glory only to fade away without anyone knowing much about them. That's because they didn't leave any literature. The same is true for families. Even letters written home and preserved can provide vital information for future generations.

Waldemar Ager (1869-1941) was an idealist who wanted to preserve Norwegian-American culture in the New World. His passion was not so much to establish a new Norway, but a "hybrid" which blended the best of Norway and America. For about thirty years, beginning in the 1890s, Ager championed the cause of a "Norwegian-American" literature in the Norwegian language. He wanted his countrymen to have a part in shaping America's future, not just providing the muscle power for construction jobs.

Waldemar was born March 23, 1869, at Fredrikstad in eastern Norway. At age thirteen the family moved to Oslo. The following year his father immigrated to Chicago as a tailor. Two years later, his mother and the three children joined him. In 1892 Waldemar moved to Eau Claire, Wisconsin, to work as a printer for a temperance newspaper called *Reform*. He spent the rest of life in Eau Claire, a city surrounded by forests and a center of the lumbering industry.

During that time, Norway was ruled by the Swedish king in Stockholm. Several of Waldemar's ancestors had served in the Swedish military and had taken part in the Swedish wars. When entering the military, they were required to have proper family names. The three brothers each took a different name. One chose "Eng" (meadow), another chose "Myra" (marsh), and Waldemar's father chose "Ager," meaning a "field."

Besides Norwegian-American culture, Waldemar Ager's other passion was temperance. At age eighteen he joined a Total Abstinence Society in Chicago and later became its secretary. It was a pledge he kept for the rest of his life.

What would move a young man of eighteen to become a total abstainer? In Ager's case, perhaps two things. First, his father was an alcoholic. Once he saw his father strike his mother. This left a deep wound on his memory which was reflected in his writings. Second, an immigrant from Fredrikstad had been converted to Methodism in America and returned to organize a Methodist congregation. His mother switched over from being Lutheran to join it, probably because of the temperance emphasis held by the Methodists. In Chicago, the Agers became active in the First Norwegian-Danish Methodist Church on Logan Square. When moving to Eau Claire, Waldemar became a member of the First Norwegian Lutheran congregation.

It wasn't long before many Norwegian Lutherans also became temperance advocates. During the immigrant days, the temperance societies provided both an advocacy against alcohol and a social club where young people could meet. My parents were not "joiners," except for the church and PTA, so I didn't experience this movement, but its influence was felt. There was never any alcoholic beverage in our home, but there was no objection to using wine in communion.

Waldemar was tireless in his writing and speaking on behalf of temperance and prohibition. He also took a strong stand against the socialist movement. He said: "If socialists had a little more respect for honest work, they would enjoy more respect themselves." There was never any doubt where he stood on issues. Nor did he back away from tangling with other Norwegians with whom he disagreed, including Rasmus B. Anderson (1846-1936), the "father of Norwegian teaching in America" at the University of Wisconsin.

In 1899, Ager married a member of his temperance lodge and took her on a honeymoon to New Orleans. They had nine children, each with a distinct Norwegian name. The Agers were a musical family and enjoyed art. One son, Trygve, became a writer and translated Ole Rolvaag's writings as well as his father's.

An excellent book on Ager is *Immigrant Idealist* published by the Norwegian-American Historical Association (1989), written by Einar Haugen. It reviews all of Ager's major writings with helpful introductions for the modern reader. Most of his early writings dealt with the temperance issues.

Ager made three return trips to Norway. He was impressed with the status of Norwegian women upon his first return in 1900 and thought they were more emancipated than American women. Their manners, he wrote, indicated that they were just as free as men. Norwegian women received the right to vote in 1913. Ager took up their cause in America, but was opposed especially by church people who felt that the place of women was in the home. Ager replied: "The question is whether she can be regarded as a human being, as men are." Ager's high respect for his mother likely influenced his views.

In 1910 Ager wrote *Kristus for Pilatus* (Christ before Pilate), a novel which won him recognition as a major writer. In this book he departed from the temperance issue as a major theme. He contrasted Christ and Pilate as a contest of love and grace versus justice and power. The idea was suggested by an 1881 painting by Hungarian painter Mih`haly Munka`czy entitled "Ecce Homo" (Behold the Man). Ager was impressed that Christ looked like a true human being in the painting, not someone incapable of being touched by human suffering. This novel caught the attention of Rolvaag, new on the faculty of St. Olaf College, who wrote to Ager: "You have precisely the qualifications for describing Norwegian-American life."

Ager opposed the American "melting pot." He saw it as a threat to the culture he loved. The "melting pot," he wrote, "was precisely made for the spiritually blunted, for those who no longer had any character by which one could see what they were or what they had been." World War I brought attacks on Norwegians in America that they were pro-Kaiser and un-American. Ethnic languages also came under attack. He believed that the Norwegian language and heritage were important and wrote "we must make our cultural contribution on the basis of it."

My favorite book of Ager's is *Sons of the Old Country*, a novel published in 1926 in Norwegian, but not translated into English until 1983. It's the story of a young man named Frederik, the son of a wealthy Norwegian business man, who went to America instead of taking over the family business. He ended up in Eau Claire where he worked in a lumber camp. Men who worked in the lumbercamps were a rowdy bunch, but Frederik managed to do the work and keep his self-respect. During the Civil War, Frederik and many of his friends joined Col. Hans Heg in the Union cause. Ager had the ability to make the reader burst out in rollicking laughter one minute and shed tears in the next.

St. Olaf College gave Ager an honorary Doctor of Letters degree in 1929. Rolvaag likely recommended it, though it also had the support of President Lars Boe.

Ager's later years were lonesome, his wife having died. This was portrayed in his last novel, *Hundeoine*, which literally means "dog's eyes," a picture of his loneliness. The American publisher entitled it *I Sit Alone*. Einar Haugen points out that *Sons of the Old Country* shows Ager as a historian, but in *I Sit Alone* as a philosopher. Knut Wefald was so moved by this book that he wrote, "I don't know if I can get to sleep to night…I have never read a book with such tenseness." In addition to novels, Ager wrote many short stories with clever plots.

To the end, Ager resisted "Americanization," even though he had become a citizen at age twenty-two. The last battle was when his congregation dropped the name "Norwegian" in 1935. At its seventieth anniversary that year, the congregation's Norwegian service was held in the afternoon. Ager sat in the balcony alone, rather than on the main floor with the others. In those years, he spent a lot of time at his lake cottage on Lake Chetek. As World War II began, he editorialized against war, referring to it as "international crime."

At his death in 1941, one eulogist stated: "He was not always right, but he was always honest." We might hope that the same could be said of us.

C H A P T E R

67

OSCAR OVERBY, "HE TAUGHT MANY TO SING"

There are a few people, maybe not many, that we wish would live forever. Oscar R. Overby (1892-1964) is one of those people on my list. He first came to my attention through the music he wrote for church choirs. These were also commonly used by high school and college choral groups.

My first look at Overby came at a Luther League Convention at Milwaukee in 1947. In those days of the former Evangelical Lutheran Church (ELC), every gathering involved a "Choral Union." In Milwaukee, Overby directed 2000 singers. His technique and charm made it fun to sing. It wasn't until 1953 that I came to know him personally. As the Executive Director of the ELC's Choral Union, he came to Bottineau, North Dakota, to hold a Church Music Institute. He had us sing hymns, both old and new, and made them exciting and unforgettable. I remember singing them in my mind for weeks afterwards.

Who was this unusually gifted and humble man? He was born September 25, 1892, on a farm along the Sheyenne River 10 miles northeast of Cooperstown, North Dakota. His parents had come from Ostmaerka in eastern Norway in 1882. The Norwegian language was so much a part of their culture that they even played baseball in the mother tongue during recess at school. A teacher offered fifty cents to any pupil who could stay away from Norwegian for a week. No one collected.

Overby completed his high school at Concordia Academy (now College) in Moorhead, Minnesota, in 1912. He went on to St. Olaf

College in Northfield, Minnesota, and to the New England Conservatory of Music in Boston. World War I called him into military service.

In 1921, Overby joined the music faculty at St. Olaf where he remained until 1948. There he worked with the famed F. Melius Christiansen. His wife, Gertrude Boe Overby (1900-1979), was from Finley, North Dakota. She was a famous soloist in her day and continued to sing with the St. Olaf Choir for many years after graduation.

In the private memoirs written for his family, Overby mentioned a few former students of whom he was especially proud. Among these are Paul J. Christiansen of Concordia College in Moorhead, John Strohm of Minot State University in North Dakota, and Frank Pooler of Long Beach State College in California. I have never met a former student of his who didn't have the highest respect and affection for him.

In 1948, Overby became the Executive Director of the ELC's Choral Union. His memoirs note two trips to Minot in 1954 and 1955. At one of these "a Danish Catholic Priest directed his boy's choir which sang 'Den store hvide flok' in good Norwegian."

4800 singers sang together for Overby in Minneapolis for the Lutheran World Federation Assembly in 1957. He called this "the super-climax of all my experiences in directing massed chorus singing."

Prof. Strohm said of Overby: "He had that unique quality of being able to communicate with everybody." Overby's own definition of music was: "Music is Christian love in search of a word." Many of us owe a great debt to Oscar Overby. He taught many to sing.

CHAPTER

68

ALVIN N. ROGNESS, "MENTOR" FOR PASTORS

I have known quite a few people of the cloth in many denominations and have learned a great deal from them. But I know of no one in the clergy profession who has been so respected and highly regarded as a mentor and role model for pastors as Alvin N. Rogness.

When I was in the Graduate School of Concordia Seminary in St. Louis, Dr. Richard Caemmerer Sr., under whom I studied homiletics, said to me: "I suppose, that pound for pound, Al Rogness is the best preacher that Lutherans have in America."

I first heard Dr. Rogness speak at an Ashram for the Lutheran Students Association of America at the National Music Camp at Interlochen, Michigan, in August 1948. I had just graduated from Concordia College with a degree in philosophy. I was fascinated by every word that he spoke. I thought: "Here is a preacher with a profound intellect, but who speaks so simply that even little children could understand him." When I returned to Luther Theological Seminary in St. Paul in 1955-56 to complete an advanced degree, Rogness had become president.

About twenty years later, I was studying a map of Trondelag in Norway, looking for a farmstead named "Eggen" where my paternal grandmother was born. I recognized a number of place-names by which people of my home community in Richland County were named. Among these were Folstad, Forness, Gylland, Sokness and Wollan. Then I spotted "Rognes," just a few miles miles east of Eggen.

I checked the "*Bygdebog,* the regional history for Storen. My hunch was correct. It was Rogness' ancestral home.

I asked Al about his family. His grandfather had left Storen in 1868 for America, settling first near Lanesboro, Minnesota. Because land was already getting scarce, they moved on to Astoria, South Dakota, about 1870. Astoria is about eighty miles north of Sioux Falls and twenty-five miles east of Brookings. Al's grandfather was a farmer, but his father started a general merchandise store in 1903. The railroad had come to Astoria in 1900. Al said that there were about 300 people in the village, 200 of them were children.

Besides salt blocks, overalls, groceries, dry goods, and such things, the store also had books. With no public library, Al would borrow books from the store and bring them home to read. Then he'd return them to the store to be sold. Born in 1906, Al attended Augustana College in Sioux Falls, graduating in 1927, then teaching speech and English for a year before entering Luther Seminary in St. Paul. Returning in the summers to work in the alumni office, he met Nora Preus whose father, O. J. H. Preus, had become president of the college. Graduating from the seminary in 1932, he enrolled at the University of Minnesota in philosophy and history for two years.

In his Ph. D. program, Al discovered Prof. David Swenson, a professor who pioneered the study of Soren Kierkegaard's writings in America. Swenson, a Swedish-American, taught math, logic and philosophy of religion. Al has many good things to say about Swenson. So have many others of his students. The story is told that when Swenson died, his wife learned Danish so she could continue his work of translating Kierkegaard's writings into English.

Al and Nora Preus were married in 1934, the year he was ordained. For the next twenty years he was a pastor in Duluth, Ames, Mason City and Sioux Falls. I attended the convention of the former Evangelical Lutheran Church in 1954 which was annually held at Central Lutheran Church in Minneapolis. At the convention of 1954, Rev. Fredrik Schiotz was elected president of the church and Rogness president of Luther Seminary. George Aus,the other candidate for the seminary, was initially declared the winner, until some late ballots came in to reverse the decision. Meanwhile, not knowing of the final outcome, Rogness had telephoned his children to tell them that they would not need to move from Sioux Falls, and then telephoned his congratulations to Aus. It was Aus who told Rogness that he was named president of the seminary. In 1950, Rogness had been elected president of Concordia College, but declined in favor of remaining at First Lutheran Church in Sioux Falls.

For the next 20 years, the seminary progressed under Rogness' leadership. First, the campus of nearby Breck Military Academy (Episcopalian) was purchased. This allowed for major development of the campus in future years. Second, Northwestern Lutheran Seminary of the Lutheran Church in America (LCA) was invited to relocate its campus from Minneapolis to the former Breck property. This eventually led to a merger of the schools under the presidency of Dr. Lloyd Svendsbye, who later became president of Augustana College. The school was renamed Luther Northwestern Theological Seminary. Today it's called Luther Seminary and is the largest Lutheran seminary in the world.

Not only has Rogness been known as an outstanding preacher, scholar and pastor, but he has excelled as a writer. He's written over twenty books, all of them produced by Augsburg Publishing House. I asked him what he thought were some of his best books. He mentioned three. *Forgiveness and Confession*, a book on spirituality, was published in 1970. Unlike most study documents written with profound meaning, it is written in non-technical language that a high school student would have no difficulty understanding.

Living in the Kingdom is an easy-to-understand explanation of Luther's Catechism which is used by thousands of congregations. I have used it for the instruction of more than five hundred people.

The other book that Rogness cited was the *Book of Comfort*. It was selected by the Academy of Parish Clergy as its "Book of the Year" in 1980, chosen as the best book written for a pastor's use in 1979. The selection was suggested by Fr. Joseph Dooley of Indianapolis, a parish priest who had been a professor at St. Meinrad's seminary in Indiana.

I have shared this book with dozens of people who were in need of comfort.

Another of Rogness' books that I've enjoyed is *The Word For Every Day*." It contains 365 readings which reflect his wide range of reading and deep understanding of the human situation. I have read this aloud to my family for after-dinner devotions. No one fell asleep during the readings. He had a knack of making difficult things easy and often drew out meaningful insights from overlooked events. While browsing in a shop in Old Jerusalem, I ran across another of his books, *The Land of Jesus*. It's an excellent book to read on the Holy Land.

For many years amidst his busy schedule, Rogness travelled to Europe and Asia to conduct retreats and missions for the U. S. Armed forces. In later years, Al and Nora lived a more quiet life in their home near the seminary in St. Paul during the winter, and at Kabekona Lake near Laporte, Minnesota, during the summer.

The Rogness children have followed in their parents' footsteps as workers in the church. Their oldest son, Michael, after twenty-one years as a parish pastor, is a seminary professor in St. Paul. Peter is a bishop in Milwaukee. Andrew is a pastor in Madison, Wisconsin. Martha is a teacher in Cloquet, Minnesota. Steve, the only one not in the ministry, is president of the Minnesota Hospital Association. Tragedy struck the Rogness family in the summer of 1960. Their son Paul, returning from two years in England as a Rhodes scholar, was struck by a truck and killed instantly just a few miles from his home.

Al Rogness died on July 12, 1993. There are many of us who have received inspiration from him. My impression is that he was never bored with life. Instead he has opened up windows of hope to many people.

CHAPTER

69

ARLEY BJELLA,
"THE MAN FROM THE PLAINS"

"A man from the plains," they called him. That's the best description for Arley Bjella, an attorney from Williston, North Dakota, who was chief executive officer of Minneapolis based Lutheran Brotherhood, an insurance company, from 1970 to 1982, and chairman of the board from 1970 to 1987.

I first met Arley in July 1948 in Fairview, Montana. The Men's Club of Zion Lutheran Church held a steak fry and invited him to speak about his experiences as a War Crimes Trial lawyer, involving the concentration camps at Dachau- Nuremberg at the end of World War II. He held the rank of captain in the Judge Advocate Division in Europe after receiving his law degree at University of North Dakota in 1941.

The Bjella story, however, starts in Aal, Hallingdal, a valley in Buskerud, to the northwest of Oslo. Arley's grandfather, Asle Olsen Bjella, immigrated to Gary, Minnesota, in 1896. Arley's father, Asle Asleson Bjella, was the eleventh of fifteen children. He came to America in 1889, the year of North Dakota's statehood, and settled in Epping, North Dakota, to become a blacksmith. Arley's great-grandfather had also been a blacksmith. Born in 1916, Arley was the youngest in a family of five. His brother Lloyd of Williston still maintains the blacksmith shop. Among the things for which the family was famous in their home community was building an automobile.

One of the sad events for the family was when Arley's mother died during the flu epidemic of 1918. Arley was just a year and a half old. Every year on May 13, his father took the children to her grave to pray, as they remembered the day of her death. The people of Epping extended their helpfulness to Asle in the rearing of his family, a kindness which Arley never forgot. It affirmed his belief in human dignity.

But Arley was not destined to be a blacksmith. In high school he was a regular on the basketball team. He also played trombone in Epping's first band, one that Lloyd organized in the blacksmith shop. It became a popular band in the community. To show that he had not forgotten his musical touch, Arley played in a reunion band in 1960 which commemorated Lloyd's twenty-five years as band director. According to Lloyd, he still played the trombone well. That was 30 years after graduating from high school.

The trials of Nuremberg, with their disclosures of inhumanity, left an indelible mark on his soul. These deepened his compassion for the suffering. After returning from the war in Europe, Arley married Beverly Heen, his college sweetheart. They have three children: Lance, Brian and Bryn.

Continuing in the law practice, he formed a partnership in Williston with Frank Jestrab. It was a booming time for western North Dakota. Rain had returned to the prairies in the 1940s. There were bumper crops and machinery dealers were busy. Then oil was struck in 1951 on the Clarence Iverson farm near Tioga. Williston became the center of North Dakota's new industry. This brought added business to their law office. His firm had much to do with the state's conservation-minded oil and gas laws.

Arley, however, didn't confine himself just to his law practice. He had some personal values that found expression in the community, serving on boards of hospitals and banks. Active in politics like his father and brother Lloyd who had been state representatives, he ran for Lt. Governor in 1950. Arley served four years as state chairman of the Republican Party. He served as president of the North Dakota State Bar Association and state chairman of the Republican Party. He is a fellow of the American College of Trial Lawyers and of the American College of Probate Counsel. The University of North Dakota's Centennial Program chose him as their chairman. In 1948, he was named the Jaycees "Outstanding Young Man of North Dakota."

The church has also been served well by Arley Bjella. While a student at the University of North Dakota, he was active in the Lutheran Student Association and arranged for Dr. Alvin N. Rogness, then in Ames, Iowa, to speak at the University. In Williston, he was president of First Lutheran Church and taught the Bethel Bible Series. He was also a member of Concordia College's Board of Regents and served on the Board of Social Services of the American Lutheran Church.

Without doubt, Arley could have stayed in Williston and had an enjoyable career among the people who were close to his heart. But other currents of history were moving. The Lutheran Brotherhood was going through some internal struggles. While he was a university student, representatives of the company had tried to recruit him to be an agent. In 1967, he was persuaded to be a candidate for the board of directors. He was elected together with a new majority that changed the operational procedures of the company.

In 1970, when the president of Lutheran Brotherhood died, Bjella was elected its chairman and chief executive officer. For the next two years he commuted between Williston and his office in Minneapolis on the Empire Builder. Long train rides give a person time to think, and I suspect that a lot of the restructuring of Lutheran Brotherhood took place over the Great Northern tracks.

Lutheran Brotherhood began as a fraternal organization on June 11, 1917, at the close of a church merger convention. Three Norwegian Lutheran groups united in Minneapolis. Jacob Aal Otteson Preus, Minnesota Insurance Commissioner, was one of the leaders. His grandfather, Rev. Herman Amberg Preus, had come from Norway in 1850 to Spring Prairie, WI, as a pioneer pastor and a founder of the Norwegian Synod, one of the uniting bodies. Preus was concerned that so many Norwegian Lutherans felt it was sinful to have insurance. However, if insurance had the endorsement of church leaders (not the denomination itself), then perhaps people would feel it was not wrong to buy insurance from any company.

Bjella and many others believed that the time had come for improvements in the organization of the company. When Bjella took over the leadership in 1970, the first thing he did was to depoliticize the company. He wanted to make sure the company lived up to its mission. Board meetings which typically lasted only an hour with limited discussion, now became open and democratic. He was known as a "peacemaker," having the ability to reconcile factions and unite them to work together.

The relationship between the insurance company and Lutheran congregations had not always been friendly. There were those who felt that the company was improperly using its name to sell their product, and that the scholarships it awarded were done for publicity rather than with a sincere interest in the work it was to be promoting. Bjella was determined that this was going to change. He did away with the congregational branch system and organized the branches on a geographical basis.

When the Nixon administration devalued the dollar by ten percent in 1973, the world mission programs of the church were in jeopardy. Under Bjella's leadership, Lutheran Brotherhood responded by giving grants totalling $375,000 to sustain the mission budgets. They've also been active in helping start new congregations and developing programs that benefit the church. Bjella retired in 1987, but retained an office in the corporate headquarters for several years.

As in North Dakota, Arley Bjella did not confine his energies just to his job. He plunged himself into a leadership role in the Minneapolis community. He is a past president of the Downtown Council of Minneapolis and has served on the board of Fairview Hospital and Healthcare Services in Minneapolis. He is also a member of the Norwegian American Chamber of Commerce and was named "Boss of the Year" by the Minneapolis Jaycees.

Bjella has been honored by his alma mater, the University of North Dakota, on several occasions, including the "Sioux Award." He has received the Knight's Cross, First Class from the Royal Norwegian Order of St. Olav. The University of North Dakota, Concordia and Gettysburg Colleges have given him Honorary Doctor of Law degrees. In 1986, the Norsk Høstfest inducted him into the Norwegian American Hall of Fame. He is also a founder of the America-Norway Heritage Fund which promotes greater understanding by the Norwegian people of the many contributions Norwegian immigrants and their descendants have made to American life.

Despite his highly successful career, Arley has not forgotten his home town, Williston. He still stays in touch with his family and friends there.

Arley Bjella was one of the most sought after lawyers in Williston, by farmers, housewives and business men. Some hoped that he'd move back there some day. At Epping, they often stop by Lloyd's blacksmith shop and say they wish Arley were back in Williston. To them he is still the "man from the plains." That's quite a tribute. He represents the best in the Scandinavian heritage.

C H A P T E R

70

THE WILD ADVENTURES OF KNUTE

Knut the Great, the Danish King of England (1016-1035), would be proud of his namesake from Spring Grove, Minnesota. Knute Lee, now of the Seattle area, has published his book entitled *Survivor: Knute's Wild Story.*

Even as a little boy, Knute couldn't stay away from danger. A gravestone fell on him at age four, killing his playmate. At age five, he teased a team of horses into a runaway. He missed death from a dynamited tree stump by seconds when ten. Its a wonder he ever survived childhood.

More near brushes with death followed him through high school and at Luther College in Decorah, Iowa, where he majored in music. While teaching school in Glasgow, Montana, Knute volunteered to be a Navy pilot and got his wings and commission in August 1942. He flew patrol planes, seaplanes, dive bombers and fighters in the war.

Knute's most bitter taste of war was off Noumea, New Caledonia, in the South Pacific. A Japanese submarine was sighted and surfaced by an American patrol plane. Out of bombs and with limited fuel, it ducked bullets from the sub until "Ace," as they called him, arrived to finish the task.

Then something unexpected happened. He thought about the 100 men who died on the bottom of the sea. He saw the faces of Japanese fathers and mothers, of sisters and wives of the sailors who perished. A deeply committed Christian, Knute grieved for their souls. The oil slick on the surface confirmed his feelings.

Dangerous landings, impossible formations and high risk carrier take-offs were a continuing part of Knute's saga. But the sub sinking on August 19, 1943, continued to haunt him. About this time, Knute decided to enroll at seminary when the war was over. He graduated from Luther Seminary in St. Paul, Minnesota, and was ordained in August 1948.

In 1946, Knute met and married Shirley Foster of New Rockford, North Dakota, then a nursing student at Fairview Hospital in Minneapolis. I knew Shirley from college at Concordia in Moorhead, Minnesota. Later I was pastor to her family in New Rockford. I had heard about Knute's wartime exploits and wondered how a quiet girl like Shirley would survive his exciting lifestyle. She has done well, earning a degree from Luther College while rearing four sons.

Besides working on farms, the railroad, driving trucks and cabs, and being a dance band musician, Knute earned a doctorate from Columbia University and Union Seminary in New York. He has also been a teacher in high school, college, seminary, and a chaplain at the Air Force Bace at Thule, Greenland. He later taught at the Seattle Lutheran Bible Institute. Even at the age of 70, he ran the half mile in 2:29 at the University of Washington's Master's Track and Field Meet. Though retired, he still runs.

ABC-TV did a movie on his World War II career. Besides the Silver Star for "conspicuous heroism," Knute proudly displays the Distinguished Flying Cross for "gallantry and intrepidity in action." There is no doubt about it, this Norwegian boy from Spring Grove would have done old King Knut proud. They would have liked each other.

CHAPTER

71

"HAP" LERWICK, FROM LUMBERJACK TO SURGEON

We first met in 1963 when he performed surgery for my brother. Dr. Everett R. Lerwick soon became special to our family both because of his outstanding medical skills and because he was a Norwegian in St. Louis.

There weren't many of us in that metropolitan area. Norwegians were so scarce in St. Louis that when we went to a fish market to buy lutefisk, the clerk said it had been shipped in from "Fargo, South Dakota!" We were lucky to find any at all. There had been a number of Norwegians who had settled in St. Louis, but they never formed an ethnic community or a congregation. There was one small Danish church and a fairly strong Swedish congregation.

Hap's father moved from Kristiansund on Norway's west coast to Oregon. As a young man, the future surgeon worked in lumber camps during the summer to earn money to prepare for his profession. It was there that he earned his nickname of "Hap" by his cheerful disposition. That cheerful disposition rubs off on to his patients. They have great confidence in his skills and express deep affection for the kind of a person he is.

Lerwick studied at the University of Oregon, University of Missouri Medical School and Washington University in St. Louis. Then followed a stint with the military in Korea (1950-52). After a plastic surgery residency in Philadelphia, he returned to St. Louis where he has been Chairman of the Department of Surgery at Missouri Baptist Hospital since 1960.

His travels for lecturing and performing vascular surgeries have taken him to Brazil, Mexico, Germany, France, Italy, Sweden and Norway. The last time I visited with him he was still excited over his 1983 trip to Stavanger to teach Norwegian surgeons.

It's not uncommon for a St. Louis newspaper to carry a story about one of Lerwick's surgeries. He designed a "Roto-Rooter that unclogs arteries. A sixty-four year old man had unbearable pains in his foot. Using the instrument called the "Hall Arterial Oscillator," he cleared the arterial plaque that was keeping blood from circulating in the limb. The man walked again without pain.

A seventy year old man was helping his son cut firewood when he was accidently pulled into a thirty inch blade which cut through over half of his body. He was able to say: "I want to go to Missouri Baptist and I want Dr. Lerwick." Hap was in a shopping mall buying a shirt when the hospital reached him. The surgery took seven hours and fourteen pints of blood. An assisting surgeon said, "This man should not have lived to even get to the hospital. I've never heard of anyone surviving such a wound." He is doing well today.

Lerwick had great appreciation for his father, also a physician. He invited me to his home so I could visit with his father in the Norwegian language. I took along our son Michael to play the violin. Our daughter Lisa also came along just to smile. He was a delightful gentleman and lived well into his nineties.

Lerwick makes surgery look easy. But he also raises cattle in hopes of developing a breed with a leaner meat. You just wonder what he will think of next.

Our cousins in Norway are always interested in what became of those who emigrated to America. When I shared this story with Magne Holten, a local journalist from Surnadal, a valley to the southwest of Trondheim, he wrote an article in the Driva newspaper speculating that the origin of the Lerwick family was from Lervik in Valsoyfjord not far from Kristiansund. However, the story was just wishful thinking. His father was originally named Johnson and thought that name too common.

Hap will be retiring in February 1996. I asked him about his future plans and learned that another trip to Norway may be a possibility. May there be many more of his kind.

CHAPTER

72

JOAN HAALAND PADDOCK, FULBRIGHT SCHOLAR IN NORWAY

It was not long after arriving in Minot in August 1974 that I met Olaf Haaland, the Sheriff of Ward County. We worked together on the Community Travelers Assistance program, helping people in need when going through Minot. In the summer of 1976, his wife Doroles worked energetically with many of us in the resettlement of Kurdish refugees.

Besides being community-minded people, the Haalands had in their family of four children a daughter, Joan, who was very musically talented. Joan was a frequently-featured trumpet soloist for musical programs in Minot. After completing high school, she went to Indiana University to continue studies in music, with the trumpet as the principal instrument.

Olaf retired from being a peace officer in 1978 and moved to Salem, Oregon, the following year. One day in the summer of 1986, Joan called at my office to ask about Norway. She had been awarded a Fulbright scholarship to study there. The Fulbright Act of 1946, an international exchange program administered by the United States Department of State, was established to increase mutual understanding between Americans and students of other countries. It was sponsored by Senator James Fulbright of Arkansas. Joan learned of the scholarship through a classified advertisement in the university's student newspaper. She had almost completed a doctorate in music at Indiana and was going to Norway to do research for her dissertation. Joan also asked for information on the American Evangelical Church in Oslo, in which she participated.

Arriving in Norway on November 10, 1986, Joan got right to work on her research project: "Twentieth Century Trumpet Music of Norway: Representative Selections with an Approach through Performance and Pedagogy." I was not aware how advanced Norwegian musicians were. However, having heard some excellent Norwegian musicians perform on summer concert tours and at the Norsk Høstfest, I shouldn't have been surprised. Joan quickly became acquainted with some of the country's leading trumpet teachers and began attending concerts and seminars.

Recipients of Fulbright scholarships are required to send progress reports to the United States Educational Foundation in Norway. These reports deal not only with the educational activities, but also with cost of living, health facilities, travelling and whatever was a part of the experience abroad. Joan shared these reports with me as information for this story.

Even with generous scholarship grants, students quickly learn how to budget their money carefully. Living costs in a university area tend to be high. Joan lived at the Kringsja Student by (student housing) where she paid 1000 kroner a month (about $150) for a room which included water, electricity, heat and local telephone. She shared a kitchen with six other people and a bathroom with one other person. It was about a four minute walk to a train which would take her to the center of Oslo.

Joan soon learned to figure out which things can be bought in Norway that are government subsidized. Among these are bread, butter, cheese, milk, fresh meats and train tickets. Norwegians make transportation convenient and economical as a way of encouraging people not to drive cars. Joan bought a coupon good for six months of train rides anywhere in the city or suburbs. Norwegian trains can be depended upon to be on time. I remember the train in Mosjoen (not far south of the Arctic Circle) being an hour late once. The depot agent apologized because there had been a snow slide which covered the track. But otherwise, you can almost set your watch by their arrival.

During her months in Norway, Joan kept busy playing her trumpet, especially in churches. Of special interest was when she played in the Hoyland Church where both of her Haaland grandparents had been baptized and confirmed and in Korgen in northern Norway from where her maternal grandmother, Barbara Watne Sullivan, has family roots. In February 1987, she gave her first concert of Norwegian trumpet music. Joan also gave trumpet lessons. In March, she was requested by the students to be the specialist that helped to prepare them for their annual concert and competition. It had been a unanimous request.

Joan was not formally enrolled in a regular class schedule in Norway, but was granted "part-time" status as a student at the Norges Musikkhogskole (Norwegian State Academy of Music). While there, she entered a music competition and won a $100 prize. To show her appreciation for the privilege of studying at the school, Joan returned the prize money. She took trumpet lessons, participated in trumpet classes and in brass ensembles.

In April, Joan was invited to be a guest at a school where her mother's cousin, Ellen Finbak Ottmar, is a teacher for the blind. Besides playing the trumpet, she talked about America and North Dakota. They celebrated her visit as an "American Day," and had a special "All-American" meal. The children loved it.

One of the fun events was a meeting with other Fulbright students in Lillehammer in Gudbrandsdal. This is where the 1994 Winter Olympics will be held. Anyone who has been to Lillehammer will not soon forget the beauty of the Lake Mjosa and its wooded countryside.

A high point in Norway for Joan was a visit to the Royal Palace and an audience with His Royal Highness Crown Prince Harald, now His Royal Majesty King Harald V. She wrote to the Crown Prince for an audience and stated that her parents would be visiting Norway in May and would be in Oslo for the Constitution Day celebration on May 17.

To Joan's delight, an invitation arrived a week later from Colonel Langlete, Head of the Palace, inviting Joan and her parents to an audience with HRH Crown Prince Harald at the palace on May 4 at 11:30

a.m. The invitation requested that she send detailed biographical data about herself and her parents.

In her reply, Joan asked permission for her parents to bring a small gift to the Crown Prince. She also offered to play a tune on her trumpet for His Royal Highness. Even though she walked past the palace daily, she asked which door they ought to use upon entering. Joan also asked about proper protocol for the visit. In the biographical information on her parents sent to Colonel Langlete, she related that her father had served in the Viking Battalion in World War II. This was the 99th Infantry Battalion Separate of Norwegian-American Ski Troops, which served as the honor guard for the return of King Haakon VII after his exile in England during the war.

The Royal Palace is at the west end of Karl Johansgate (Karl Johan's street). At the east end of the street is the Storting or parliament building. This is the famous street where a much photographed "Syttende Mai" parade takes place every year.

Joan and her parents entered through the main entrance and, after questioning, were escorted up red carpeted stairs to the office of Colonel Veil, adjutant to His Royal Highness. Upon arrival, the Crown Prince greeted them with a handshake and they were seated around a small table. They began their conversation by bringing a special greeting from the Norsk Høstfest. The Haalands presented their gift to the Crown Prince and then gave him a copy of my book, *The Scandinavian Heritage*.

HRH Crown Prince Harald asked Joan about her trumpet studies and work with Norwegian composers for her Fulbright project. Her father, Olaf, spoke to the Crown Prince in his Stavanger dialect and was surprised to have him reply both in Norwegian and English. Commenting that the Crown Prince could speak perfect English without any Norwegian brogue, he replied, "Vel, I can turn it on ven I vant to."

They talked about a number of items, including Olaf's service in the Viking Battalion and the Crown Prince's time in America during World War II. Their fifteen minutes went by quickly and comfortably. Then His Royal Highness escorted them to the door and wished them well on their visit in Norway. He also sent a special greeting back to Minot. They thanked the Crown Prince for the visit and expressed best wishes to the Royal Family. On the way out, her parents were photographed by the King's guard. Joan said, "Our royal visit is one we shall never forget."

When the Minot Symphony Orchestra gave its 1988 Høstfest concert, Joan, now married to Paul Paddock and living in McMinnville, Oregon, was guest trumpet soloist. She played selections by Norwegian composers. Those of us who knew Joan while she was a high school musician, could only be amazed at her relaxed poise and flawless performance before an appreciative audience.

CHAPTER

73

AN AMERICAN AT THE UNIVERSITY OF OSLO LAW SCHOOL

I've known Brad Peterson since he was in third grade. In the meantime, Brad has graduated from Minot's Magic City High School and Minot State University.

In the summer of 1989, after completing two years in the University of North Dakota Law School, Brad spent seven weeks at the University of Oslo's Law School. The University has an exchange program with UND. Brad was part of a group of ten UND students attending a special program concentrating on International Law.

They arrived in Oslo on May 16, the day before "Syttende Mai," when Norwegians around the world celebrate their Constitution Day. Brad considered himself fortunate to have arrived in time for Norway's most colorful celebration on May 17. He said the parade down Karl Johans Gate (Street, pronounced "GAH-the") from the palace to the Parliament (Storting) took four hours, beginning at 10 a.m. He noted that King Olav V appeared in a business suit and not in military uniform, while he stood to salute each group. Norwegians pointed out that the parade did not have a display of military equipment, only the honor guard was in uniform.

There were two parades. The first was the adults wearing their festive clothes (bunads). The second parade was made up of students. Technical school students were dressed in red and the business students in blue. The people lined up on the streets were all dressed up in their Sunday best.

The law students were feasted with a smorgasbord breakfast before the parade, complete with aquavit. Brad thought the aquavit tasted a little like kerosene. But they had a choice spot at the Palace to watch the parade. He was definitely impressed. Brad liked King Olav, having gotten to see him four times during his stay, including the closing of the Parliament with its elaborate pageantry.

Norway hosted a famous visitor while the Law School was in session. Pope John Paul II came to Oslo in early June. Brad noted that there was little local publicity about his arrival in Norway, though large crowds of tourists came especially to see him on the first-ever visit of a pope to the Scandinavian lands. The crowd, estimated at about 100,000, heard the pontiff speak on the Akershus Castle grounds. Security, Brad said, was tight. Copters hovered overhead, metal detectors were used for checking people at gates and sharpshooters were watching crowds from trees. King Olav V, as head of state, was dressed in his military uniform for the occasion.

The summer law students got an in-depth briefing on the Norwegian constitution as a part of their program. And they learned about King Olaf Haraldsson (St. Olaf - died 1030), Norway's "eternal king."

They were taught by a prestigious law faculty who were well informed about international law. After the constitution, they received a thorough briefing on Norwegian legal history. Brad pointed out one basic difference between how law is practiced in Norway and in America - Norwegian law is based on "code" rather than the study of "cases." They also have two laymen (non-judges) sitting on the bench with the presiding judge. They have the power to override the judge's decisions. They move a lot faster than in America. If a case is heard on Tuesday, there will be a decision by the end of the week, instead of weeks later as happens in some places. The Supreme Court has seventeen judges.

The one thing that Brad liked about Norwegian law is that there is just one system for the whole country. The law student doesn't have to become knowledgeable in fifty-two systems like in America: federal, one for each state and the District of Columbia.

Apart from the classroom, Brad enjoyed getting to meet students from Norway and other countries. He found that the European students were more liberal in their political views than his. They thought he was too conservative. When asked if there were other students in America with such conservative views, he said, "Yes, I know of five or six more." He confirmed to me what I had learned from some friends in Norway that the Soviet Union is running a propaganda campaign to change its image in Norway. Many of the younger generation feel quite comfortable having the Russian Bear for a neighbor. Another difference noted by Brad was that Norwegians aren't so interested in the private lives of their public officials as we are in America. They're more concerned about performance than image. The scandals that often ruin public officials in America were more apt to be ignored in Norway, he noted. And while Norway prides itself on its openness and lack of ethnic prejudice, Brad observed that there was resentment against recent immigrants from Turkey and Afghanistan.

People read more newspapers in Norway, according to Brad. They don't have as much radio or television. Since radio and television are publicly operated, they don't have advertising.

One of the biggest differences in comparison to the American system is that students are not required to attend class lectures. Some of them obtain the reading lists and study the required bibliography, and then write their examinations. Brad didn't care much for that as he felt there's value in dialoguing with a professor in class. The law school takes a minimum five years in Norway, though a student may stay longer and take the tests whenever ready.

Competition is keen and the flunk-out rate is high. Fifty percent of the students admitted to the Law School are not advanced at the end of the first year; thirty percent at the end of the second year; fifty percent the third year; twenty percent the fourth year; and ten to twenty percent at the end of the final year. The students, however, are not dropped from Law school. They may continue to attend until they graduate. The grade on the re-take wipes out an earlier lower grade. Examination papers are scored by professional readers rather than the professors. There were almost 3,700 students in the Law School in 1987.

I asked if drugs were a real serious matter in Norway. He indicated that they are not, but that lot of alcohol is consumed by students.

There was some social life for Law School students. Having heard that not many professors attended the student's social events, the Americans went out of their way to invite them and twelve of the fifteen Summer School professors showed up. Their next strategy was to break up the faculty groups and get them to visit individually with small groups of students. It worked, and the faculty went on to have a jolly good time, unlike most of the parties to which they were invited on campus. This socializing was a surprise to the Norwegians.

The University was founded in 1811 by King Frederick VI, who ruled from Copenhagen. It began near Karl Johans Gate near where the Palace and the Continental Hotel stand today, but was moved away from the city center in the 1930s. Only the Law School has remained on its original site. The Nobel Peace Prize is awarded at the Law School. The permanent staff of the University totals about 3,300 persons. There are seven faculties: Theology, Law, Medicine, Arts, Mathematics and Natural Sciences, Dentistry and Social Science. The Department of Nursing, established in 1985, is an independent unit. Tuition at the University is free, but students pay a modest semester fee which is used for welfare purposes.

This was Brad's second trip to Norway. I asked if he'd like to return again. Without hesitation, he replied "definitely." I asked, "How soon?" He replied, "any time." There's no doubt that he was enthusiastic about his summer in Norway.

CHAPTER

74

THE FOUGNERS MEET IN MINOT

They came from all directions. Descendants of the Fougner and the Leom families travelled from nineteen states, two Canadian provinces, plus eighteen1 relatives from Norway, to meet in Minot, North Dakota, June 25-26, 1988. They represented more than 1200 people of Norwegian ancestry who trace their roots back to Eystein Paa Jorstad (1270-1328) and his wife Aase who lived in Faaberg Parish, Gudbrandsdalen, Norway.

This reunion was a gathering of the descendants of the seven children of Hans (born 1817) and Ane (born 1825) Gudbrandhaugen, six of whom immigrated to America. The Fougner name comes from two farms near Follebu in the Gausdal area of Gudbrandsdal about fifteen miles northwest of Lillehammer. The Fougner name comes from two farms in Gudbrandsdal. The Leoms (also spelled Leum and Lium) were part of the family who did not take the Fougner name. This story will use "Fougner" to indicate both Fougners and Leoms.

A map in the family history book indicated that North Dakota was home to 249 Fougners. Minnesota was second with 124 and Wisconsin was third with 110. British Columbia, Alberta and Saskatchewan claimed 193. As to be expected, there were a number in California - fifty-nine. They list 127 of the family in Norway. The majority of them immigrated to America.

In his book, *Saga In Steel and Concrete*, Kenneth Bjork lists several Fougners who have distinguished themselves as engineers in America. They include Herman Fougner, a graduate of Trondheim's Technical College in 1897, who pioneered the use of reinforced concrete for building. His work includes buildings at West Point Military Academy. His brother, Nicolay Fougner, also a Trondheim graduate, pioneered the use of concrete in ship building, designing the first such ships for the Standard Oil Company of New York.

It's no accident that the family reunion was well attended. Robert Fougner, an architect in Minot, showed me the planning that went into the event and the well kept records that were researched to contact family members. Robert and Agnes Leom Cushing worked for about eight years and invested thousands of hours in preparing the family history getting ready for the reunion. They, however, gave lots of credit to the others on their committee.

Gudbrandsdal, the home of the Fougners, is a beautiful valley north of Oslo running from Gjovik on the south to near Dombas on the north. The highway and railroad tracks follow Lake Mjosa and the Lagen River. To the west one can see beautifully snow-capped mountains. They are also a spectacular sight from the air.

Gudbrandsdal means "Gudbrand's valley." Gudbrand was an important man who lived there in St. Olaf's time. When King Olaf arrived about 1015 with his "hird" (about 400 armed men), he gave people a choice of either becoming Christians and being baptized, to leave their homes, or fight Olaf's men in battle and having their homes burned. Seeing successful resistance impossible, Gudbrand yielded to the king's demands and adopted the king's religion. As a reward, Olaf had a church built in the valley. Visitors to Norway can see what buildings used to be like in Gudbrandsdal by going to Maihaugen, a beautiful outdoor museum in Lillehammer.

Robert Fougner traces his ancestry through his father, Ingval, born in 1899 at Clifford, North Dakota. In 1906, his parents moved to Bonetraill, north of Williston. During World War II, Robert was a radioman on the USS Terror, the flagship of the Pacific Mine Fleet. When a Japanese Kamikaze suicide plane dived into it, he was, fortunately, below deck in a safe place. There were heavy casualties from the attack. After the war, Robert went to North Dakota State University in Fargo and graduated with a degree in architecture.

Agnes Leom Cushing was born in Follebu, Gudbrandsdal and immigrated with her parents when she was only eighteen months old. She learned Norwegian well, however, and Bob told me that she was an invaluable translator of family records when writing the family history.

The gathering in Minot was held at the North Dakota State Fair Grounds. Meals were catered. An advance registration covered the costs, including the building rental. Identification badges, indicating the branch of the Fougner family to which they traced their roots, were prepared in advance.

I conducted a family worship service at which Gene Fougner of Prescott Valley, Arizona, was pianist and a solist sang "Den Store Hvide Flok." That's a favorite hymn of Norwegians written by Hans Brorson (1694-1764), one of Denmark's greatest hymnwriters. The words are set to music arranged by Edvard Grieg (1843-1907), based on an old folk tune from Heddal. On my first trip through Gudbrandsdal, while looking at the snow-capped mountains, I kept hearing this song in my mind.

One of the special features were T-shirts ordered for the event. They identified the family and had flags of the United States, Canada and the third flag was supposed to have been Norway. The logo designer, however, made a mistake on the colors. The result was the flag of Iceland instead of Norway. But it didn't matter. All the shirts were quickly sold out.

A lot of baking had to be done, including lots of lefse and other pastries. The week preceding the reunion was one of the hottest on record and this made for discomfort in the kitchen.

One of Robert's concerns was the children. It turned out that they had as much fun as their parents and grandparents. Alvina Skogen came to the rescue and kept them entertained with games. There were also displays of various artifacts related to their heritage, including a genealogy chart.

Robert was busy with general arrangements and regretted that he didn't get to spend as much time as he wanted with the guests. Agnes, however, took care of the registration desk and met everyone. Since she spoke Norwegian with some fluency, she could also meet the guests from Norway comfortably. Once in a while, however, Agnes told me she started talking Norwegian to Americans who couldn't understand a word of it.

This was the first meeting of the Fougner clan. In fact, most of the people from the seven branches of the family didn't know that the others existed. It was Agnes and Bob's patient research that uncovered the family tree, something like a detective story. Will they meet again? Robert thinks so.

The relatives from Gudbrandsdal invited their American cousins to visit them in the Old Country. This has been done by at least ten of the family. Bob's reaction was: "What a beautiful country!

Celebrating heritage is a good experience. It helps people realize who they are and the strength that has made them what they are. One reason for including this story in a volume on Norwegian heritage is to call attention to a family whose careful planning resulted in a great celebration. Their hard work can become a model for others who are planning such gatherings. What was the reaction of those who attended? They said it was great fun.

CHAPTER

75

THE "AMERICANIZATION" OF NORWEGIAN IMMIGRANTS

ORLD WAR I NOT ONLY BROKE UP the German Empire, but also brought an end to the dream of a "New Norway" in the United States. I grew up in the aftermath of those days and remember heated discussions that went on in Norwegian-American Communities.

The earliest immigrants from Scandinavia were eager to become Americans and readily intermarried with Yankees and other ethnic groups. But after the Civil War, the flow of immigrants became so heavy and concentrated in some areas of the Midwest that there was little reason to learn English except to pass grades in public schools and get a loan from the bankers.

Norway's independence from Sweden in 1905 lifted Norwegian pride to new heights. By 1914, when the centennial of the Constitution was celebrated in both Norway and America, you'd have thought that the Norwegian-Americans were going to treat English as a second language forever. The Norwegian language newspapers were going strong.

The ""Big Three" were *Scandinavian* of Chicago, the *Minneapolis Tidende* (Times) and the *Decorah-Posten*. The Chicago paper printed both daily and semi-weekly editions. The Decorah paper boasted a circulation of 41,000 even though the city had but a few thousand people living in it. There were other papers too, the *Nordisk Tidende* in New York is still publishing. The *Decorah-Posten* sold its subscription list to the *Western Viking* in Seattle which is still going strong. Normanden of Grand Forks was the leading North Dakota paper with 10,000 subscribers and the *Fram* (Forward) in Fargo was in second place. They merged in 1917.

The University of North Dakota in Grand Forks established a Scandinavian studies program in the early 1890s. Teaching Norwegian at the University is mandated by the state constitution for "perpetuity." This is the only state with such a clause in its constitution. Teaching Norwegian as an elective in public schools began in 1913. Fargo, Grand Forks, Minot and Valley City were among those establishing these programs. Every May 17th the excitement for Norwegian-Americans reached a feverish pitch, especially in 1914, when Governor Hanna represented the state in Oslo for the unveiling of the Lincoln statue in Frogner Park.

My parents, however, spoke only English to me, fearing that I'd have a speech handicap when starting school. My father sang to me in Norwegian, but there was no conversation in the language of the Old Country. As long as she lived, my mother answered me in English whenever I talked to her in Norwegian.

There were six Norwegian Lutheran denominations using the mother language, all competing with each other and printing their own papers. Religious instruction in the Norwegian language was a the rule in most congregations into the 1920s. A few brave congregations used the word "English" in their names.

Some other denominations also had Norwegian publications, notably the Methodists, Seventh-Day Adventists and Mormons. There were a number of independent publications too, one of them in Minneapolis entitled "Gaa Paa" (Forward) which promoted Marxian socialism. Up until the beginning of World War I, ethnic pluralism was accepted as a part of the American life.

The war changed all that, especially for the North Europeans. Germans were hit hardest. It was forbidden to teach German and even to hold worship services in the German language in many places. Scandinavians, having a long standing relation with Germany, were especially suspect of being pro-Kaiser in the war years because of their common bonds of culture, trade and religion.

The Scandinavian countries maintained official neutrality during the war, though Sweden and Denmark favored the German, while the Norwegians leaned towards the English cause. Norway's Queen Maud was an English princess. Norwegians in America followed the lead of their homelands in backing neutrality. A Gore-McLemore resolution in Congress advised Americans not to book passage on armed belligerent ships. This was aimed against the British. Administration pressure and Republican influence defeated the measure. However, all the Minnesotans in Congress, except for one, backed it. The *New York Times* angrily declared that the Minnesota delegation was composed of "eleven Kaiserists and one American, and a mighty fine one, Senator Knute Nelson, born in Norway." Nelson broke rank with most of the people who elected him. They were for neutrality. The German-Americans actively supported the neutralist position until America entered the war on the side of the Allies.

The United Norwegian Lutheran Church adopted a neutralist position at its 1915 convention and was severely criticized for it. This added fire to the fuel in suspecting that Scandinavians had not severed allegiance to their homelands. My grandfather, Ole Fiske, when petitioning for naturalization at the court house in Wahpeton, North Dakota, on February 7, 1910, was required "to renounce absolutely and forever all allegiance and fidelity to any foreign prince, potentate, state, or sovereignty, particularly to Haakon VII, King of Norway." This was eighteen years after his arrival in America.

There were a few Norwegians, however, who became vocal in support of the Kaiser. Peer Stromme was one of them. He was said to have known more Norwegian-Americans than any other living American. Stromme "stoutly defended Germany and with even more fervor denounced Great Britain. This didn't sit well with the Anglo-Saxon spirit of America. His weekly column in *Normanden* was suspended in 1917-1918. In support of his position he said England was the only country of the many he had visited where Americans had been consistently treated with contempt and scorn. By contrast, he claimed, his experiences in Germany and with Germans on both sides of the Atlantic had been uniformly pleasant. He particularly recalled his years studying under German professors at Concordia Seminary in St. Louis who he said were "fine people."

Anxiety among immigrants began in 1907 When a literacy test was proposed for immigrants. Racism and religious discrimination showed itself especially against Catholics, Jews and Italians. Such a law passed Congress, but was vetoed by President Taft. It passed again in 1915 but was vetoed by President Wilson. If this legislation had stood, most Scandinavians would have been denied entry into the country. They were literate, but not in English.

The war hysteria brought demands on the immigrants to show their undivided loyalty to the United States. Theodore Roosevelt popularized the term "hyphenism," saying that "the hyphen is incompatible with patriotism." This was a direct attack on the immigrants calling themselves "Norwegian-Americans, "German-Americans," etc. Roosevelt was not against immigrants, but launched a strong campaign for military preparedness and a firmer stance toward Germany. Wilson also opposed the literacy law, but reminded the immigrants that when coming to America, they were "leaving all other countries behind."

In 1915, a Federal Judge delivered a stern lecture to an Austrian immigrant against the hyphen: "Remember, and remember well, that you are no longer Austrian, nor Austro-American, but wholly and solely American., He charged the immigrant to be American "without hyphens either in front or back."

The hyphenist question became a hot item among Norwegian immigrants. They were agreed on their loyalty to their new land, but insisted that the government could not dictate cultural orientation. They were split, however, on the language issue. But by the early 1930s, the Norwegian language was a lost cause for the second and third generations in most places. The Norwegian Lutheran Church of America changed it name to Evangelical Lutheran Church in 1946. There was more opposition by Norwegians who were not members of the denomination than from those who were. My father voted for the change at the national convention.

Tempers have cooled since World War II. The Germans are our allies and friends again. Since 1945 a large influx of new immigrants has entered our country, many as political refugees.

By now the Scandinavians are fully accepted as part of the American scene and are even referred to as "white Anglo-Saxons." The pendulum of the war hysteria of 80 years ago has swung the other way. Proof of this the is the success of the Scandinavian ethnic festivals. They have become a symbol of pluralism and ethnic pride for many. An excellent book for further study is *Ethnicity Challenged: The Upper Midwest Norwegian-American Experience in World War* by Carl H. Chrislock, published by the Norwegian-American Historical Association (1981).

CHAPTER

76

AMERICA AT THE "END OF THE FRONTIER"

I just have faint recollections of my grandfathers, both having died before my fourth birthday. There are many things I'd like to have asked them. My maternal great-grandparents, Ole and Kari Bakken, who emigrated from Hallingdal died long before my birth.

I'd like to have known more about the America that they encountered. How did they get along without knowing English? Did they experience prejudice and racism? What were people talking about? My great-grandparents arrived just after the Civil War in 1867. Grandpa Hellik Thompson arrived from Numedal in 1877 and Grandpa Ole Fiske arrived in 1892. Grandma Beret Eggen Fiske arrived from Storen the following year. All my progenitors emigrated from Norway to America in just a twenty-six year span. 1890 is regarded by historians as the "end of the frontier." There are plenty statistics and bare facts about the times, but the real issue is how did America look through their eyes?

America was well established by the time my family arrived. Not all the issues of the new republic had been solved, but the issues for the 20th century were coming into focus.

The years after the Civil War (1861-65), called the "Reconstruction," were turbulent. The rise of the Ku Klux Klan in the South to frustrate the Civil Rights Act of 1866 for Negroes was probably the most extreme form of racism in our country's history, but it wasn't limited to the South. In the western states, the Indian wars were heating up. There was resentment against the Chinese, especially in California.

The purchase of Alaska in 1867 brought better times to the Eskimos, but this did not protect them from exploitation.

The immigrants from Europe were in demand for their skills but were not welcomed into the power structures of the New World. Signs in Chicago shop windows saying "Irish Need Not Apply," were common. Epithets such as "dumb Norwegians," and "dumb Swedes," as well as "Kikes," "Dagos," "Polocks," "Wops," etc. were part of Yankee vocabulary.

But what were people talking about? In the western lands called the "Great American Desert," there was a movement to plant trees. Carl Schurz, an immigrant from Germany who was Secretary of the Interior from 1877-1881, called for a national forest policy. It finally resulted in the planting of shelter belts under Franklin D. Roosevelt's administration in the 1930s. In 1939, our farm near Colfax, North Dakota, was the second one in Richland Country to get a shelter belt. Tree planting is still a long way from completion in the state.

Water distribution, like today, was an issue. John Wesley Powell wrote an article in *Century* magazine in May 1890 stating that "the waters must be divided among the states, and, as yet, there is no law for it, and the states are now in conflict." He wrote that "the waters are to be divided among the people so that each man may have the amount necessary to fertilize his farm, each hamlet, town, and city the amount necessary for domestic purposes." This is still not resolved.

Farmers were in trouble. The Grange was established to organize farmers and the Populist movement was on the rise. Theodore Roosevelt wrote in 1888 about the need to "Americanize" the immigrants. He returned vigorously to that theme in 1915.

"Barbed wire" brought struggle to the plains between the cattlemen who wanted open range and the farmers who wanted to do selective breeding of livestock and to grow wheat. This meant the end of the cattle drives and dependence on railroads. The "fence cutters" were ready to murder to keep the open range.

Religion was an issue. President Grant gave a speech in Des Moines in 1876 pleading for the continuation of the separation of church and state. Robert G. Ingersoll, Attorney General of Illinois (1867-69) and an avowed agnostic, militantly campaigned against the churches of the land.

Public schools were an issue in some states, such as Illinois, where it was feared that Catholics and Lutherans threatened the existence of the public school system. Archbishop John Ireland addressed the National Educational Association in St. Paul in 1890, to "declare unbounded loyalty to the Constitution of my country." He further stated "I am a friend and an advocate of the state school. In the circumstances of the present time, I uphold the parish school. I sincerely wish that the need for it did not exist. I would have all schools for the children of the people to be state schools." Ireland, who had been a chaplain in the Union Army and was a founder of Catholic University of America in Washington, DC, was seeking public funds for parochial education.

Red Cloud, chief of the largest tribe of the Teton Sioux Nation, gave an eloquent speech in New York City in 1870 to appeal for reason and justice in the relations of the red and white races. Though a critic of government policies and Indian agents, he opposed war. He said, "We do not want riches, we do not ask for riches, but we want our children properly trained and brought up." Carl Schurz called for justice in the nation's Indian policies in an article published in 1881. He laid the blame on the inability of the government to control "the restless and unscrupulous greed of frontiersmen who pushed their settlements and ventures into the Indian country, provoked conflicts with the Indians, and then called for the protection of the government against the resisting and retaliating Indians." By contrast, Gen. Philip Sheridan said "the only good Indian is a dead Indian."

In California there were anti-Chinese demonstrations. By 1882 about 375,000 Chinese had immigrated to America, San Francisco being the heart of the settlement. This resulted in Congress passing the Chinese Exclusion Act in 1882. A fine of up to $500 per person was imposed on any vessel which brought Chinese to America.

It was also a time of Anti-Trust legislation. The financial success of the Standard Oil Trust resulted in the Sherman Antitrust Act of 1890. But because the law did not define "trusts," it was ineffective. The laws passed regulating child labor and compulsory attendance at school, however, gained support.

It was the time of new technology. The reaper revolutionized harvesting and the telegraph wire did the same for communications. Medicine was beginning to making great strides.

The purchase of Alaska from Russia in 1867 for $7,200,000 was laughed at as "Seward's Folly." But the Secretary of State was undaunted. Two years later, he went to Sitka and delivered a speech in which he looked forward to Alaska becoming a state in the Union.

I find the music of the times interesting. The Negro spirituals, revival hymns and cowboy songs were the people's music. They sang "O Bury Me Not On The Lone Prairie!" "The Old Chisholm Trail," and "Good-Bye, Old Paint." But during the "Gay Nineties" in New York's Bowery they sang of the fallen maiden, "She Is More To Be Pitied Than Censured."

What about the Scandinavian immigrants? What kind of a reputation did they establish for themselves? After the war, the South needed people to rebuild its economy. A. J. McWhirter, President of the Southern Immigration Association, encouraged Southerners to cooperate in drawing immigrants to the South. In an address at Vicksburg, Tennessee, in 1883, he said "The Scandinavian peasantry are born farmers - farmers from instinct - and for industry, sobriety, economy, and general intelligence are not surpassed by any class or nationality seeking homes in free America." Concerning the situation in Texas, he said: "A thousand educated Germans or Scandinavians thrown into the state of Texas would do more for its development and bring it more actual wealth out of its resources than could ever be hoped for from the native Texan."

For the most part, Scandinavians stayed north of the Mason-Dixon line and settled in communities of their own people, where they have preserved much of their culture. The amazing thing to me is how they retained their love of the homeland with a determination to be patriotic Americans. Even though my grandparents spoke English with a foreign accent, they were clear on this point. America was the land of their choice and the place where a new adventure would begin.

CHAPTER

77

"NEWS FROM NORWAY"

News from Norway used to mean a letter from the "Old Country" to the family in the "New World." Today it is a newsletter issued ten times a year by the Royal Norwegian Embassy in Washington, D. C. It is available without cost.

This publication has interesting reports about the latest information on Norwegian culture, politics, economics and industrial development. It also lists titles of English publications of Norwegian interests. It even contains recipes.

Since there probably are as many Norwegian-Americans as there are Norwegians in Norway, it's of special interest to the government in the "Motherland" to maintain the friendliest of relations with the United States. There are no countries in the world where America is held in such high esteem by the people as in Scandinavia, even when the press and government disagree with some of our economic and foreign policies.

When Norway became an oil exporting nation, its economy was infused with a surge of new wealth. Rather than pump all the new money into the nation's business, large amounts were set aside to help Third World Countries with their development. This helped hold Norway's inflation down.

Exporting is important to Norway. Of the 13,000 industrial firms in the country, 1800 are active exporters. I was surprised to discover a relative in Oslo, Thor Fiske, who has a position in this business. A country like Norway needs to export its goods to survive in the modern world.

Norway encourages Americans to study in their universities and colleges. They also invite American high school students to attend Camp Norway in Sandane, operated through the Minnesota Department of Education and Augsburg College in Minneapolis. At Voss, there's a summer school of fine arts for high school students. For students who want to spend a full school year in Norway, there are scholarships to attend folk high schools. Scholarships for advanced study and research are also available. *News From Norway* contains information on such study opportunities.

Short-wave radio schedules are printed in the newsletter. Radio Norway International sends out a half hour program in English called "Norway Today" every Sunday evening besides the regular Norwegian broadcasts.

Norwegians are strong believers in their young people. They strongly supported the 1985 International Youth Year, a program of the United Nations. One interesting thing I learned from this publication is that sixty-three percent of unmarried Norwegian young people between 20 and 25 have savings accounts. Norwegian youth have strong feelings for the youth of poorer nations. They participate in "Operation One-Day-Work" which sends money to help refugees in southern Africa. In Norwegian schools there is time set aside between classes for discussion and outdoor activities. This allows students to be relaxed while in school. They believe that stress inhibits learning. All this information is in *News From Norway*.

If you would like to receive this newsletter, write: Royal Norwegian Embassy, 2720 - 34th Street, N. W., Washington, D. C. 20008-2721.

*Royal Norwegian
Coat of Arms.*